LOGIC'S DICTATE

PASSION AND POWER COLLIDE IN THIS UNFORGETTABLE INTERGALACTIC SAGA

STEVE GIBSON

MINDSTIR MEDIA

Published by MindStir Media, LLC
45 Lafayette Rd | Suite 181| North Hampton, NH 03862 | USA
1.800.767.0531 | www.mindstirmedia.com

Printed in the United States of America.

Paperback ISBN: 978-1-965340-93-6
Hardcover ISBN: 978-1-963844-84-9

For Drizzle,
my little fall of Rein.

CHAPTER 1

THE VIEW FROM ABOVE

The ship departs FoldSpace around Pluto. The Merkian captain thereafter executes the hyperdrive and lands at a high orbital position above Earth and Earth's satellites. From there, the captain also sees to it that protective shields, both for defensive purposes and for camouflage, are engaged.

Having arrived again within Earth's solar system, Cliven prepares for the continued examination of Earth. "I've just about had it," Cliven says. "You have asked me—heck, all of us—to study Earth and try to understand it. We've come light years from our home with the hope that Earth can join with the advanced civilizations, but I just don't see it."

"Patience," Rein urges.

"I get it. I shouldn't get annoyed with the little stuff. There are obviously the bigger issues: senseless spending on munitions and the related wars, religious divisions, myopic selfishness, and lack of environmental planning are amongst a few of the larger issues."

"Yes, I agree with all of those."

"I know we should focus on the big issues, but the common stupidity on the little stuff is beyond annoying. For example, explain to me how the phrase 'fuck you' makes any sense," Cliven replies.

"First, as we discussed, they are working on the bigger issues, but I can see how the little things bother you. They bother me too and your example is a good one. It is true that they equate 'fuck' with sex, and they understand that sex, when done well and even when not done well, is a great thing. It is not clear why they then turn it around and use this word meaning sex as part of the worst insults they throw at someone else, but I still think we need to be patient with them," Rein says.

"Well, you're not helping much," Cliven blurts in complete frustration. "You know, it's some of the little things that demonstrate their overarching personalities that are also indicative of the larger problems. They appear not to think."

"As cultural attaché, you must admit you need to be a lot more tolerant of these sociological variations and anomalies," Rein insists.

"I understand, but there's more," Cliven says as he opens up another set of data files about Earth, specifically the United States of America.

For seven years, a team from the planet sector known as Merk (with the planet Merk at its core) has been charged with Earth Assessment and Study ("EAS"), and, somewhat unfortunately, Rein has been put in charge of that project. Needless to emphasize, it has been one of the most challenging worlds Rein has ever dealt with. While other worlds have their oddities, Earth's culture, in some ways, goes beyond not making sense. Nevertheless, this Merk team has been assigned to determine whether Earth should be approached for inclusion into Merk: a group of advanced planets in the galaxy that only allows new entrants after they demonstrate a level of sophistication, maturity, and understanding of the need to prioritize peace and cooperation.

"I agree, but there's also no question Earth is capable of some of the most amazing achievements—Tschaikovsky's music, Herbert's literature, and the food in Paris or Chicago, to name a few. On the other hand, the level of stupidity is also galaxy-class: lingering in the left lane on an expressway, the illegalization of public nudity, and praying for rain."

"Yes," Cliven agrees, "the fact they outlaw being nude in public is just silly. First, they agree that a beautiful human body is something great to look at, and then they say don't look at it. Little old ladies think being naked is horrific, but then they gobble up romance novels with more sex than an X-rated movie and more public displays of flesh than a European beach."

"And then they say to those people dressed in clearly pleasing attire, 'leave a little to the imagination,'" Rein adds, "virtually admitting that they want to see the nakedness they have been imagining all along. That being said, I've seen some people on Earth who should never be seen without lots of clothes on, and I could make an argument that that level of human ugliness is immoral, but probably not criminal."

"Well, not everyone looks like you, Rein. Maybe you need to be the one with more tolerance. Although, I've got to agree that praying for rain, and other things, makes even less sense."

"I don't know. I mean, asking for divine intervention as a last hope maybe isn't totally insane," Rein replies.

"Hold on a second, you cannot be serious. They believe God knows everything and is all-powerful, and then they believe they can change God's ecological plan with a small prayer?" Cliven criticizes.

"Well," Rein replies, "I guess they think it does not hurt to ask, and maybe the prayer was part of the plan."

"I'm not letting you off that easy," Cliven pounces. "First, if they believe God's plan is set because God cannot make a mistake and therefore whatever God has predestined is immutable, then they should know that asking for a change through a small prayer is fruitless. It's also hard to understand that a prayer asking for ecological change is rational as it does not take into account the holistic worldwide ecological environment."

"But they think they have free will despite their God being all-knowing and that free will can itself effect change," Rein mutters, inviting further pouncing.

"C'mon, as you well know, they can't believe in free will if they believe God both knows everything and is all-powerful. If those two things are true, then God knows what has happened, is happening, and will happen. If God perfectly knows the future, then the future cannot change based upon free will. Moreover, praying for rain is not a manifestation of free will but further intervention by God, so that does not even make sense. Anyway, I think you already know this and are, once again, being overly generous to these Earthlings in giving them some glimmer of a chance that they make sense."

"Maybe so, but not all of them are confused about God and free will. The agnostic movement has arguably reached a majority in most developed countries on Earth."

Cliven concludes, "That's my best hope for these folks. The agnostics are closer to Merk than anyone. The people of Merk are more advanced in the study of the universe and believe they still have unanswered questions. How can Earthlings think they have all the answers with their current level of scientific development?"

"I know," Rein says, finally sharing in a less-than-generous mentality. "This contention that 'You should just have faith' really bothers me. Faith in what? And then those who appeal to faith invariably argue that their understanding of what they have faith in is the only answer and that all others are wrong, thereby creating division, prejudice, and ultimately war. Religious division has not only killed more people on Earth but has plagued the galaxy equally through the years."

"Thankfully, those days are over for all of the planets in the Merk sector," Cliven concludes.

"Listen, we've got to run and meet the captain, but don't lose that thought . . ." Rein says as they both get up, understanding they need to hustle and traverse the full length of the ship to make it to the captain's dinner on time.

Their ship is one of the best in the fleet. It has state-of-the-art food fabricators, a full, real kitchen for certain meals, and temperature-controlled, correctly contouring, true massage-enabled beds that are heaven to stay in. Of course, that doesn't include the navigational and flight capabilities. Although their mission is one of peace, the ship is also outfitted with defensive and offensive armaments sufficient to take on anything known in the galaxy.

EAS had been going on long before this Merk team had been deployed. Earth has been a subject of interest for hundreds of years, but only now has it become the subject of a more intense focus. That focus was not the least brought about by one American who seemed to get it: Andrew Brock. Merk has been following Andy since at least high school. Andy posted an amazing article on the internet during his sophomore year, and he set forth many contentions in the article, but a specific one really caught their attention: "The world spends trillions of dollars a year on the military. We divert our attention from starvation, homelessness, and the need to irrigate wide areas of drought-suffering land so that we can focus on the military-industrial complex. Will we change? No. Can we change? Yes. What will it take? The key is incentives. We need to harness the selfishness of humans to convince humans these diversions are not in our selfish interest. How do we do that? I have a plan. Read on."

Andy's plan ingeniously created a carrot-and-stick approach incorporating US-led (but joined by allies) incentives to join in lessening military-industrial expenditures and diverting some funds to particular projects on an incremental basis. It also incorporated new fusion technology for energy development as part of the carrot. While not the plan of ultimate sophistication one would imagine of a global think tank, for a sophomore in high school, it was pretty impressive writing.

Andy also found a way to point out the historical hypocrisy of the then-current administration's policies toward education. The administration insisted on maintaining a policy of state-controlled, high student-teacher-ratioed classes along with a plethora of useless course studies. Andy reflected on his own education at the private institutions run by his father, Edward Brock, and thoroughly cut through the bullshit of the status quo.

Andy, now himself a candidate for president of the United States of America, has revealed an array of policy positions that have uniquely brought the country together—as much as possible.

Andy is also simply an amazing human being: fifty-five years old with the body of a very fit thirty-five-year-old, beyond intelligent, charming, funny, focused, slightly impatient with colleagues who do not think things through, but otherwise a born leader. Somehow, he finds time to prepare chef-level cuisine, sing like Sinatra, and can kick just about anyone's ass in racquetball. With an IQ north of 160, Andy's main talent is a policy savant. He has an intuitive sense of sociological, economic, and political dynamics. He's driven by logic, but also has a natural empathic capability. You might think of him as a combination of Spock, Deanna Troi and Picard rolled into one. Some petty men who have experienced Andy think he is unrelatable and too perfect. Most women find him exactly what they would ever dream about. What Merk has observed is that he simply seems to make more effort at applying logic to the data set available and somehow includes vast sociological dynamics in his decision-making. He does it at a policy level, a business level, and a personal level. While some might consider that unrelatable as a persona, Merk believes that he is no more unrelatable than Mozart in the music arena or Einstein in physics. It just so happens that Andy's talents spill over into very practical areas of life. The reports state, like Einstein, that he works harder than anyone else. Combine talent with work effort and you get a superb human result.

All of that has caught Merk's attention. Merk found Andy's ability to lead, coupled with his policy positions, to potentially shape Earth into a planet that could become part of the community of civilized planets within the galaxy. Merk also found Andy's objective deployment of logic-based reasoning with his empathic capabilities to be remarkably unique on Earth and maybe even in the galaxy.

Andy Brock was, in a word: promising.

CHAPTER 2

IOWA

"I mean, listen. I don't smoke, drink, or use drugs, but don't force me to give up my breakfast at the Chicago House of Pancakes," Andy tells Tom Kynes, his campaign manager.

"I get that," Tom interrupts, "but starting the day with Cream of Wheat with lots of brown sugar, followed by pancakes, scrambled eggs, four strips of bacon, and coffee, is not exactly going to keep you fit and healthy."

"Ah, but you left out the freshly squeezed orange juice that is to die for," Andy forcefully retorts.

"Alright, alright, I have to admit this is the best breakfast in the world taste-wise, but, well, it just pisses me off that you eat this stuff and your muscles are harder than rocks."

"Listen, Tom, keep your jealousy in check, and let me have my one indulgence. By the way, what time are we leaving for Davenport?"

"Well, we are scheduled to leave in two hours, but the driver is already at the Silverstone, and everything should be ready as early as one hour from now," Tom observes.

Andy decided long ago that the best way to travel certain distances was by motorcoach and, more specifically, a fleet of Candor Silverstones. Andy is frugal, but not to the point of being impractical. The forty-five-foot motorcoaches are, in his opinion, the best mix of luxury and value on the market—and have been that for as long as Andy could remember. They are the starships of the road. With over

600 horsepower engines, massive torque, and tech-controlled every-thing, they drive like a race car but live like a luxury hotel. They are, quite simply, perfect. Full kitchens, master bedrooms and bathrooms that make luxury hotels jealous, as well as home theatre and computer station arrangements that keep Andy entertained and engaged, are all features that make the Silverstone his favorite—particularly at the price. Sure, he could spend more on another coach, but why? He likes to update his fleet and at the price point of the Silverstone, he could safely and practically buy new ones every few years. Moreover, while Andy has a private plane, he still finds that his fleet of Silverstones for his team, especially for short-travel engagements to Iowa from Chicago, are far better than navigating the airways.

"Hey, Tom, did Lisa finish the last part of the speech on health care?"

"Not yet. In fact, she has a few questions if you've got a second."

"Hmmm, have Lisa join me on Silverstone One on the trip to Davenport, and we will go over it together."

"OK, well, then, I see you still have two more papers to read anyway, so let me get going and get the team on Silverstone One, assuming I can wind my way out of this crowd—I still can't believe you can focus on as much as you do while having breakfast at a public restaurant, but I know you love the Cream of Wheat here . . ."

"Enough about the breakfast; leave me alone," Andy rebukes.

Andy not only loves his breakfasts but also the newspapers that come with them, particularly if he is in Chicago. While he, obviously, can access the *Tribune* online anywhere in the world, Andy still feels that reading the real thing, the paper version, is somehow different. He tries to find time to read four papers a day: whatever local paper is available in the city he is in at the time, the *Chicago Tribune*, the *WSJ*, and the *Japan Times*. His breakfast time is, therefore, special. It is his time with the news and his thoughts. While the news isn't nec-essarily the truth, it carries a truth of its own—the viewpoints being espoused. While Andy's politics are national, if not international, he understands that politics are also very, very local, and one needs to be in touch with those viewpoints in order to lead.

Lisa Black is waiting (but working) on Silverstone One for half an hour before Andy arrives. Lisa, by all measures, is the best political operative around. Now, "political operative," by most connotations, has a negative impact, but in Andy's eyes, it is, with Lisa, all positive. She seems to intuitively understand the policy positions Andy advances. She also senses the ethical compass Andy follows. Perhaps more importantly, Lisa also believes the ultimate goal of advancing humanity that Andy could achieve is actually within reach. All of this made Lisa—who, by the way, could write like no one else in Andy's orbit—invaluable.

"So, how are we going to pay for this, Andy?" Lisa asks, somewhat indelicately.

"I thought you spoke with Dempsey on the defense policy side," Andy probes.

"Not yet, but by your comment, you don't need to say more. I remember the aggregate policy position and should have factored that into the tie-in on the medical side. May I assume the thirty billion dollars will be reallocated from the military budget?" Lisa correctly observes.

"Yes, but don't forget that that reallocation won't be more than a temporary feature given the midterm savings we'll get once the project build is finished," Andy instructs.

One of Andy's health care fixes is typical Andy: frugal, practical, and inventive. Andy's plan is to launch medical center builds in sixty of the biggest metro areas across the country in phase one. Each medical center build would be approximately five hundred million dollars on average. The thirty billion dollars will be a good start for phase one of the buildout. In larger cities, the cost would be more expensive; in smaller metros, costs would obviously be lower. The builds would consist of a main hospital, a teaching hospital, medical offices, and an administration center. The hospital would take patients on a means-tested basis and would enjoy liability limitations. Not only would this project support significant construction employment around the country, but it would also begin to provide a medical infrastructure that is unequaled in history. Each medical center would recruit medical professionals from around the world, have intensive training programs, and work cooperatively with each other to advance medical practical science. The medical centers would also deploy purchasing economies of scale and leverage practice efficiencies. After the conclusion of phase one, larger phases would be instituted so that by the end of twenty years, an entire array of government-private medical centers operating on advantageous ground would be serving the entire country.

Although Robert Dempsey, Andy's chief defense policy advisor, is not completely happy with it, the thirty billion dollars initially taken from defense is paltry by comparison to the total defense budget. The US continues to spend twice as much as the next largest competitor in the rest of the world on defense. The military-industrial complex is bloated and inefficient. Andy's plan is to attack that structure with this reallocation as a shot across the bow.

Tom sits down next to Lisa and chimes in, "You understand my concerns about appealing to the broader electorate in the primaries, right?"

Lisa agrees, "Seldom does a candidate win by fighting from the middle."

Andy had this conversation with them and others on several fronts but feels confident about his approach for several reasons: He is way ahead in the polls, his approach is completely different, and people like that he tells them the truth. He also isn't fighting from the middle. The policy positions he has taken are not readily classifiable as left, right, or even middle. They are different. Government has a role. The marketplace should be left to operate freely, but that does not negate a proper government role. Things such as education, the environment, energy, creative medical care, and the like are all the proper provinces of an incentive-based government level of interaction.

"Listen, guys, I know it hasn't worked since Clinton, and he was hardly a pure centrist, but I'm actually attacking the election from a completely different angle that has no real precedents. My policies, while rooted in traditional Republican philosophies, apply a practical role for the government and dispense with the religious right's sanctimonious nonsense. I'm also damn good for the minorities because my plans advance not only the economic interests of the country but creatively devise how we can gain truly better opportunities for the folks out there who need some help. Moreover, the African American community knows clearly that I will fight racial bigotry with every fiber of my being. Besides, we all believe that the free market must be kept free and that economic competition and incentives are the best way to do this. We don't want a government-run economy, but that does not mean there are not some special boosts the government can do to work with the private sector to achieve some positive ends. Moreover, dealing with the bloated military-industrial complex, horrible medical service industry conditions, and education plans are core competencies of the government. Logic dictates the approach I'm taking, and I trust my instincts that these policies will be appreciated by the voters as well."

Lisa understands the concepts, but putting them into a speech that will sell at the Iowa State Fair isn't easy. That being said, if there is one thing she knows Andy can do, it is sell it and sell it convincingly.

Right as they turn onto I-80, despite Andy's confidence, MSNBC airs "breaking news" that Chinese President Chen Aiguo invited Andy's chief Democratic competitor, Lance Como, to China for a conference, and when doing so, decried Andy's Taiwan recognition stance. President Chen also rattled sabers, claiming that Andy's plans would bring about World War Three.

"So, it looks like I lost the China vote," Andy muses. "That's about a billion and a half voters. Oh, wait a second, they aren't registered in this country—yet. I guess they won't be registered until China wins the war they claim is going to happen."

Dempsey calls in and is put through the central speaker system. "Let them blow smoke; they don't have the cards, and it is about time they stop bullying the Chinese Nationalists in Taiwan. And hell, it's a different world since the US first recognized the One China policy. Russia is now a truly democratic country, the Koreas are reconciled and joined on their peninsula, India is a formidable competitor to China, Japan is militarily restrengthened and prepared to use it, and the Middle East is behaving itself given the massive energy realignment. Moreover, our strategic missile defense won't let any nukes through. The only option China would have is to try and send a half billion men over on boats, but our navy wouldn't let them through."

Dempsey, who has a first name but nevertheless prefers being called by his last name, is mostly right. NATO is no more because Russia actually became a modern country of the West. After Putin, the Russians, having had enough of strongman rule and the failed invasion of Ukraine, revolted and demanded free and fair elections. Nothing could have been better for the country as Russia's economy blossomed and Russian international trade doubled. Russia has actually become a manufacturing hub for electric cars—cars that somewhat compete with the lower-level Teslas.

The second key country keeping China in check is Japan. Japan shed itself of its decades of economic stagnation by really putting its mind to the energy sector, which had two real benefits: It gained relative energy independence, and it turned itself into a reborn industrial powerhouse by manufacturing energy-sector technology.

Another country that's giving China fits is India. India outstretches China's population, and its own tech sector helps bring more of those folks into the middle class. While still struggling compared to the leading economies, India has made major strides, and its ground force military is no slouch. Indeed, India has upped its acquisition of high-end aircraft to such an extent that it could reasonably defend against a Chinese ground assault.

Moreover, while still powerful, China has finally come to grips with the reality of its demographic and environmental problems. On the demographic side, the population inversion is becoming almost intolerable: too few new people to work to support the older, larger population. And that total population is no longer inclined to work for a pittance to support an export engine. That export engine also for years degraded the Chinese environment to the point where a significant percentage of government spending is allocated to trying to clean up the air and water.

Independently, Chinese arrogance is at work. While China always claims to play the long game and patiently wait for the Middle Kingdom's rise to global dominance, that goal now seems completely unrealistic, which has put enormous pressure on the Chinese administration to act desperately. Adding fuel to that fire is Andy's policy of saying "enough is enough" and announcing that if elected, he would recognize Taiwan as independent and arguably the rightful government to retake control of the rest of China.

This Support Taiwan policy is politically risky. It does not do a whole lot to garner US votes as there is not a huge Taiwan constituency, but sometimes doing the right thing does pay off. The polls

STEVE GIBSON | 13

show that the voters really like a few things about the policy: They are fed up with China, and they like that Andy has some real balls. They also detest the continuing human rights abuses that the Chinese government allows and even administers. That being said, not everyone is willing to risk war, and therein lies the rub.

Andy asks Lisa to add an entire section to his next Iowa speech about China and instructs Tom to get him some time on the news channels to discuss these issues. Unlike most other historical Republican candidates, not only does Fox treat him well, but the mainstream media has given him a fair shot. They like his balancing of free market principles with incentive-based government programs to boost certain sectors and help minorities. It also doesn't hurt that some of Andy's criminal justice and education reforms are creatively far better for minorities than any Democratic Party-based programs. Andy is beating the Democrats at their own game and helping minorities far better than they are. Andy's record in fighting discrimination and relating to the African American community is impeccable. That makes Como a desperate candidate and also makes Andy formidable.

As suspected, Andy's speech in Davenport is wildly well received. Andy is able to get to the heart of the issue and relate. There is a protester in the audience who becomes quite loud concerning national health insurance, and Andy sees the opportunity. He responds to the protester, "Sir, may I have your name?"

"My name is Reginald Dawkins."

"Mr. Dawkins, I understand your concerns. I'll make you a deal. Join me for dinner tonight, and let's discuss your complaints. Now, I'm not going to extend this deal to everyone who interrupts my speech, but something tells me you deserve particular attention. Will you join me later, but let me finish now?" Andy asks.

"Yes, sir," the protester says in a near state of shock and with more respect than anyone expects in the crowd.

Andy ends his speech with, "OK, I've got a couple of extra seats at the dinner table. I hope a few members of the press can join Mr. Dawkins and me for dinner. We're eating Italian tonight, so I have no doubt you'll be happy with the food, and I hope the conversation is enjoyed as well."

Of course, members of the press are more than happy to attend dinner. Two cable news reporters and three major newspaper reporters are invited.

Later that evening, Mr. Dawkins and the reporters are seated at the dinner table in Mario's Italian Bistro's private back room. Shortly after, Andy enters and sits at the head of the table.

"Mr. Dawkins, you had some thoughts on medical care in the United States. Please elaborate. Oh, sorry, here's the waiter. Please, everyone, place your orders first."

With all of the orders placed, Mr. Dawkins says, "The Democrats seem to understand a lot better the struggle in this country to get care. Man, I just can't afford it for me and my family. Obama helped but did not go far enough."

"I agree," Andy says, then patiently goes through example after example of how government-run programs and bureaucracies are inefficient, ineffective, and wasteful. He explains that if you don't have an incentive-based system, then people just aren't motivated. This has been proven historically, time and again. Andy then goes on to present his hybrid plan of building medical centers that would be public-private partnerships with incredible legal benefits to the health sector. Andy explains that no Democratic candidate ever came up with a reallocation of defense spending to support such a massive infusion of healthcare infrastructure into the US system.

The protestor, an import from LA, learns that there are already plans to build a medical care facility within two miles of his own home in East LA and that he and his family can finally go to a facility and receive exceptional healthcare for a fraction of the cost of what he is currently paying. At that point, all concerns from Mr. Dawkins are erased.

The media at the table eats it up because they have to. The reports after the dinner are glowing.

The protestor vows to vote for Andy. The fact that Andy has him over for dinner and takes the time to listen boosts Andy's lead in the polls even more. The only thing left for the win in the Iowa primary is the candidates' debate, which is next week.

Over the years, there have been some changes in the ordering of the primaries. It ended up that folks liked the old days better, and the order of the states holding primaries went all the way back to the days of Trump and Biden/Harris. This resulted in reinstating the historical order. What did not change was the fact that debates would be held before the primaries.

Debating is not something Andy shies away from. He was on the debate team through high school and college. He just couldn't help but be on it. Most people think of debate as two people standing up, like Lincoln and Douglas, and slowly trying to convince the audience of their position. National Forensic Debate is nothing like that. Competitive debate is more physically and mentally challenging than any activity Andy has ever engaged in. Understand, Andy was taught martial arts since he could walk and talk. He has won karate competitions since the sixth grade. Debate is harder. First of all, the faster (and clearer) you speak, the more arguments you make. The more arguments you make, the more the other side has to respond to. If they fail to respond, they will usually lose. Andy usually won and has eight years of school-based debate experience to call upon. While in a political debate, you couldn't (and wouldn't) talk that fast. His experience with talking fast means he is also able to think fast on policy grounds. In thinking fast, he is able to quickly and comprehensively respond to the arguments that are posed and in such a concise and convincing manner that his competitors are left in the dust.

The week flies by, and it is time for the debate. His main Republican rival at the debate, Alexander Simpson, thinks he will attack Andy on Andy's prized educational policy. Simpson knows that Iowans are proud of their educational system and will likely buck at the mention of change. The moderator attacks Andy's policy indirectly by asking Simpson to address whether Andy's policy will result in certain current educators losing their jobs. Simpson pounces, or so he thinks. "Of course this policy will. How can you force the great education system of Iowa to change in the manner that Mr. Brock proposes by changing the curriculum and not see the loss of a large number of educator jobs? There's no way that you get rid of certain programs and not lose people."

The crowd, going against the rules, applauds.

The moderator invites Andy to respond, and he does. "Mr. Simpson wants to perpetuate a fundamentally failed system, and he left out a key feature of my program: I'm going to decrease the teacher-student ratio from thirty to one to fifteen to one. I'm going to fund the building of new school facilities to reach that goal. Not only am I therefore going to virtually double employment of educators, but I'm going to add construction jobs to the Iowa economy and I'm also going to make Iowa's students more internationally competitive so that they have great jobs when they graduate. Moreover, for the first time I'm going to throw federal money at this effort. Mr. Simpson has no plan to match. By the way, this will help Iowa's minority populations like nothing else. Join me, and let's get this done."

The crowd, forgetting their previous applause in favor of Simpson, explodes in cheers for Andy.

Andy wins Iowa by a huge margin. And, yes, Iowans are happy that they finally shifted their failed caucus structure to a primary.

CHAPTER 3

DO WE INTERVENE?

R ein, sporting the typical Merk uniform designed for women, sat on the deck of the ship, awaiting the call for the captain's dinner. The dark grey bodysuit was made of high-quality Merkian fabric, and while not transparent, it leaves little to disguise Rein's features. She stands five foot three, with 107 pounds of mostly muscle. Merkian women have less body fat than Earthlings, and Rein's body is exemplary as far as Merkians go. Her bodysuit reveals ample and perky breasts, a slim waist, and curved hips. Her ass is, in a word, tight; her abs even tighter. The fact that her beautiful body is generously revealed by the bodysuit is not something that makes Rein self-conscious. Merkians are simply not ashamed of their bodies. They generally work hard at keeping themselves fit and do not suffer from religious guilt in having their bodies shown or known.

There is no religious-based guilt because Merkians, due a level of galactic sophistication that developed over ten thousand years of civilization, do not adhere to any religious faith or atheism. They are class agnostics. Merkians humbly concluded, nearly uniformly, that they simply were not, even with all their technology, experience, intelligence, and scientific advancement, able to deduce that there is a divine being, let alone what that divine being is. Merkians have not ruled out the prospect that there might be one but have yet to furnish a definitive answer on this crucial issue.

This led to a lot less societal trauma than that experienced in worlds like Earth. With no religion claiming that they are the chosen ones or that they are right and everyone else is wrong, there is no religious basis for conflict or societal separation. There are no jihads. There are no crusades. Merkians simply do not appreciate fighting to defend religious dogma: There is no dogma to fight over. This allows Merkians to channel their energies into the advancement of society.

However, this does not mean that Merkians do not have a sophisticated philosophical grounding and a profound ethical code. Epistemologically, Merkians believe in the universal truth known on Earth as *cogito ergo sum*. I think, therefore, I am. It is at that epistemological point that Merkians' agnosticism kicks in: They have concluded that their system of ethics must operate out of that one universal truth. So, instead of the golden rule, which is a subjective belief that you should do unto others as you would have them do unto you, the Merkians apply a much more objective ethical test: Don't assume you can interfere in another's life without their consent.

This one rule resolves all ethical questions.

Is murder wrong? Yes. Murder is the highest form of interference with another's life.

Rape is wrong for the same reason.

Theft is also resolved on that basis.

Prostitution is ethical and, therefore, legal because there is consent.

Drug use is legal because taking drugs does not, in and of itself, interfere with another's life. However, if you interfere with another person's life because you can't control your drugs, then there are severe consequences. That being said, the Merkian government invests in extraordinary educational programs concerning drug use and has always developed tremendous drug treatment facilities, which has generally resulted in relatively minimal drug abuse. Drug legalization also means there is no drug-based crime, which creates massive tax revenues.

It took Merkians some time to deal with the subject of abortion, but they ultimately recognized that there are two lives involved, and both lives need to be respected. Merkians are, therefore, neither pro-life nor pro-choice in the language of how the people of Earth perceive this issue. Merkians generally say that both sides are wrong on Earth. One cannot, according to Merkian thought, disrespect the right of the mother to control her body, but also cannot disrespect the life of the growing human inside the mother. Killing that human life at any point is a slippery slope. Is abortion OK one minute before birth? One month? Six months? Where to draw the ethical line?

Fortunately, Merkian technology saved the day. If the mother desires an abortion, then the government mandates that the human life be removed from the body, at government expense and in a manner that will preserve that life. Remarkably, even the most incipient form of human life is susceptible to growth and maturation by way of Merkian technology. This means that a removal from the mother's womb at any point in time allows the child to develop and ultimately live a full life, all with government-supported institutions that give any child a fine chance at happiness—even without their biological parents being involved. Strangely enough, Merkians found that in over 95 percent of the cases where there was this kind of government intervention, the biological parents ultimately and successfully resumed their role in the child's life.

Remarkable to the Merkians is that Andy holds all of their same ethical positions—it just took him thousands of years of societal development shorter to get there. This makes Merkians more than just intrigued about Andy. It also makes the prospect of potential intervention in Earth to optimize Andy's success a real possibility.

Like most other developed societies in the galaxy that are able to watch episodes of *Star Trek*, the Merkians find the show somewhat amusing, but find the ill-developed Prime Directive a bit off the mark. While *Star Trek* gets it somewhat right by mandating the Prime Directive (and usually following it), it is not entirely the correct policy. Merkians choose not to get involved because they want the separate world to develop on its own. Primitive and undeveloped cultures are just a pain in the ass to deal with. Such cultures also pose incredible ethical dilemmas regarding when and how to intervene. That being said, if a deserving world requires intervention, then there is no directive to stop it. A world that faces apocalypse might very well be saved under the right circumstances. And it is the combination of a war with China coupled with Andy's truly remarkable prospects to lead Earth toward a level of galaxy-class sophistication that offers a real possibility of Merkian intervention.

Realizing this intervention is possible, Rein considers the circumstances within which it might occur. She has these thoughts on her way to dinner at the captain's table.

As she heads to the dining room, Rein cannot rid herself of her thoughts of that one thing on Earth that Earthlings have no idea is so valuable: garlic. Earthlings truly have no idea how lucky they are, as their planet is the only source of garlic in the known universe. While other planets have it, they had to secretly steal it from Earth, and it has not only been hard to get but even harder to keep—the growth of Earth-based garlic is hard on most other planets. It can be grown, even hydroponically, but it does not taste exactly the same. Moreover, for whatever reason, replicators experience difficulty synthesizing the taste of natural garlic.

Thankfully, the captain chooses his favorite meal tonight, all prepared in the ship's chef's kitchens, and none of it is replicated. Rein can't wait to eat the rosemary and garlic beef stew accompanied by bread and butter so expertly prepared from scratch that if Rein believed in heaven, she could only conclude she would be there as she devoured this meal. The beef in the stew is tender and infused with flavor because each piece is specifically pre-seasoned before being cooked in the broth. The roux for the stew has a wide array of Earth ingredients that do not appear to make sense together, but oh, do they work: tomato sauce, tomato paste, mustard, red wine, and the previously mentioned rosemary and garlic, to name but a few. Of course, the potatoes, onions, and carrots are plentiful and mouthwatering. It is funny: Conversation usually flows during the captain's meals, but not when experiencing this beef stew.

The captain is clearly enjoying the meal. He is certainly the leader from a travel, defense, and offense perspective. His job is to get them there safely, and if that requires military defense, then so be it. It almost never requires offense. Rein thinks this captain, at least tonight, is exceptional, if for no other reason than his choice of cuisine.

Politics and world intervention, however, are not in the captain's purview. These issues are left to the administrators of EAS—Earth Assessment and Study. Rein knows that, as the person in charge of EAS, she has the ultimate power to decide whether intervention will occur. The captain will need to support that decision whenever and however it's made.

The conversation at dinner that does ultimately occur, after the attendees have sufficient beef stew to allow a return to thought, does not disappoint.

A conservative group led by Cliven, the team's diplomatic liaison, is opposed to intervention. They feel China will not be able to inflict catastrophic losses to the point that Earth will not recover. They argue that Merk did not intervene in World War II and thus did not take down Hitler. They also argue that Merk did not intervene against Stalin and the millions lost to his atrocities. While those were tragic losses, they were not necessary to allow for the successful development of Earth as the more enlightened parts of society won the day.

Another group led by Sorcen, the team's sociobiologist, argues for substantial preparations for intervention. Sorcen maintains that even with the American strategic missile defense, the radioactive effects of that many nukes going off in the atmosphere could be catastrophic, if nothing for the enduring radioactive residue. Many current nuclear armaments are programmed to detonate automatically after leaving friendly geography upon substantial engagement, such as any meaningful attempt at being shot down. Even the Merk ship would have a heck of a time sweeping the atmosphere to clear it out. Sorcen is an even bigger fan than Rein of the beef stew and says, "You know, one big concern is the possible impact on garlic production if war were to break out."

Rein, certainly influenced by the argument for the preservation of garlic, is, at this point, torn. Rein sees that the allies arrayed against China are powerful, and while many lives would be lost in a conventional war, those allies are likely to succeed. On the other hand, the prospect of that many nukes going off is not to be discounted as unviable for the survival of Earth. Rein also ignores, for the moment, the apparently sarcastic fixation on garlic.

"Cliven, what's the likelihood that the Chinese would launch nukes?" Rein inquires.

"The Chinese have become not only desperate, but arguably unstable. Part of it is their amazing arrogance that they should ultimately lead the world. While historically the Chinese maintained that they could outwait eternity as the Middle Kingdom, the current Chinese president has decided that his own personal destiny is more important,"

Cliven informs. "This makes the possibility of an attempted first strike a meaningful reality. That being said, I believe that the American allies could sustain such an attack—albeit with heavy human losses—and the garlic production facilities will not be wiped out."

"Enough with the garlic. Although I appreciate that in times like these, a little humor goes a long way," Rein diverts.

"That's understood, Cliven," Sorcen replies, "but a first strike could be catastrophic. We've never really been able to fully contain or control this many nukes in this confined of a space. While I've got to admit there's a good chance of Earth's survival, there's also a real possibility of global catastrophe. And, just having taken my last bite of tonight's stew, please forgive me if I add that garlic production would no doubt be affected as well."

Rein does nothing more than give Sorcen her look, ending the garlic discussion. "Well," Rein concludes, "I will take this all under advisement, and I want everyone on high alert to assess any material changes in the strategic dynamic. We will revisit this discussion tomorrow at noon. Until then, let's all enjoy the salted caramel gelato, but if anyone starts in with the prospects of sugarcane losses, I will likely end the conversation there and then and just make a decision.

"However, let's turn to another front, and that is the question of how an intervention might occur," Rein redirects the focus. "There are really three levels of intervention that seem possible here: First, role-played participation as part of the US team on the one hand and the Chinese team on the other; two, massive direct intervention to stop the conflict; or three, post-conflict intervention to remedy the effects of the conflict. It would seem to me that pre-conflict role-playing would not only require the least use of resources but should prove the most efficacious."

"So, Rein, who are you planning to send to China? I think we know you are planning to 'interact' with Brock," Cliven interjects.

"Let's keep our focus on the mission, guys, and keep the snide comments to a minimum. Yes, I will obviously be the one to handle the US side if that's what we decide, and we'll send Krin to China. Cliven, get Krin prepped for cosmetics, and we will regroup for mission objectives, as I stated. We will decide which direction to go in at that point."

CHAPTER 4

THE BEST PRIMARY DEBATE

"**O**K, so why exactly are we doing ten reps at a lower weight than eight heavier reps?" Andy presses on Jeb, his personal trainer.

Jeb stands at a solid six foot two and weighs 205 pounds. He is also a Rhodes Scholar with an online personal training empire. Andy helped finance the beginnings of that empire and still pays Jeb six figures a year to provide Andy with personal training. Jeb is that rare combination of street smart, book smart, and down-to-earth. Jeb knows he is indebted to Andy for getting his start in the business. He also realizes what a great gig he has: having the ability to keep a steady income with Andy while also leveraging this online fitness empire. It also does not hurt Jeb's business that Andy is his client—one whom he can publicize.

"Andy, we've gone over this a couple of times. I'd like to instill muscle confusion, and at your age, I want more toning than muscle build anyway."

"Let's make our way to the nearest racquetball court and I'll discuss with you there whether I'm too old to build muscle," Andy threatens.

Tom Kynes, Andy's campaign manager, is no slouch himself but physically quite different. A Boston Southie, Tom is unmistakably American-Irish with a thick Southie accent and attitude to go with it. He graduated at the top of his class in political science at Boston University and was near the top of his class at Harvard Law. At five foot eight and 150 pounds, he is shorter than most but never lets anyone who matters believe that. His pure force of personality makes it clear that no one should ever think his shorter physical stature will be the subject of disrespect at any time.

Tom enters the travel gym, having overheard most of the conversation. He urges Jeb not to fall into the Andy racquetball trap and pleads with Andy to return to debate prep. Neither man listens.

"Tom, if I don't grab lunch in Silverstone One, I won't be able to complete my muscle build from this workout session. Just ask Jeb."

"I guess when a guy gets older, he gets real sensitive," Jeb jibes.

"I thought trainers were supposed to be supportive, positive influences," Tom argues.

"Well, if Andy will stop questioning my training methods, then I'll let up. Until then, all bets are off," Jeb counters.

"Since it appears I don't need to be here for this conversation about me, I am going to get my lunch. Toni is starting out with her garlic sautéed zucchini. You know, Toni has more recipes involving garlic than any other. I'm not sure if that is because she knows what I like or she makes what she likes. I guess it doesn't matter because garlic really is the source of most happiness. Don't you guys agree?"

"While I agree that a discussion of cuisine is always critical, Andy, maybe we can sneak in a little discussion of the fate of the world that will be the subject of a debate someday," Tom prompts.

"True, because if we don't save the planet from the ravages of war, the garlic crop could be put in jeopardy," Andy responds.

"If the public heard your priorities, Andy, I'm pretty sure you'd lose," Jeb observes.

"Not if the voters tasted Chef's garlic sautéed zucchini!" Andy debates.

"Alright, can we at least discuss Jackson's recent attack on your business history over lunch, Andy?" Tom asks.

Given Andy's massive victory in Iowa, Sen. Mike Jackson, one of Andy's primary competitors who did not compete in Iowa, decided to throw his entire war chest against Andy in New Hampshire and decided the best subject to focus on was Andy's business history.

Andy made his fortune in the content rights arena. He saw early on that the growth of wealth was going to be in intellectual property—the stuff you can't touch but is very valuable anyway: movies, photos, music, software, and books, for example. Andy decided to buy rights to these things and license them to others.

In the same vein, Andy also goes after those individuals who believe that republishing without permission or otherwise taking or using these properties without permission is acceptable. It is not acceptable as such use or takings is against the law. Andy also helps other owners protect their rights.

Andy's company, RightHouse, not only holds billions of dollars' worth of property, but also recovered billions of dollars against the infringers of those properties. RightHouse then expanded into content production, including movies, music, books, and software. RightHouse is the largest movie producer in the world, and Andy is at the helm of it.

The problem is that a large number of folks who feel unhindered by legal constraints and who like to take stuff without paying for it do not enjoy RightHouse coming after them and forcing them to pay for what they've stolen. They also don't care for the extra monies they have to pay as, effectively, a penalty. It is these folks, both Democrats and Republicans, whom Sen. Jackson is appealing to.

"Tom," Andy says while finishing his rack of lamb with a mustard glaze, "one, I just don't think there are that many voters out there who support theft, and two, I think there are a whole lot more who don't support it."

"I get that, but let's at least work on our response to this."

"Got it, but what's the latest on the Korean border?" Andy asks.

Interestingly enough, Andy's defense policy adviser, Robert Dempsey, also comes from strong Irish roots—this time, though, Chicago-Irish. Dempsey grew up in the former Mayor Daley's neighborhood in Chicago, a stronghold of Irish Americans. He is an Irish Catholic who went to DePaul University and Georgetown Law

School and yet really does not have much of a faith in the Catholic religion. To Dempsey, being Catholic is more of a cultural and social identification and practice than a strict religious adherence. Not entirely ironically, Dempsey, much like his often attributed but false namesake, is quite the boxer. He can fight with the best of them on an amateur basis in the ring and can intellectually fight toe-to-toe with them on a professional basis.

Dempsey, who is just getting started on French apple Pie à la Mode, joins in, "China has now amassed a total of 300,000 troops. They've also added a complement of tanks and armored carriers to the mix. Amazingly, they are now starting to amass another 200,000 troops on the Nam border. They are doing this while maintaining 500,000 troops on the Indian border and a healthy complement on the northern frontier. They are not happy with your Taiwan stance."

"When is Como going to China?" Tom asks Dempsey.

"It looks like next month, but with these Chinese provocations, no travel is particularly clear."

"What is Chen thinking?" Andy asks. "I mean, he's got two billion Indians to his south and is otherwise surrounded by Asian and European powers that are not supporting his antics."

"Well, China still does a lot of trade with those powers and is not without influence. Those powers are not going to attack China and would probably not come to Vietnam's aid if China tried to take Vietnam over. Heck, they might even let China go into Korea," Dempsey argues.

"And then there is the Taiwan deployment. What's the situation with Chinese naval movements in the area?"

Dempsey's concern is visible. "It's not good. It seems like every time you give a speech about recognizing Taiwan, they add another deployment. They have even been more threatening to the Philippines of late."

"Polling on these issues is split," Tom segues to the debate. "While there is that segment who just does not want conflict, there is the other side who can't stand how obnoxious China has been and wants to put an end to it. The good news: We are on the better side of the poll."

"Alright, well, we certainly have some points we need to make at this debate that might be a little hard to get across," Andy acknowledges, "but that's half the fun."

The New Hampshire debate has only three candidates in attendance: Andy, Mike Jackson, and Governor Laura McDonald, out of Florida. McDonald is not too far off the political spectrum from Andy and is a fierce competitor. Jackson is a more traditional Republican.

The debate moderator, Felicia Oswald, has spent years as the lead news anchor for PBS. Oswald is a pretty neutral journalist but secretly harbors a real liking of Andy's policies—and can't help but have a secret liking for Andy as well, who is the world's most eligible bachelor.

Felicia starts the debate. "Welcome to the Republican primary New Hampshire debate. My name is Felicia Oswald, and I will be tonight's moderator. Tonight's debate may be a little different from what you are accustomed to. I will attempt to keep the flow going by asking follow-up questions to the candidates and will do my best to ensure they answer the questions being asked. I ask the audience to hold their applause to two occasions: soon, when I introduce the candidates, and at the very end, when the debate has concluded. Now, please welcome the candidates."

With that, McDonald enters the stage first, followed by Jackson and then Andy.

"The first question is to Senator Jackson. Senator, you are against abortion except in the context of rape. Please explain whether you believe that a toddler who was born as a result of rape may be murdered without consequence."

Jackson replies, "That's a ridiculous question. Of course you can't kill a child after it has been born, regardless of the circumstance."

Oswald follows up, "OK, then what about a minute before birth? Can you abort the human life then?"

Jackson responds, "Well, no, that would be about the same as right after birth."

Oswald adds, "OK, where do you draw the line—three months after conception, six months?"

A visibly flustered Jackson tries to answer with, "Well, it's hard to draw any line in the sand, Felicia. I just think we should have a rape exception."

Oswald concludes, "Well, Senator, I don't think you have answered the question, but I need to move on. Governor McDonald, the next question is for you. The candidates on the Democratic side are calling for immigration amnesty, in other words, allowing the thirty million undocumented immigrants to be able to gain citizenship. What is your position?"

"I'm against amnesty at any level. There needs to be fundamental respect for our borders, and these so-called 'immigrants' came over the border without permission."

"So, do you want to send them back where they came from?"

"Well, I believe we, as a country, have every right to do so, but not at the cost of creating problems for ourselves. That's a lot of money we're talking about in terms of tracking them down and sending them back. It is enough that we do it on an incremental basis and have them live under the fear of deportation."

"Mr. Brock, what's your position on this question?" Oswald asks.

"Most, if not all, of these immigrants have formed a substantial bond with our nation. Heck, a substantial amount of positive economic activity is associated with these folks. While I agree with my colleague, Ms. McDonald, that our borders need to be respected, I believe that a more rational policy would be to continue to enforce border security but have a path toward citizenship for the people who are here and are positively contributing to society. We could then pass some fundamental and substantial citizenship requirements, have them pay a tax on the illegal nature in which they arrived, and otherwise have them demonstrate that they deserve to be here. If those measures are satisfied, then our nation will be better for it. As you see from the demographic experience of first Japan and then China, the lack of reasonable attention to population growth has, in the case of Japan, seriously diminished their growth as a nation and, in the case of China, created such societal pressures that they are looking outward to capture some sense of progress. Our immigrants continue to be a source of strength for our country, and both logic and a sense of humanity demand that we should recognize the same."

"OK, let's take this up a notch. Mr. Jackson, DNA evidence demonstrated last week that Noel Valenzuela was falsely convicted of murder and put to death in the electric chair. You are a proponent of the death penalty. What do you say to Mr. Valenzuela's family, who is in the audience with us today?"

"Our criminal justice system is imperfect, and I mourn the loss of Mr. Valenzuela. I would only ask the family to remember Heidi Sparks, who was raped and murdered by two men last year, who both happened to be named Valenzuela. There was video evidence of what they did. I saw the video. Unfortunately, certain members of her family saw the video. What happened to her was horrific, and those two individuals who committed that horror did not deserve to live. It would be unjust for them to live after what they did. That is why I am for the death penalty under the right circumstances."

"Mr. Brock, do you agree?"

"Yes and no. I agree that those who commit the kind of heinous crimes that Mr. Jackson just described do not deserve to live. I disagree that the government has the right to take those lives for the very reason that I do not trust the government, or anyone, to be perfect in effecting the execution. It's also a slippery slope. Let's say that the death penalty is instituted for treason. Now, I agree that treason is a serious crime, but it is also subject to too much abuse by those in positions of authority. People can get framed for all kinds of things. Until we have a perfect system for adjudicating fault, we cannot have the death penalty."

"So, Mr. Brock, I regret to say that we all know about the circumstances of your wife. You often appeal to the raw logic of circumstances. In fact, I think I've heard you use the word 'logic' more than any presidential candidate in history. Are you going to apply raw logic to those circumstances and not conclude that they are the exception?"

At the mention of his wife, Andy's body stiffens, and he hesitates considerably before answering. "A president cannot have double standards. Yes, a drunk driver crashed into my wife's car on the expressway and killed her. Yes, I cannot ever forgive that man as a husband. Stephanie was and is the love of my life. We had a marriage that others could only dream of. As a man, I cannot forgive him. As a president, I could not justify a double standard of applying the death penalty even in the case of my and my wife's extreme personal tragedy. I hope we can put this issue to rest. I am not a big fan of dwelling on my personal life in terms of discussing policy. I understand it is necessary at times, but I would ask that this incredibly painful memory and circumstance not continue to be the subject of discussion. My wife's life should be honored. She was a great woman. Her death is something of my own personal mourning, and I ask that it remain there. I do apply logic as much as possible, but not in an inhuman manner. However, it would be illogical and unfair to have a double standard."

Utter silence falls over the auditorium, lasting for an unusually long period for a debate. Finally, the moderator indicates that a new subject is up for inquiry.

"Ms. McDonald, under what circumstances, if any, would you call for a preemptive nuclear strike against one of our adversaries?"

"There are circumstances, but the best policy is not to show our cards to anyone and describe the circumstances of when we take military action. Unpredictability is critical in all phases of military involvement. The worst thing we can do is telegraph our intentions to our adversaries just to win some points in a presidential debate."

"Do you agree, Mr. Jackson?"

"I do, actually. Pounding our chest now for the sake of winning some votes is what politicians do. Good public servants, and presidents, do what is right. And what is right is to not signal to our adversaries under what specific circumstances we would do a preemptive strike. We need to keep the option open, but not describe the circumstances under which we would exercise that option."

"Well, Mr. Brock, your colleagues seem pretty firm on this point. May we assume you agree with them?"

"No. In many circumstances, I would agree with my esteemed competition. Keeping your enemies guessing is often a good policy. But think about this one: If your adversary thinks you might make a preemptive strike and they don't know when you'll do it, then they have no choice but to plan for a preemptive strike themselves. Then it comes down to who plans best in making a preemptive strike. We have relied on mutually assured destruction for a long time. Our enemies know that if they push the button, then we will push ours. The better policy is to tell our adversaries to not ever, ever push that button. Don't ever think about a first strike. You don't need to because we will never be the ones that will do it to you. Our nukes are a defensive mechanism only.

"Moreover, no one wins in a nuclear war. The more likely result is total global devastation. We only keep nukes to ensure that some idiot on the other side never believes they can successfully deploy them.

"Lastly, our strategic nuclear defense is superb. We have finally achieved the Star Wars defense that Ronald Reagan dreamed of. Now, while we can probably defend ourselves against direct hits, that does not mean the radiation residue that might occur and might stay in the atmosphere, depending upon the nature of the attack, would not create devastating problems for the globe. Ironically, an attack on us would probably come back to haunt the attacker as much as us, given that the possible radiation cloud, once again, depending on how the attack went, could travel as much to the attacker as stay over us.

"We just need to play this right and not motivate any enemy to believe they need to strike first. The mere threat of a preemptive strike that my colleagues on this stage make may very well be the trigger our adversaries use to launch their own nukes first."

At Andy's last answer, despite being instructed not to applaud during the debate, not only did the audience applaud, but they stood up and cheered – for five minutes. While McDonald did not do horribly, Jackson was a train wreck. That being said, Andy's answers and confident presentation completely destroyed both of them. The debate was effectively over, and every pundit concluded afterward that the nomination for president was in Andy's complete control. Only a complete strategic flop or something hidden in Andy's closet would allow anyone to defeat him at this point.

CHAPTER 5

A COMPETING INTEREST

D ressed in a cashmere-and-silk-blend sweater and modal pants, the man says, "Well, well, Brock seems unstoppable. You'll agree he will put us all out of business, right, Esteban?"

"First, I have to say you look incredibly comfortable in what you have on, but without one of my cigars, it's just not a completed effort at luxury. That being said, I'm pretty sure you are not too worried about my business, but that his consolidation of power with his policies will likely put you out of the kind of business you do."

"You know, most men would not comment on another man's wardrobe unless they are truly confident in their manhood. I am comfortable, and if more men took the time to understand how to dress, then they would not be so stressed. It is amazing how modal feels against the skin. However, we did not come here to talk about fabric choices. It is true that Brock threatens my business, and that is why I have brought you fine people together. We need to stop him. Of course, it can't get back to us, and he can't become a martyr."

Ping adds, "First, I'm not sure we have control over whether he becomes a martyr, but we should be able to control whether it gets back to us. By the way, whoever set this meeting up in Makati did a great job. Being so close to the Peninsula Hotel has made the trip all the more worthwhile. Their service is really excellent, as is their food. By the way, did you buy those clothes here in Makati?"

"We needed somewhere convenient that was on the way back from China for Parisi and otherwise allowed for confidentiality. Frankly, I also like the service, the food, and that I can still get legitimate massages from very pretty ladies in my hotel room for less than ten bucks an hour. Now, I'm not saying the massages do not conclude in a very pleasing manner, but they are designed to be legitimate. By the way, enough about the clothes."

Parisi adds, "So, we understand that what I'm concerned about, along with the very powerful group I represent, is that Brock's ascension to power will likely mean war, and that is not good for anyone. I am a patriot. I don't believe in the kind of thing we are discussing, generally speaking. But if we are talking about risking the future of the US, as well as the world, then I think we need to take action. Heck, I dislike the Chinese government as much as the next guy, but going to war with them is not a bright move."

Weinstein, who is preoccupied with finishing his menudo, says with half a mouthful, "I concede that Makati was a great location, and by the way, the fact they added the perfect mix of tomatoes and garlic to this menudo is spectacular. Less importantly, the man will seriously eat into our business profits—he's the only guy who can possibly bring us to war and actually reduce military expenditures. He's really pissing me off. That being said, you should have come to me about your clothing purchases. If you think for one minute that a man with my background can't find bargains even on luxury, then you should think again."

"Jesus, enough about the clothes already. Anyway, I'm going to give the go-ahead on this. It has to look like a nutcase hit, so it's not like we are using a paramilitary group. I put the likelihood of success on this operation at seventy-five percent. We do have Plan B, however."

CHAPTER 6

A DATE

A ndy wins New Hampshire handily.

McDonald withdraws from the campaign as she really only had a chance of capturing a vote from the female majority, which is now poised for a landslide in Andy's favor. The problem is that McDonald's target female vote ends up liking Andy both on policy grounds and for a handful of more conspicuous reasons.

Jackson captures enough of the traditional Republican vote to hang on in hopes to get more of the conservative Southern vote in the upcoming primaries.

"So," Lisa says, "Jackson basically is handing Nevada to you."

"Yes, it looks like he's putting all of his eggs in South Carolina. You know this means we might have a little time this weekend to work on a keynote speech for South Carolina."

"You are typically not this obvious. Of course we need to work on that speech, and we should do it this weekend as we typically would do, and when I say 'we,' I mean 'me.'"

"Whoa, you aren't giving me any credit for speech development participation?"

Lisa blushes. "No, I just mean that if you were implying I was unaware of the need to put pen to paper this weekend, well, I was aware."

Andy is not unaware of anything. He is not unaware that Lisa looks particularly amazing today in True Religion jeans, his favorite on her, with the buttons on each back pocket to accent her ass. She has unabashedly paired them with a white crop top. True to her attitude toward society, which matched Andy's views, she also refuses to wear a bra. Her wardrobe choice is often the subject of news commentary, but that made Lisa's position even stronger. Regardless of that debate, Andy is the current beneficiary of Lisa's stance.

Like Andy, Lisa is steadfast in her gym routine. She shares Andy's personal trainer and uses the road gym when she isn't busy managing one of her numerous responsibilities. Lisa's arms are toned, her legs are amazing, and she has rock-hard abs to go with them. Like many successful A-type personalities, she works hard and plays hard.

While nothing has happened between Andy and Lisa since she joined the team, given Andy's and Lisa's personalities, there was likely little hope of some attraction not being there.

"Lisa, I think it is time we expressed some thoughts we have both been thinking, but as, arguably, your boss, I have to be real careful here, and I hope you'll make it a little easier for me."

"Well, Andy, you are more than just arguably my boss: you are my boss, and I don't know what you are saying I have been making hard."

Andy thinks but does not say exactly what she has been making hard.

"So, it's not going to be easy. OK, Lisa, I like you and feel a growing connection. I want to take you to Chicago this weekend, have an official date, and maybe get a little work in on the speech if that's OK with you."

Lisa finds Andy attractive but never imagined that the soon-to-be most powerful man in the world—maybe the most powerful man in history—would find a woman twenty years his junior to be someone he could see himself with. Maybe she did subconsciously avoid personal interactions. She's thought about the attraction for some time, but she never imagined that anything could happen. Then there's the political ramifications of dating him and what would happen if the "date" did not go well. Would she lose her job? On the other hand, the chance to actually be with Andy was too hard to pass up for a woman like Lisa: go for it all or go home.

"Andy, I'm just not sure that you dating me will be safe for your candidacy. Listen, there are a billion women out there who would die to go on a date with you, and I'm probably understating that number by several billion."

"I'm not interested in other women. I'm not built like that. It's not like I'm going to go on a dating app or hit the bar scene. Throughout my life, I have dated very few women and always dated one at a time. The only women I have ever dated were women whom I came to know through the course of my life, not by way of some hookup. I do know we have a connection. You are amazing, in every which way. And I know there would be at least two billion men who would kill to go on a date with you, and I'm probably understating that by a great margin. I also don't give a damn about what people think of my personal dating habits. My personal life is my personal life. I have nothing to hide, and I am not going to do a poll to determine whether I can go on a date with you."

As usual, Andy made a compelling argument. Lisa wonders how she could possibly think she would not be persuaded by the most persuasive man on the planet. She is also intrigued by what this date would be about.

"So, what do I need to bring with me to Chicago in terms of clothes?"

"I took the liberty of placing some recently purchased items in a suitcase, all of which should be to your liking."

"What?! That seems a little presumptuous and arrogant."

"C'mon, Lisa, you are worth the risk. I'm worth billions, and you are going to begrudge me a little convenience in packing for you ahead of time?"

"Alright, but the clothes better fit."

"You're a size 8 for pants and a medium up top, right?"

With Lisa being, at the largest, an extra small everywhere, she has no response at this point but to throw a cushion at Andy.

"We are wheels up at 10:00 a.m."

Andy and Lisa fly to Chicago on Andy's private plane. From Midway, they drive in Andy's limo to his penthouse condo on the eighty-seventh floor of the new Marina City in Downtown Chicago, which is located right on the river. The old Marina City has been completely rebuilt. Instead of two corncob towers made of deteriorating concrete, the new Marina City comprises of two gleaming glass and steel towers with a state-of-the-art marina underneath—which, of course, houses Andy's yacht.

Lisa wonders about the proposed sleeping arrangements and is not disappointed. Andy shows her to her bedroom, which has a view of the Loop and the river going west. To say the bedroom was stunning is breathtakingly unfair. The floors are marble but with the softest rugs on the market. The technology in the bedroom was to be expected—voice-automated lighting, shades, temperature, audio, television, and service. If Lisa wants crepes, all she would have to do is speak, and the building's caterers would appear within half an hour with the most delicious crepes she could desire.

So far, it has been the best "date" she has ever had, and it really hasn't even started yet.

Lisa opens her suitcase and finds not only every amenity she might need but also exactly the kind of apparel she would choose if she had weeks to shop at her favorite stores. The sweaters are cashmere-silk blends, and the leggings are modal, to name a few items. Lisa decides on a white sweater that does nothing to hide her nipples and black leggings that do everything to show off her form.

Despite having caterers for room service from probably one of the best gourmet restaurants in the city, Andy likes to go out.

Lisa walked out of her bedroom, and Andy could not help but react to her appearance, which Lisa noticed. Despite the obvious reaction, Andy is also hungry.

"I hope you are hungry. May we step out to eat?"

"Absolutely. Where do you have in mind?"

"Well, it is one of my favorite places that creates real problems with making choices—I have trouble deciding what to order at times, so I am going to solve the problem another way."

"Hmmm, I don't doubt that you have a solution, but I'll just wait and see what's going on."

Andy has a first-floor garage that houses several of his vehicles. On this occasion, he chooses a twenty-five-foot Destiny RV, which has a full-sized bathroom, Murphy bed, lounge seating for meals, a full kitchen, and some of the best imaginable seating for both driver and passenger. While the Destiny is not as large as the Silverstone, it is no slouch with its home-theater seating and home-theater audio-visual capabilities.

Andy and Lisa head to the drive-through at Luigi's in River North. Strangely enough, it is a known fact that this restaurant, where you get your food by standing in line, has the best hot dogs, chili, pasta, bread, and chocolate cake you can find. Andy solves the problem of having to choose by ordering everything he has a craving for. After ordering and filling up the RV, the two depart from Luigi's and head south. While the drive was short, it was long enough to fill the vehicle with the delicious scents of the food placed in the kitchen. Andy finds a spot in Grant Park, and they make their way to the dining table in the RV together.

"Andy, this is delicious. You know, you never cease to surprise me. I half expected some high-end restaurant, but I should have known better."

"Lisa, it is your turn to make a move. You're keeping me waiting."

"Listen, this food is amazing, and it's unfair to push me to move when I'm preoccupied with my chili."

Andy and Lisa are playing Scrabble on Andy's internet pad during lunch. They made a deal—whoever won was then able to ask the other to do a task. Any task that is lawful was on the table.

Lisa wins.

"OK, what's it going to be?" Andy asks.

"I want to hear you sing tonight. Karaoke at the Red Toad— your song, 'My Kind of Town.'"

Lisa, being from Chicago, loves the sound of Sinatra. She cannot wait to hear Andy sing it, as it is one of her favorites.

"Well, for someone concerned about keeping us a bit of a secret, me singing at the Red Toad tonight is hardly inconspicuous."

"I've had a change of heart. If we are going to do this, then we are going to do it."

Having finished their lunch and game of Scrabble, Andy decides it is time to return to his penthouse. In Andy's spa room, two massage therapists are set up and are waiting to provide a shiatsu-Swedish combination couple's massage for the two of them. That massage lasts two hours. Lisa was in desperate need of a good pampering.

Two hours had flown by without either of them realizing the time. After freshening up, Andy and Lisa head to dinner at the top of the new Worthington Building, a restaurant named "The 105th," for an obvious reason.

Andy, donning a white turtleneck and black suit, expertly matches Lisa. Andy strategically provided her with a tight, black mini-dress through her suitcase. Lisa does not complain, and neither does Andy.

At this point, the press had been made aware of the situation, and the photojournalists had their dream evening ahead of them.

From dinner, they make their way to the Red Toad. It is not every day that restaurants or lounges host a celebrity of Andy's status. That is particularly true for karaoke venues. The Red Toad cannot contain itself. Despite Andy being a Republican and the Democrats still having a stronghold on Chicago, Chicagoans know that Andy is a different type of Republican, and they love him for it. He also loves Chicagoans. This is, then, a perfect storm of loving.

Andy, of course, does not have to wait long for his turn to sing. The Red Toad's new audio system is concert-level in quality, and Andy's version of "My Kind of Town" sounds amazing. If there are undecided Chicago voters in the restaurant before hearing Andy sing, they are no longer ambivalent afterward.

Lisa and Andy are also now known as an item, and they are only half-done with their "date."

Lisa knew that dating Andy was going to be amazing, but the reality was finally starting to sink in. She cannot help but love the man, even though they have more to learn about each other. Lisa appreciates that very few men, if any, buy their date a suitcase worth of clothes and amenities, fly them on a private plane to Chicago, take them out for great meals, arrange for them to have a massage, and then sing like Sinatra during the evening. This isn't a date; it is the best frickin' day of her life with a man who treats her like a queen. He's funny, charming, and sexy to boot. *Enough!* she thinks. Her constant other thought is: *Can this be happening?*

Andy starts to realize that asking Lisa out was a great decision. She is smart, beautiful, considerate, charming, and sexy. Damn, does she take his breath away. Moving on after his wife's accident has been tough, but with loyal, steadfast women like Lisa at his side, Andy is feeling more assured than he has in a long time.

Focusing on the South Carolina speech this weekend will be challenging for sure, but if any couple can multitask, it's them.

CHAPTER 7

SOUTH CAROLINA

S omehow, by the end of the weekend, Andy and Lisa polished off the speech for the South Carolina stop of the campaign trail. Together, they make a formidable team and thoroughly enjoy the work, as well as the time spent together.

Without a shadow of a doubt, the press is having a field day. The world's most eligible bachelor is courting a gorgeous staff member. It is sexy, politically dangerous, and right in front of them.

This is also all in the environment of having to win the conservative vote in South Carolina. While Andy is well positioned in the general election to carry crossover and independent votes in South Carolina, the more conservative primary vote is another matter altogether.

Andy refuses to concede that vote and believes that his policy positions are designed, at least in part, to carry that conservative vote.

Lisa was often with Andy on the campaign trail but now is a fixture by his side. She is on the podium with Andy in the auditorium in Charleston, and the plan is for her to uncharacteristically join Andy at the lectern right after his speech. That has never happened before. Andy is not just not hiding Lisa; he is putting the relationship right out front.

The speech Lisa wrote for Andy is magnificent and beautifully targeted for the South Carolina audience.

Andy delivers it not just like a pro but with a level of conviction and passion that comes right through the TV into voters' living rooms.

"Mr. Jackson argues I'm too moderate for South Carolina. Really? Mr. Jackson is prepared to back down to China. Is that conservative? Mr. Jackson does not have faith in our military to deal with the Chinese threat. Is that conservative?

"Are my policies new? Yes. That does not make them outside the line of the Republican Party. We believe that the government's role should be appropriately limited. We believe in the free market. We believe that government should not involve itself in our personal lives any more than is absolutely required. These are conservative ideals.

"Government involvement in education is not a change. Public education is critical. We just have to do it right.

"Drug decriminalization is a new policy, but it makes sense that the government should not control what we do. Government, however, should tax it, educate against it, and take the criminal element out of controlling it.

"I'm the true conservative. I believe that limited government should come in where necessary to improve our lives, but for the most part, stay out of our lives. I believe that government should limit the regulation of our lives and instead incentivize positive behavior.

"I also happen to believe that our criminal justice system is not only broken, but completely missing the point. My vision is not to have prisons that cost us a ridiculous amount of money. Create reform communities where convicts are offered the opportunity to be provided housing in a farming environment. They will be responsible for growing food in a commune. They will be responsible for making clothes. The food and clothes they grow and make will not only feed and clothe themselves but will also be given to homeless folks across the country. Next to the reform communities will be communities where the homeless will be provided the opportunity for a new life. These communities will be in the previously barren Southwest desert areas that will be the subject of the new irrigation programs by way of water pipelines from the Midwest and by irrigation lines from the Pacific—all solar-powered. This will save conservative voters money. This will make conservative voters safer.

"Do I just stay put with traditional Republican policies? No. Do I just sit back and complain about liberal Democrats? No. I'm going to take it to another level. I know you are going to join me. There is a new Republican majority out there. Heck, there is a new America out there. I just happen to be a Republican because that's where my policies are best seen. But I want every vote in America, and I intend to fight for each of them.

"Now, I know the folks in South Carolina have been loyal to the traditional Republican Party. I know some of my ideas are mixing things up. I also know that the people of South Carolina are smart enough to know that not only do we need to be strong against China, but we need to make our country as strong as it can be. Join me. We will win, and the 'we' will be America."

The room goes crazy, though it is not clear what they appreciate more: what he has said or the way he has said it. Andy has this ability to move people. Reagan was seen as a great communicator with a quiet manner about him that was very appealing. Andy modulates his voice in just the right way and at the right time. His vocal prowess makes it almost impossible not to be moved.

The gunman is uninterested in Andy's speech. He was also not informed that Lisa was going to join Andy at the lectern after the speech. The gunman is instructed to take the shot at the time of the pandemonium at the end of the speech. This is out of courtesy to the gunman— to give him a chance to hide and get away. Holding Andy in his sights, pandemonium is beginning. The gunman is actually concerned about being seen by the crowd, now engaged in an activity that was not predicted: They are not rioting with joy, but it is close. The gunman knows he needs to act. Twenty million dollars is on the line if he gets the job done today. The gunman does not see Lisa stand to the side of Andy just as he takes the shot. Thankfully, he thinks he gets Andy even though Lisa is somewhat in the way. Unfortunately for Lisa, he also gets her.

CHAPTER 8

TIME TO GO IN

"Well, this changes the dynamic of how and when I go in," says Rein.

"I would like to say they would never be so stupid as to try to kill humanity's best chance for survival and success, but given their history, I'm not surprised. Just imagine if Lincoln, Martin Luther King Jr., and Jack and Bobby Kennedy all lived to see it through to the end of their careers," says Cliven.

Cliven is one of Rein's most cherished colleagues. He is recognized on Merk as one of the greatest writers on the subject of new world inclusion. His books on the subject are considered nearly doctrinal. Cliven's manner of speaking is akin to that of William F. Buckley Jr.—slow, methodical, articulate, and compelling. Rein once showed Cliven a recording of William F. Buckley Jr., and Cliven was immediately taken with the Earthman's arguments and comportment.

Sorcen is Cliven's near twin in demeanor. Another intellectual, Sorcen prides himself on his compassion as much as his logic.

"The question is whether Earth deserves our attention at this point, given what they have done. They have an incredible generational leader, and they try to kill him. He's not just generational. If his policies are enacted, he has the chance of transforming his country and maybe the world," says Sorcen.

"Hold on, guys, we have had our own development problems over time within the Merk," Rein observes. "You know this.

Moreover, the fact that Andy got as far as he did means that they are prepared to recognize the intelligence needed to take the next step. I mean, he is absolutely controlling the election. He is winning primary voters at a greater percentage than anyone in history in a contested environment. The people are reacting. Let's not give up on them. Andy's alive. Lisa is dead. Andy not only needs a protector but a speechwriter. I can do both."

"Rein, I understand we don't have the constraints of some kind of Prime Directive, but don't you think that writing his speeches is a little aggressive? I mean, you will be smack in the middle of everything, then likely asked into the administration. I think we may be a little myopic here, right?" asks Cliven.

"Listen, they're Andy's ideas and philosophies, so if I'm only putting them down into appropriate words, then I don't think that's such a big deal. Anyway, the understanding is that Andy controls the ultimate draft anyway, and I would not expect that to change with me. I'm not going to motivate him on any policy change or policy position. Of course, that is if I even succeed in having him hire me as the speechwriter. As far as being part of the administration, that's far down the road, and I never have to accept such an offer. I can claim I want to go back into academia."

Cliven and Sorcen look at each other and laugh at that. Not only is Rein one of the most compelling females in the galaxy from an intellectual and sensual perspective, but she also has an X factor that everyone realizes is impossible not to want to be around. If Andy can resist Rein, that would be a first.

Sorcen responds, "You'll not only get the job, but he'll beg you to be part of his administration."

"Well, maybe, but anyway, in that regard, I assume my credentials are in order, and we have configured all security systems as well?" Rein asks.

"Yes," Marsen, the group's logistics manager, answers. "Thankfully, the acclimation time you put in at the University of Chicago and then at Stanford is really going to pay dividends now. The degrees you received, even in the record time you received them, are relevant enough to allow you to claim you are qualified to be a speechwriter, and part of that reason is that a speechwriter does not come with a specific degree requirement. Of course, the donations you have made to those institutions aren't hurting anything as well. Independently, your real Merkian education, of course, makes your Earth studies child's play by comparison. The CV is contained within your travel packet. Six security agents will be within proximity at all times on a three-way rotation. Their names are also in the travel packet. We should not have let the attack on Andy happen, and nothing like that will occur again unless something truly unforeseen and utterly weird strikes."

"Thanks, Marsen. Good job, as usual. The only question is whether I can stand to be constrained, again, by all the clothes they wear on Earth. I really loved Lisa's wardrobe, but even that was a bit much for me. During my acclimation period, I was able to get away with a lot, but I wasn't in front of the cameras then. It was also a bit of fun creating some real tension with my acclimation wardrobe. While I understood I did not want to be unduly noticed, I was happy to have a little more freedom, and I did not risk too much. Now, it appears I will need to be more conservative. At least, thanks to Lisa and her trailblazer attitude, I won't have to deal with wearing a bra."

CHAPTER 9

RECOVERY

"**M**r. Brock, you really should rest another day. Even though you were shot in the buttocks, we need to monitor you for any signs of infection," the doctor says.

"I'm here one more day, but that does not mean we don't work the issues from this room. Tom, has Stacy started with what we need to do for Lisa?"

"Yes, Andy, while her family was not exactly poor, Stacy has put together the financial package for everything from the funeral to a full retirement plan for every blood relative we could find, and when I say retirement, I mean that each one could retire today."

Stacy is Andy's chief administrative assistant and has assumed the same role within Andy's companies for years. While some would call her a personal assistant at some level, Stacy's business acumen makes her much more than that. The other reason not to call Stacy a personal assistant is that Andy maintains two personal assistants who divide various functions not so intimately involved with business matters.

"Tom, where is . . ."

"I'm right here. I was just in the hallway clarifying with the doctor that we have set up medical facilities at your home and office that make this hospital look like a MASH unit. I know you want out of here, and it will happen quite smoothly tomorrow," Stacy says.

"Tom, what's the status of the campaign?"

"Your already high numbers are now through the roof. At this point, there is really nothing left but the convention and to pick a VP. Jackson dropped out after you won South Carolina, and that really leaves no one else. I mean, you should still show up in some of the rest of the states, but it's effectively over. You were already winning, but the circumstances of the attack have had the result of having even people who were marginal come over to your camp. I guess it's human nature to treat you sympathetically or heroically in this situation."

"Well, as we are going to the convention, I will need to make a speech, and while I have written my own speeches in the past, I have become accustomed to having a speech writer. No matter how hard it is for me to talk about it, it is something we need to address."

"Andy, I'm glad you brought it up because I honestly did not know how to do it, but now that you have brought it up, I have identified a few candidates for the position," Tom says.

"I have a schedule of interviews set for tomorrow," Stacy interrupts. "There is one candidate whom I think you will find very compelling."

"I can't imagine that after losing Lisa, I'll find any candidate compelling. Tell me a little about this candidate."

"First of all, when I video-conferenced with her, it was the most amazing audio-visual experience I ever had in a videoconference. The signal was crystal clear, the audio was studio quality, and the background was an unbelievably futuristic setting. It was like she was on some kind of movie set. I wanted to focus on the substance of the interview and did not ask about these environmental attributes, but they were spectacular."

"That's real interesting, Stacy, but are you willing to tell me anything about this candidate?"

"Her credentials are impeccable and her background check is pristine. Her articulation is superb, her writing samples make your own speechwriting skills look like you draft in crayon, she's funny, and, even though I'm not into women, I'm sure any man alive will find her gorgeous."

"Crayon, huh?"

"Well, maybe I overstated that. You are not a bad speechwriter, as far as I've seen."

"Tom, have you whittled the total candidates down to three at least?"

"Yes, but I believe Stacy's gorgeous lady is the only one you need to interview."

"What's going on here? Is she really that good?"

"Yes," Tom and Stacy say at the same time.

"Stacy, what's the status of the gunman?"

"He got away from the auditorium, but the FBI tracked him down. He's dead. They found a suicide note complaining about Taiwan. The thought is that it was a fake note. The further thought is that it was and is a conspiracy. The FBI and Secret Service have enhanced security beyond anything ever seen before."

"You are pissing off so many vested interests out there that it does not even make sense to spend time figuring out which group wants you taken out," Tom observes.

"I agree; let's let the security folks do their job.

"All right, well, let's get me out of here tomorrow, and then I'll meet this wonder of a person you guys are bragging about."

CHAPTER 10

PLAN B

"Any real chance they can trace the gunman back to us?"

"Not really. I don't think they'll buy the suicide note, but we covered our tracks really well."

"Have you found your subject for Plan B?"

"Yes, and I have high hopes. I think even the unsuccessful Plan A will provide the means for a successful Plan B."

"OK, well, let's get it done right this time. It's a shame he wore a vest, and that woman got in the way. How lucky to just get shot where he did. It is not ironic. The guy is really a pain in the ass, even his own."

"By the way, could you pass me over more of the adobo? You know, I may never want to leave the Philippines, given the food and the massages."

"Well, we need to move out soon if Plan B is going to work."

CHAPTER 11

THE INTERVIEW

om escorts Rein to Andy's quarters, where he reads over the most recent edition of the *Chicago Tribune*. Still recovering, he has all of his medical facilities stationed in the room across the hall. Despite his doctor's suggestions, he remains firm that he will hold all work-related matters in his library. "Mr. Brock, I'd like you to meet Miss Annie Chandler."

Rein enters the luxuriously appointed room. Andy somewhat sits and somewhat reclines on a chaise lounge. Rein is invited to sit across from Andy on a well-appointed oversized leather chair.

"Mr. Brock, it is a great honor to meet you," Rein says.

"Forgive me for not getting up and for my posture as I am recovering from a shot in the butt."

"No apologies needed. I am sorry for your loss and your circumstance."

"I've heard a lot about you already, Miss Chandler. So, you have degrees from the University of Chicago and Stanford. Which institution did you prefer?"

"You may think this is pandering, but I honestly preferred Chicago only because I preferred that city over the other. That is not to say the Bay Area isn't great. I just liked the Midwestern feel better, and strangely enough, I love snow."

"How closely have you followed my policy positions?"

"I would like to believe there is very little I don't know about your policy positions."

"Hmmm. So, what's my view on abortion?"

"You believe, effectively, that both sides are wrong: We need to respect both the human life inside the mother's body and respect the mother's rights, and ask such removal of the baby can occur at any time so long as that removal does not occur in a manner to diminish the then-existing life prospects of the baby."

"I'm not sure I could have said it any better. How about prostitution?"

"Once again, a person should be allowed to do with their body what they will. Government does not have the right to moralize about sexual conduct. What I haven't heard you advocate is that such a position is grounded in the First Amendment."

"Well, then, you haven't heard everything as I believe that the expression rights and no establishment clauses directly relate to that position. You did pretty well, though. OK, how about tax increases?"

"You believe we are taxed enough. Government needs to become more efficient and smarter. Period."

"How do you feel about my policies?"

"They are magnificent."

"I take it you do not care to elaborate."

"Any elaboration would be redundant."

"Is there any policy position you disagree with?"

"No."

"For a speechwriter, you are a lady of very few words."

"The best speech is punchy and pithy."

"What's your favorite book?"

"*Ender's Game.*"

"What's your favorite movie?"

"*The Sound of Music.*"

"If you could go back in time just once and meet one person, who would it be?"

"Jesus Christ."

"Why?"

"I'd want to get a better sense of how much of the story was true."

"How do you feel about Lisa's death? In other words, do you have any fear of being around me?"

"That was really two questions. The answer to the first is I thought it was horrific and gut-wrenchingly sad, and the answer to the second is I have no fear of being around you. You are pursuing exactly what this country and this world needs."

"Do you think it wrong of me to have dated Lisa?"

"No."

"Do you have any questions for me?"

"Yes, why do you need me, given that it is clear that you are fully capable of writing and giving great speeches?"

"I'm capable of doing a lot of tasks that I delegate. A good leader delegates as much as possible."

"What's your favorite book?"

"*Dune.*"

"Why?"

"Fear is the mind-killer."

"What's your favorite movie?"

"*Patton.*"

"Why?"

"Perfect matching of actor, script, director, and story. I also liked some of his approaches."

"I liked that movie as well. I guess I only have one last question: Am I hired?"

"Yes."

"Then I guess I have one final question: When do I start?"

"About fifteen minutes ago."

CHAPTER 12

MERK'S CHINA

The aftermath of the interview left Rein reeling. Meeting Andy was an entirely weird experience for her. How is it that an Earthling is not only so compelling, but also such a match? They didn't just meet; they collided metaphysically. Rein finds herself a bit distracted.

As part of being distracted, Rein's mind flows in a random pattern, which is unusual for her. As part of her random thoughts, while preparing to return briefly to the ship, Rein also thinks about how silly the construct of the transporter system was in *Star Trek*. First of all, the notion that technology will deconstitute and then reconstitute animate matter is just scientifically nonsensical. It would require effective death and then rebirth. The truth about how people are transported is that they are closer to folding space. What is, however, somewhat consistent is defining the matter that is the subject of the fold. Merk technicians and physicists don't actually understand why it is not good to transport inanimate matter with animate matter, but that is just how it works. The transport of both animate matter and inanimate matter is possible, but there is also a risk of transport residue, and therefore, it is not a good practice. If absolutely necessary, one could transport fully clothed, but it is best not to do that as a matter of habit. Part of the problem is suspected to be the relocation of matter within a defined space and ensuring said relocation does not occupy the same space within the transport context. While FoldSpace obviously occurs at a larger scale and transports mass structures and the people within, the technology of the Send and mass transport FoldSpace operates a bit differently in the microcosm application. In any event, no Send generally occurs when a person carries a weapon or wears clothes. Using the Sender thus requires nudity, which is not a problem for any Merk, so long as the places traveled are reasonably temperate. Regardless, a Send requires an immediately subsequent Send for provisions along with clothing.

In any event, Rein uses the Sender to attend a critical meeting back on the ship. The Send Room on the ship is temperate, and the Send Crew stands ready to provision with clothing any person who is the subject of a Send who desires clothing before heading back to their respective quarters—unless, for some reason, there is an immediate second Send with the clothes removed pre-Send.

Generally speaking, the ship is temperate enough not to require clothing, although most people find wearing some clothing to be more comfortable than constant nudity. Clothing is also required in all food preparation and food consumption areas, for obvious reasons. Other than that, however, there is no mandate that clothing be worn in any Merk location—shipside or otherwise.

Not entirely coincidentally, the Merk discovered the Send technology fairly contemporaneously with faster-than-light (FTL) travel. Merk learned that that was true for other advanced FTL worlds. What is also true about most FTL worlds is that they are not only advanced, but indeed civilized. In other words, they are smart enough to understand that conflict is not productive.

The Davark is, unfortunately, an FTL world that does not share the customary belief that conflict should be avoided and is not what Merk would consider civilized. The Davark believe that they are superior to other worlds and that their rightful place in the universe is to dominate others. The Davark are religious conservatives as well, which leads them to profoundly dislike the agnostics of Merk. Even more surprising is that the Davark hold these beliefs despite advanced technology. One reason the belief structure is in place is due to the government's promulgation of religion as a method to retain power. The government leaders preach that they have been anointed by God and, therefore, rule with divine guidance. There are a myriad of explanations by the government regarding evolutionary advances, all coming back to divine intervention. The government has also instituted a heavily discriminatory structure regarding women, strangely articulated to emanate from religious beliefs. According to the government, women are subordinate to men, and God made it that way. No woman can become a minister—that is the province of men.

After decades of military conflict, Davark was able to steal much of its technology from other worlds. Relatively recently, the Davark leadership set their sights on Merk.

Indeed, the Davarkian leadership is power hungry and willing to expand its power beyond its current borders. The situation with the Davark is one of the key reasons Rein is forced to return to the ship so quickly.

While preparing for the upcoming meeting concerning the Davark, Rein is grateful that other FTL planets within the Merkian sector have joined the Merk in an effort to contain and generally deal with the Davark. Containment of an FTL-enabled enemy is not easy, however.

Lately, the Davark have become more aggressive in their skirmishes with their peaceful neighbors. A report just reached the ship that the Davark successfully attacked a Merk outpost, killing thousands.

Rein is brought back for several reasons, the most important of which is to join in the assessment of whether further Earth-related activities might need to be cut short. If the Davark continue in any level of success, then every ship might be needed and every strategist required.

Presently, it is generally believed that the Merk team could continue in their important Earth-related activities, but that remains a close call.

An independent problem is that more than a few Merkians feel that the Merk lacks effective strategic leadership, particularly in military operations.

As the Merk are peaceful in orientation, they do not expend much energy in military strategic thought. While they are intellectually advanced, their instinctive nature is oriented toward diplomacy and peace.

One aspect of military strategy is to attempt to know one's enemy—to be able to think like the adversary. While no Merk has hope there is anyone out there like the Davark, the belief is that a greater community of thought on this is critical. Therefore, one of the current plans is to potentially recruit someone from another world who can be trusted to consult with the Merk on military strategy and might see things a little bit differently from Merk strategists. Having a truly outside view of the Davark could be helpful. Merk has employed this strategy in the past to great success. The important quality is an independent strategic mind that will look at the problem through a fresh, different lens.

Of course, that search will not be an easy one, but nevertheless, it will likely be quite worth it.

As Rein puts on her typical Merk attire after getting through the Send, she continues to prepare for the meeting that will address these subjects and begins to think about who in the universe might be a good candidate for strategic thinking.

"We appreciate you returning so quickly, Rein. We know you are in the thick of it on Earth right now," says Sorcen.

"Listen, the Davark are a concern for us all and must be treated as a priority," Rein responds.

"I think the situation will require expedited treatment, but the latest report is that the situation is somewhat contained for the moment. It looks like Davark was treating this as a shot across the bow, as they say on Earth, even if thousands lost their lives," the captain reports.

"I agree that it looks like we are in a midrange planning mode if I am calculating things correctly and if I believe what I have been hearing from my colleagues closer to the action," says Cliven.

"OK, so unless someone tells me we need to return to Merk, then we will stick it out awhile longer on Earth. Do you agree, captain?" Rein asks.

"Yes. I appreciate that your jurisdiction, Rein, is making decisions about Earth, but, as you implied, if I decide we need to get back to Merk, then we are going, understood?"

"Yes, captain," they all reply.

CHAPTER 13

PREPARATION FOR THE CONVENTION

R ein takes a Sender back to Chicago. The campaign team is gathered in the Chicago headquarters in order to accomplish two main objectives: the choice of a vice presidential candidate and the preparation of the final speeches.

Rein notices that Andy looks not only remarkably stylish for a man of Earth but also incredibly comfortable. While Andy can afford any style of clothes he wants, he is partial to suits that fit like athletic wear but are nevertheless very well-tailored. DukesMen is a good source for these suits, although LaRange is coming on strong in this department. While Andy can have anything custom-made, he doesn't know why he would go through the effort as those stores made them readily available.

Rein feels a little self-conscious and worries that her attire does not match up well enough. She wears a black jacket over a white top with black jeans. Her top ends shortly below her breasts. She feels a bit concerned about a bare midriff in this company but believes it won't be a problem.

It ends up not exactly being a problem. Tom does a good job of appearing not to look at her stomach. The other men in the room are not as successful as Tom, though Andy is a pure pro. As he joins

Rein at the café stand in the conference room, he looks her in the eye and says, "Are you sending us a signal that we should be viewing everything as black and white?"

Rein thinks a moment and responds, "What I wear is not intended to send any message, unless it is a statement. I choose to put on whatever I happen to like at the moment."

"Well, it appears you are not the only one who likes what you wear, evidenced by the reaction from the room," Andy observes. "If you were any more distracting, we'd have to delay the convention by a few months just to get things done."

"I don't understand it. How does a little skin showing make any difference? It's actually kind of insulting. Am I only interesting if I show my belly?"

"You don't seem to quite have the whole male psychology thing down. I'm sure most men might find you interesting even if you did not show a little skin, but by showing some skin, you certainly incite certain male instincts into a higher gear."

"You don't seem to suffer from that same level of being incited," Rein surmises.

"I suffer from the task of keeping everything professional and on track. Therefore, right now, I can't afford to get distracted. I'm a little disappointed with my colleagues, frankly. They should be better at focusing as well."

With that, Andy calls to the room, "Guys, the food is here, so let's plate up and get to work. My hope is that the feast for your eyes that Annie has apparently provided can be replaced, at least for a moment, with actual food."

Dempsey mutters quietly to Tom a completely indelicate remark about having no problem eating the subject of their previous and ongoing attention. Tom refuses to disagree.

Rein (aka Annie Chandler) finds herself enjoying her Earth surroundings more than she expects. The accommodations are remarkably comfortable for not being Merkian. The chairs are supportive yet cushy, the temperature is pleasant and just humid enough—and the food is excellent. There is the immature treatment of certain issues, but she knows she can't expect Earth to be Merk. She is remarkably happy with the creature comforts of Earth.

One of those, again, is food, which she recognized long ago. Simply put, Earth does food well. Part of that is ingredients, and part of it is the attention Earthlings dedicate to preparation, or at least some Earthlings. Today's lunch starts with a cucumber-tomato-onion salad with Kalamata olives. The dressing is a balsamic mixture that isn't bitter and is actually a little sweet. Because it was Andy, she supposed, there was a gentle hint of garlic in the salad, which was so well seasoned that she did not need to add salt or pepper. The main course is chicken Marsala with a side of rigatoni Bolognese. The Marsala is not overpowered by the wine. Rein finds herself extremely comfortable in this room, with these people, eating this food. Despite being objectively foreign, it is subjectively close. It feels like home—not her home, but somehow someone's home. Maybe her second home. On second thought, she feels it is simply homey. She then feels that that is a strange thought since this "home" is so unlike her real home or homes on Merk.

"I know you do a lot of things well, Andy, but I have to say that food is probably at the top of the list," Dempsey admires.

"Thanks, but Toni should get the credit."

"True," Dempsey responds, "and, by the way, anyone know whether that magnificent lady is married?"

"No, and I was just discussing that fact with her boyfriend," Stacy informs. "I am sure he'd be happy to discuss her single status with you. By the way, he is six four and probably 230 pounds, and I don't know what he does for a living, but I know he is no stranger to the gym."

"I think I will wish Toni and him the best of luck together," Dempsey, a master tactician, quickly observes.

Andy is growing a little concerned that his team is becoming complacent. Yes, he has the nomination wrapped up. Yes, he is ahead of Como in the polls. The way to victory, however, is to plan for the worst. Moreover, this election is not about him. This is not about him becoming president. People need help, and not only Americans. The world is in serious jeopardy. There is also tremendous opportunity. Andy senses there might be a real chance to bring a central vision to the world that it could generally adopt. China is the outlier. That being said, if he can revamp US policy and solve China, then he wonders what else might be possible. End hunger. Colonize Mars. Lasting peace. He feels the need to remind his team that the stakes— his stakes, their stakes, and the world's stakes—are so much higher than what folks have seen in any other election.

"Alright, everyone, if we can stop fantasizing about a match with Toni for one moment due to her magical use of garlic and other seasonings and try not to focus on Annie's midsection, then maybe we can focus not only on the matters at hand but also maybe saving the world. Seriously, there have been moments throughout history that tested humanity in such a profound manner and determined the very course of not only survival but who we are at our core. It is not even a bit dramatic to say that we are now in one of those times. It is not just the conflict with China that matters. I suspect we'll get through that. What we have before us is evolutionary: Will we advance to the next level of what we can be? Will we evolve into truly civilized beings? That is what is at stake. Will we become truly sentient?"

Rein listens. She almost cannot believe that this man possesses such an advanced mentality—one that spans the galaxy with its significance. How does he know the ramifications of this time? There are moments in time when people find they feel so strongly about another person that they tell themselves they are in love. Rein has never understood such claims of feelings toward another, but the combination of everything that is Andy erases much of her uncertainty. She is moved. She finds him compelling. He touches her at the core of her being. He is inescapable. Her prior studies of Andy seemed to reach unrealistic results. The reports appeared overblown. No man of Earth or Merk could possess the talents that Andy possesses, yet here, in his presence and by interacting with him, she feels that the reports and studies she has pored over for months and months do not do him justice. Remarkably, he is more compelling than any Merkian she has ever met—and that is saying a lot. *Well*, Rein thinks, *I guess this is it. Hmm, what to do now?*

"Annie, I'm sure whatever you are thinking is interesting, but I would prefer if you would join our discussion. I'll ask again: do you see this vision with respect to my acceptance speech?"

Annie looks up at Andy. "Yes, sir."

"Good, but let's first turn our attention to the VP pick. Given my recent experience, we can all agree that the VP choice is critical, right?"

There is a universally unspoken yes to that question by way of body language. There is not a soul in the room who fails to recognize that the loss of Lisa is still palpable. What recently happened to Andy was the same event that took Lisa from them. It is kind of strange, however, that there are no negative feelings about Annie. No one blames her for being here. No one feels she is in Lisa's place. It is more as if Annie has carved out a place of her own. It is also felt that Lisa is, in her own way, irreplaceable.

"OK, so let's go over our final list. I trust everyone in the room to keep this in the room. I feel truly lucky to be in a position where I can trust everyone here. Historically, the VP choice committee has been much more limited. I consider this too important to limit the participants, and given this team, I have no concerns about leaks," Andy posits.

Tom intervenes, "We've got McDonald out of Florida, Gatlin from California, and Engel from Arizona. In case anyone forgot, Gatlin's a Democrat."

"We've had McDonald and Engel come in to meet everyone. I think it's time we bring in Gatlin. Tom, please set that up now, and then we'll reconvene. Annie, let's go over the acceptance speech parameters next." With that, Andy thanked everyone, and then he and Annie headed to his private den to discuss the speech.

"Here's the problem as I see it: We need to save some thunder for the inaugural address. While I want the nomination acceptance to fire up the base, I also want it to be inclusive," Andy starts.

"I don't see that as a problem. There is so much we have on the table in terms of policy advances that I think we can save some real oomph for the inaugural and still get our points through in the acceptance. I want to add, if I may, that choosing Gatlin will give you a huge excitement factor at the convention, and, frankly, from what I've seen, he's the closest candidate within your policy mix," Annie ventures.

Rein and the EAS thoroughly studied various VP candidates. The EAS looked upon Jack Gatlin as someone nearest to the potential of Andy Brock. Jack had advanced tremendous policy positions of his own, revamped California government, and was the most conservative Democratic governor of California since the Republican Reagan administration.

"Good observations, but the risk of picking a Democrat is huge," Andy responds.

"You've already passed those risks given your policies. Your numbers are through the roof. The people love the changes you are planning to bring, and maybe for the first time ever, you will be able to lead not from the edges but three-dimensionally. Moreover, Jack's policy positions align with yours very nicely. He's actually a remarkable fiscal conservative while retaining socially liberal stances. Sound like someone you know?" Annie asks.

"Maybe, but what do you mean by 'three-dimensionally'?"

"Historically, Republicans and Democrats maintained policies that were flat. Republicans have been for less government, strong defense, and were socially conservative. Democrats were effectively the opposite: more government, less emphasis on defense (even though Democrats tend to get us into shooting wars), and liberal on social issues. Your policies don't fit that mold. They rise above the traditional framework to another dimension: a third dimension. You agree with a market economy that is a hallmark of less government intervention but, by the same token, have policies that will have the government intervene to incentivize and actually build out important economic functions. You are willing to take some money from the military in order to do that. By the same token, you are also strong against China (the strongest, in fact) and support the principles of respecting Taiwan. No one has done that. You are socially liberal and will not allow discrimination, and you will not stand for any adverse treatment of religious groups. You are a maverick and your policies just don't fit a traditional mold. You are a third dimension. Who else will build out entire communities for prisoners and the homeless and try to have those communities be profitable additions to the GDP and save taxes?"

"Are you sure you don't want to be my VP?"

"I'd love to, but I'm pretty sure the electorate will like Gatlin better."

"I'm not so sure about that. They are more familiar with Gatlin, but I'm pretty sure they'd love you."

"Love me, huh?" Annie asks the question with body language that is playful enough to cause Andy to pause.

"Yes, love you. You present very well publicly, as you are well aware, particularly given the reactions you received today alone. Let's not be coy."

"Anyway, I think we can have the inaugural focus on the international and the social and have the nomination acceptance focus on economics and infrastructure, OK?"

"That makes sense. When can I see your draft?"

"Tomorrow at 9:30 a.m."

"You do understand the importance of this speech? I'd give yourself a little room for comfort on the timing."

"Ah, where I'm from, that is a luxury of time. Sorry, I did not mean to come off as arrogant or glib. Let's just see if I can do it by then. I suspect I can."

CHAPTER 14

THE VP CHOICE

L as Vegas has come a long way. Once the town of a few casinos and motels, it is now not only the entertainment center of the world but also an economically diverse and sophisticated metropolis of over four million people. The city is also home to the Aces, the Golden Knights, the Raiders, and the A's, and, important to many, a championship-level major league soccer team.

Las Vegas is a prototype of the future that Andy envisions. In addition to the rest of Nevada, Las Vegas has already funneled vast resources into education. They have built hundreds of new schools, reduced the student-to-teacher ratio by nearly half, provided free lunches and breakfasts, and focused on a core curriculum. While not perfect, Las Vegas and Nevada have become the most advanced pre-college educational centers in the country.

Las Vegas is also a glimmering showpiece of modern architecture now. While the skyline used to be dominated by massive hotel resorts, there are now glistening towers of multiuse buildings that combine offices with condos and other uses. Las Vegas claims to have one of the greatest skylines in the world, which has been helped at some level by an ample water supply. Southern Nevada has found a way to optimize water supply through a combination of retention, conservation, and sourcing. While not as robust as the water pipeline envisioned by Andy, Southern Nevada's strategy is a template for how great water management can yield amazing results. Indeed, there are now at least fifty buildings with over fifty stories and numerous buildings with over one hundred stories. One tower is particularly amazing. The three-thousand-foot-tall Sierra West Tower houses virtually everything: offices, a hotel, condominiums, a grammar school, a junior high and a high school, a grocery store, a vertical mall, several gyms, and plenty of restaurants and nightclubs to keep everyone fed. At the base of Sierra West Tower is a convention center that will be holding the Republican National Convention in a few days' time.

It is no accident that the convention is taking place not only in Las Vegas but at the Sierra West Tower. Andy foresees his possible victory and is certain that Las Vegas and the Sierra West Tower are married to his vision and his campaign. They are an example of the vision he seeks to become more of a national and even global reality. Ronald Reagan spoke of a shining city on a hill. Sierra West Tower is in and of itself a shining city full of what the future promises.

The Sierra West Tower is also wonderfully convenient. Andy and his team are able to book an entire floor of the tower that comes complete with conference rooms, a dining hall, and a gym. The floor is completely secured from external access as well. Not only is key card entry required to enter the designated elevator, but thumbprints are also required to get through the floor's foyer. Lastly, each room is also interfaced with thumbprint and facial recognition. Of course, all of this comes at a steep price, but the price is worth it.

Each room has a TV that doubles as a computer interface. The interface displays the day's events and meetings and also reveals alerts for various events. The same audio-visual system also enables announcements and paging independently.

The view from the 250th floor is spectacular. Andy's personal space has a bedroom suite, an office suite, a dining room, and a conference suite, with two bathrooms and a powder room. At 2,500 square feet, it is the size of a decent, middle-income home. Each member of Andy's team is outfitted with a bedroom, an office suite, a dining area, and one and a half baths. Room service is security-cleared and, more importantly, provides delicious selections. The audio-visual system allows for online food ordering with delivery ETAs computed within twenty minutes after placing the order. There are five menus to choose from: standard American fare as well as Chinese, Japanese,

French, and Mexican cuisines. Andy opts for the standard American breakfast and the Japanese yakiniku for dinner. Rein is over the moon with the coq au vin—which has just the right amount of garlic. To say that everyone is comfortable is an understatement.

An alert goes off for the 9:30 a.m. meeting in the main conference room. This alert, however, only goes off in Tom's and Rein's rooms. Andy is already in the conference room and wants only the highest-level meeting for the convention issues he intends to address. Tom, of course, is well-trusted by Andy at every level. He has demonstrated through the years a level of skill, discretion, and intelligence that justifies the position he holds as campaign manager. Annie has been proving herself as well. In fact, Andy finds Annie to be as significant an intellectual force as he has ever met. In a state of potential arrogance, he allows himself the privilege of admitting he has met his match. Quite candidly, he is also finding himself enjoying her company. Annie is starting to warm up a bit with isolated bursts of sarcasm. Andy knows that carrying off well-placed sarcasm is a sign of both smarts and discretion. Thankfully, Annie's sarcasm fits within that description. Andy has to stop himself for a second. OK, here he is about to be awarded the Republican nomination for president of the United States. He cannot get distracted at this moment by romance. Yes, he probably found a worthy companion in Lisa and is still mourning her death, but Annie is amazing. There is no doubt that Lisa was beautiful, smart, witty, and charming, but with no disrespect to her, Annie is mesmerizing. There is something about the X factor that cannot be described; it is only experienced. Andy finds himself experiencing it and begins to think Annie is feeling the same sense as him. Until he met Lisa, he had not found interesting female companionship since his wife's death, but his time with Lisa was painfully brief. To now find himself even interested in another female so soon struck Andy as odd, if not miraculous.

Tom enters the conference room first. "So, it's to be Gatlin, huh?"

"Well, let's wait for Annie," and before he can finish, she walks into the room. "I was just saying we should wait to discuss the VP choice till you got here."

Andy does not quite know what to think. "Annie" is wearing a light-grey bodysuit. It is readily apparent there is no underwear to encumber her. On the one hand, what she is wearing is perfectly legal. Everything is covered. Also, this is not a public meeting; it just being Andy, Tom, and her. Moreover, both Andy and Tom are certainly dressed casually—business casual but still casual. On the other hand, the bodysuit would never be worn at a standard business meeting. However, she had just traveled down the hall. It isn't like she has traversed through an office building. Maybe the problem (if there is one) is the way she looks in the bodysuit—which is to say, stunning. What catches his eye this time in particular is how well-formed her thighs are—muscled, yet still feminine, and they form the perfect curve toward her midsection. It is also how gracefully she moves. Part of it is posture; she holds her shoulders back and sometimes tends to glide across the room.

Tom, as usual, does not fail. "So, I trust that you have made yourself quite comfortable at Sierra West?" he asks Annie.

"I am comfortable almost anywhere I go," Annie replies.

"Really? Well, you should try a Japanese boardroom someday," Tom provokes.

"I find, Tom, that comfort stems from within, and no matter what the external circumstances, I can find peace in any environment."

Andy suspects that Tom knows Annie is winning this exchange, but Andy also knows that Tom is no slouch.

Taking a more direct approach as he fears being outmaneuvered, Tom says, "Listen, I was trying to be politely indirect, but don't you think your attire is a little aggressive?"

Annie bursts out in laughter. "How so?"

So, she isn't going to make this any easier on them. "C'mon. It looks like you jumped out of a very, very R-rated Jane Fonda video. I don't generally see people wearing bodysuits unless, one, they are very comfortable with their bodies, and two, they are going to the gym."

"Let's get this straight. One, I am very comfortable with my body, so let's check that one off. Two, if you are uncomfortable with my body, then that's your problem. Three, what I wear is none of your business. Finally, your navy blue shirt and black slacks really don't color match, so you have a lot more problems than I do with clothing." Annie makes her speech while holding her hands on her hips. Nothing is hiding in her physique. Her nipples are erect and apparent through the bodysuit, and while there is no camel toe, there is a pronounced thigh gap that makes it quite clear how fit Annie is.

Controlling himself at some level, Andy decides to come to Tom's rescue as Tom is clearly in need of help. "Annie, you know you are unusual and independent—and unusual in your independence. Tom, I'm sure, did not intend to insult you, but you can't begrudge him a little surprise at your unusualness."

"Really? No, I can't accept that. I also can't believe we are taking time to discuss what I choose to wear when we have many more important things to address. You both need to get over yourselves, and we need to focus," Annie replies.

Tom and Andy look at each other. Andy says, "She's right. Get over it."

Rein has studied the people of Earth, especially the males, for some time now. In these studies, she has learned that the men of Earth, generally speaking, have trouble keeping their egos in check. It is rare for men to admit they are wrong and that any woman is right, but Andy does not hesitate to do so.

Not to be completely defeated, Tom concludes, "OK, so maybe it is my problem, Annie, but you've got to know that your sensuality is distracting."

"Tom, you're a very handsome man yourself, but I force myself to overcome my sexual stirrings toward you somehow and focus on work. Maybe one day I will fail and thrust myself at you."

Andy broke in with a gut-level laugh. No one would call Tom the world's sexiest man. The thought, let alone the image, of Annie ever throwing herself at Tom is hysterical.

"OK, Jack will be with us shortly to go over his final interview. I'd like both of you with me for that. Annie, how are the final revisions to the acceptance speech coming?"

"I have it ready right now. I have a clean version for your review and a markup to show the most recent changes."

Andy had not expected the revisions until later today. They had only reviewed the final version very late last night. This woman is a true force of nature.

"OK, let's go over that after we meet with Jack."

The "Jack" mentioned is Jack Gatlin, the governor of California, who is immensely popular both in his state and across the country. Years prior to Jack being in office, California suffered from high taxes, heavy regulations, and population losses. Jack has been recognized by the press as a conservative Democrat who institutes policies that look Republican in nature but can only be instituted by a Democratic-controlled government in California. Jack did, in fact, reduce taxes, lighten regulations, revamp the education system, and tackle the homeless problem with creativity and practicality. Jack, when asked about Andy, commented favorably about Andy's policies and wondered aloud whether Andy was a closet Democrat. Andy often took the opportunity with the press to ask the same question in reverse about Jack. Both Jack and Andy are political mavericks and admire each other. Andy wants a VP who can lead the country, if necessary, although the thought of a Republican-led ticket winning California in the general election is also quite tantalizing.

"Tom, I just received a prompt that Jack is here. Please have him brought in," Andy says.

As Jack walks into the conference room, Rein sees how easy the energy is between Jack and Andy. When Jack shakes Andy's hand, it is warm and energetic but not overdone. There is a sheer absence of apparent psychological competition between the two, which is remarkable since they are both type-A personalities of the upper tier. The palpable positive energy between them goes beyond mutual respect. They seem to intuitively understand each other.

"Jack, thanks so much for visiting," Andy announces.

"Andy, my pleasure, although the press seems the happiest. Our meetings certainly are red meat for the reporters."

"Listen, Jack, despite being a politician, I actually don't play politics. Even though the team has not made a final decision, you are my number one choice, and I think the press is right about this one: We'd not only make history but more importantly, we'd make one heck of a team. I told my team I'm ready to go with you, and I'm prepared to do so at this meeting. This is such an important decision for both of us that I just wanted to go over a few of the final concepts, if that's OK."

"Andy, we have a remarkable opportunity, so whatever you need to get comfortable with, then shoot."

"Great. Well, you are an asset to the country who should not waste away just waiting to take over in case I get shot again. Therefore, I wanted to make sure a certain division of labor worked for you, just so long as I don't relegate ultimate control to you as I take the oath seriously."

"I get that you want to delegate certain issues to me and maintain ultimate control over those. The delegation should enable me to get the job done, but in a manner that does not diminish the notions that I ultimately report to you, keep you informed, and with discretion, ask for your direction on key points."

"Well said. Are you okay with daily calls and weekly lunches?"

"Heck, not only am I okay with it, I would love the access to you."

"Listen, even on the issues you don't more or less control, I'm still going to involve you. There will be very few decisions I make that I am not going to want your input on. Jack, you are going to be a busy man. While we are going to have our daily calls and weekly lunches, I predict you are going to be in the vast majority of my meetings. More importantly, while we are in those meetings, I'd prefer it if you were the more vocal one between the two of us. Sitting back and listening is more helpful to me than directing the inquiries. I mean, I won't be shy about chiming in, but my hope is that you can weed out the responses while I evaluate. How's that sound?"

"Wow. I'm pretty breathless. You are even more the man and executive than I imagined. Andy, this is an almost unbelievable situation you and I and the country find ourselves in. First, we are in different political parties, yet you are not only inviting me into the White House but also inviting me to be a more significant part of your administration than any prior VP. The only thing I guess I can say is that you are doing exactly the same thing I suspect I would do if I were in your position, and I am not saying that just to make you like me. You know, before I met you, some people told me that you were too perfect, unapproachable, and unrelatable. I think those people simply never met you. Yes, you apply logic and rationality more than the average person or even above the average person. Those who envy you probably don't take the time to make the effort to think things through. What they also are missing is that you don't ignore the human element when striving for the logical. I think that we may need to work on ensuring that the world comes to know Andy Brock the person, or they might misunderstand that the level of your talent does not diminish your humility and generosity."

"Jack, thanks. I do try to relate, and I agree that we need to help lead people to strive for logical rationality while also maintaining a deep sense of humanity. In any event, Annie, let's go through the parameters of Jack's first areas of control."

"Jack would be in charge of each of the following: the administration of the water pipeline from the Midwest to the Southwest, the educational buildout, and the prison reform into farming community opportunities."

"Anything left for me?" Andy asks.

There is general recognition in the room that Andy will have plenty left: handling possible war with China, federal judge appointments, the overall economy and tax policy, environmental improvements, the federal budget, and the medical facility buildout, to name a few.

"Well, my hope is to steal more away from you under the radar," Jack says.

"Annie, please keep your eye on this guy," Andy implores.

"I don't know, Andy. I kinda like him better than you already," Rein says.

"Tom, please keep your eye on both of them," Andy says.

"I am afraid if I keep my eye on Annie, then she'll have me shot, but I'll do the best I can," Tom replies. "Just joking, Annie. Please don't start in on me again. I can't take another round," Tom finishes.

"Gentlemen, I hope we can agree that any further comments from anyone about my physical attributes are inappropriate. Enough said?" Annie concludes.

"Well, for me, I get it, but I won't be walking on eggshells. If anyone—whether it is you, Tom, Andy, or anyone else—appears in a happy mood, is wearing a pleasing outfit, or is scented with nice cologne, then I will not be prevented from commenting favorably," Jack says.

"See, Tom, that's the way to handle it," Annie says.

"Wow, I guess the intricacies of these interactions are above my pay grade. That being said, Annie, let me be the first to say how pleasant your choice of outfit is today," Tom says while looking at Jack.

"Why, thank you, Tom, and may I reiterate that your color scheme simply does not work. I'm so glad we can spend this valuable time with the soon-to-be most powerful men in the world discussing sartorial issues," Annie replies.

"I think we understand each other's points. Jack, I hereby offer to you the status of my choice to be nominated as vice president of the United States. Do you accept?" Andy asks.

"Yes, it would be my honor, sir," Jack replies.

"Well, then, welcome to the team," Andy says. "As you can probably tell, Annie has quickly become one of my most important advisers and is the best darn speechwriter I've ever had, which says a lot, as you all know. For purposes of continuity between our two acceptance speeches, I'd like her to at least review and comment on your speech. If you'd like to have her manage the first draft, that's OK too. What say you?"

"I'm already impressed with Annie's acumen on several levels, and I'm not talking about her bodysuit, so, yes, I'd love to have her punch out a first draft. Annie, let's schedule some time to go over the parameters, OK?"

"Sounds good, Jack. How about we start at 4 p.m. and have a working dinner if necessary?"

"Where shall we meet?"

"Let's use the war room down the hall. It's the small conference room called 'Meadows' a few doors down from here. See you at 4."

"Jack, we'll let you go now as I have to punch out the final version of my own speech with Annie. Let's get together tomorrow at 10 a.m. to go over strategy, OK?"

"Andy, sounds great. See you then," Jack says before exiting smartly.

"Andy, this is going to be one helluva team you are putting together and an incredible package to manage for the campaign. You always said it was going to be exciting, but this structure takes things to another level," Tom says.

"This is only the beginning. Tom, I know you've got more con-vention logistics to work out, so we'll let you go now. Annie, let's see the marked version of the acceptance speech," Andy directs.

Andy and Rein finish the acceptance speech through their lunch. Despite the two of them clearly having a growing sense of attraction to each other, when the job has to be done, then they, amazingly, are able to maintain exclusive focus on the task. Once they are done with the speech and Andy is on his way to the gym for his daily workout, they leave each other with a look—one that each feel is trying to communicate something other than merely goodbye or thanks. It is a look that most people would interpret as a moment, but with intellects as advanced as Andy's and Rein's, it is a look that could have a number of possible meanings. Neither Andy nor Rein is ready to express themselves on the subject, but it is becoming clear to both of them, inwardly and quietly, that someday something is going to give. Rein does not know how that works with an Earthling. Andy does not know how that works again with a member of his team. They both only know it is going to have to be explored at some level, or the tension will only increase to the point of distraction.

CHAPTER 15

A BIT DISTRACTED

A ndy's workout goes fairly well. Today is leg day, and Jeb, his trainer, feels Andy is a little distracted. "Hey, Andy, what's up with you? I've seen you with a load of stuff on your plate work-wise, and I know you've got the convention and all, but you seem a little out of focus on your training. What's the scoop?"

"Really? I'm about to be nominated as a presidential candidate, and I've got a bunch of issues I've never had to handle before. You can't understand I'm a little preoccupied?"

Jeb responds, "Yeah, you're Andy Fuckin' Brock, so don't tell me you can't handle a little thing like a political convention."

"First, my middle name is 'Danger,' not 'Fuckin',' and second, you're right. Let me ask you a question: What do you think about the fact I had a relationship with Lisa? Was that so wrong?"

Jeb doesn't bite. "This isn't about Lisa, is it? I've known you long enough to know where this is going. The answer is everyone can see the amazing fit, and therefore, if you feel it is wrong to make a move on Annie, then get some balls and do what is right, regardless of what you think other people might think. Who you have a relationship with is your own fuckin' business."

Somewhat shocked, Andy responds, "I haven't said a word to anyone about whether I have any feelings for Annie. Like Lisa, she's way younger than me as well. Hell, I just can't believe I was falling for Lisa, and now, so suddenly, people are thinking I could fall for Annie."

Jeb is ready for that comment. "Well, given how old you are, you should probably act your age and stop the high school nonsense. Was it your fault some idiot shooter murdered Lisa? No. Is it your fault the most amazing woman in the galaxy fell into your lap and appears to look at you like you are some kinda god? No. I'll give you three days, and if you don't make a move, then I'll consider it open season on Annie. Hell, there should be no question to any woman out there that I am a whole lot sexier than you are anyway."

Andy actually feels a little pang of jealousy but doesn't let it show. "You don't even have to wait. Make your move. And you're right; you are sexier than I am. In fact, I've thought about making a move on you for quite some time—that's exactly how sexy you are."

Jeb moves back a little and says, "Do you have a calculator 'cause I'm having trouble adding up how much money I will get for black-mailing you on that last comment. The Democrats and the press would love to hear about your latent homosexuality."

"Well, I'm not gay, but even if I were, then I'm not sure it would be worth blackmailing me about. Anyway, I get where you're going with this. Annie is pretty special, and if there's something there, then I shouldn't hold back. I get it. Now, bend over slowly when you pick up those barbells so that I can get the full measure of your sexy ass."

Jeb backs away some more and says, "I'm going to pay for that homosexuality remark for a while, right?"

Smiling broadly, Andy says, "You've got that right."

CHAPTER 16

JACK'S OBSERVATIONS

Meanwhile, it was 4 p.m., and Annie and Jack started their meeting to talk about Jack's acceptance speech. Jack asks, "So most people I know are at least a little intimidated by Andy. You don't seem even the least bit intimidated. If I am right about that, then may I say, I'm goddamned impressed."

"You know, I think Andy is misunderstood. I also think, quite humbly, from my perspective, he almost never intends to be intimidating. Yes, if there is an adversary out there who requires Andy to ratchet it up, then hell yeah, he can be intimidating. That's at least my take on our limited experience together. But for the most part, Andy is one of the most rational, objective people I've met. That is the opposite of being intimidating. If you know a person will treat you reasonably and intelligently, then there is great predictability in the interaction. That should not be intimidating if you are a contemplative person. Typically, only bullies try to intimidate other people to hide their own inadequacies. Andy does not need to bully anyone. He might intellectually overpower another person, but that would be the nature of the interaction, not Andy being mean or nasty."

Jack thinks a moment, then responds, "He's lucky to have you. Hell, we're lucky to have you. I guess I feel the same way you do about him, which is one reason I think we—and I now mean the three of us—can work well together. In fact, I can't wait for you to meet my wife. Brenda and I share the same sensibilities. We obviously love each other but also work well together out of a great sense of mutual respect and understanding. I know that should be expected in a marriage, but sadly, I think the divorce rate argues against it. I'm lucky to have Brenda. Andy is lucky to have you, but I'm not suggesting you are in any way romantically oriented toward him."

That last comment forces a bit more of a pause in Rein's psyche than she is prepared for, but she still has enough force of will to respond. "Of course not. Our relationship is merely professional. I mean, I'd like to think we are friends, but . . . Okay, so on to your speech, I think we don't go in the typical direction of the VP 'attack dog' approach. Let's benefit from your status as a Democrat and use that as the bridge to inclusion. I say you compliment the opposition as much as possible—rise above it and stay positive."

Jack shakes his head and says, "You know, I was hoping you and Andy would adopt that approach. This relationship keeps on amazing me. Okay, so let's focus on why this relationship works, why our philosophies are tied together, and why this brings a positive advance to the country. Sprinkle in some key policy positions I'll be responsible for, add in my experience as governor, and if you can—and I'm not sure about this—put in some humor as well."

Annie, not taking the bait, replies, "I'm not sure I'm capable of the humor part, but other than that, I think we are on the same page. I'll be done with the draft tomorrow, and if you come to me on bended knee and apologize for the 'humor' remark, then maybe I'll show it to you."

Jack heads out the door and, at the same time, says, "I take back the humor comment and look forward to going over the draft with you tomorrow. By the way, I also take back the remark about anything romantic between you and Andy. Anyone with any ability to read a room can sense that you and Andy are two of a kind. I'll keep that between you and me, but I would be shocked if you and Andy don't admit to each other what no doubt everyone else in the world sees or will see . . ."

Rein begins to protest, but Jack is already out the door. *What is it with people?* she thinks. *Anyway, I've got to get to work.*

CHAPTER 17

THE CONVENTION

True to her word, Rein finishes the speeches. The convention is going as planned, and Andy and Jack are nominated as a formality, given the results of the primaries.

The positive press and the bump in the polls are as predicted coming out of the first days of the convention, but the real reaction will only come about after the candidates' speeches. Faster than it seems it could happen, it is time for Jack's acceptance speech.

The stage is impressive, with tech blue and silver colors and a modern but warm feel. The crowd is primed for a historic speech by a Democrat being nominated on the Republican ticket.

Jack begins, "I come before you, not as a Democrat. I also can't really say I come before you as a Republican. I do come before you as an American, and in that capacity, I accept your nomination for vice president of the United States."

The interruption of applause lasts longer than anticipated.

"Andy Brock and I see a future for our country that is not restrained by party lines. We see a future that unites Americans based upon policies that do not fit into neat little baskets of division. The future you will enable through your vote for us is a future based upon creative and practical changes that serve you. In the past, we have spent billions, even trillions of dollars, with nothing to show for it. It will cost something to build the water pipeline that will allow the

American West to be irrigated, but why in the world have we never done that before?"

Sustained applause.

"It will cost relatively little to initially advance prison reform with communal farming communities that are secure, but those communities will actually pay for themselves. Why has that not been done before?"

More applause.

"It will cost relatively little to build medical facilities across the country that will advance healthcare in this country as never before. Why has that not been done before?"

Yet more applause.

"What you are seeing with the Brock-Gatlin team is something you've never seen before. These are policies never before even mentioned by politicians in either the Republican Party or Democratic Party. These are your policies. Your vote is not for Andy or me. Your vote is for the advancement of the future that you deserve."

Of course, more applause.

"I'm not here tonight to bad mouth our competitors in the other party. You know what? They are fine people and great Americans. Running for any office is hard. Running for the highest offices is even harder. Andy and I are confident that we will win this campaign. It is at that moment we will ask everyone, including those running against us and those who foolishly did not vote for us, to join us."

Yet more applause continues to interrupt Jack's speech as he goes on to describe where he comes from, and there is more policy discussion and more discussion of the vision he has for the country. Jack concludes with, "Perhaps more importantly than anything, Andy and I are going to join the party of Lincoln with the party of Kennedy. We will not tolerate racial injustice. We will not tolerate discrimination of any kind. Our policies will be designed to advance the interests of all people, no matter their color or creed. We will not disfavor those in the majority, but our policies will provide opportunities for those who want to work. We will not give handouts. We will provide incentives and platforms to succeed. A great man once had a dream. That dream is coming true and it will be a reality you will have earned with your vote."

The convention center erupts, and the crowd reaction is overwhelming. Jack's delivery is spot-on. There are real questions in the press corps about how Andy is going to improve upon Jack's speech. Heck, there are also real questions of whether Jack should be heading the ticket rather than second on the ticket. Everyone has to wait one more night to think about that question.

The whole team gathers in the main conference room afterward. Everyone congratulates Jack on hitting a home run. Jack makes it clear it is Annie who deserves the credit. Annie, who is wearing a pencil skirt that would generally be viewed as more traditionally professional than her bodysuit, is a focus of attention for the congratulations on her writing skills, but also, probably subconsciously by most, her raw magnetism. Andy is proud of Jack, Annie, and the rest of the team and says as much, but he has some other news to report: "China is not happy. I've actually been briefed by the administration. China flew numerous sorties over Taiwan, Korea, and Vietnam. They did not fire, but they have disrespected the airspace of others like never before. Annie, we've got to rewrite some of the speech."

Sooner than Andy thought possible, it was his turn. The anticipation in the convention hall is thick. It actually works out that the press makes Andy's job easier by universally concluding that Jack's speech cannot be topped by Andy.

Andy begins, "Who wants Jack Gatlin to be president someday?"

The convention hall erupts.

"Give me a little credit. I'm the guy who chose him.

"Well, before some folks change their minds even more after hearing Jack's speech, I am going to hurry up and now accept your nomination as the Republican candidate for president of the United States of America."

It erupts again.

"Some of you may know I got shot. Like many of our veterans who know this, getting shot does something to you. It helps remind you of your own mortality. With the possibility of my own mortality happening at any moment, I rest easy knowing that if I am elected, then maybe the better man on the ticket is ready to take my place in the Oval Office. More importantly, we will be a true team from day one. There will be a division of labor. As President Truman said, the buck will stop with me, but I'll hold Jack responsible for more than any other VP in the history of this country. I also know you'll be okay with that, knowing the great man Jack clearly is."

Sustained applause. The commentators are already preparing their thoughts on how Andy wins over the crowd with his humility while hitting them over the head with his smarts. Andy is well on his way to outdoing Jack's speech the previous night.

"Everyone told me my choices would stop me from being here. You can't win the nomination if you don't embrace the religious right. You can't win if you appeal to minorities. Republicans don't spend money on water pipelines and education, they told me. Guess what? I'm here. And I'm here not because of me. I was going to go my own way on this campaign, no matter what. I felt it was the right thing to do. So, it wasn't me that got me here. It was you. You are making the future that should have always been possible. Your votes will achieve the greatness we are capable of. So don't applaud Jack. Don't applaud me. You know what, go ahead and applaud yourselves."

Even though it seems like pandering to the crowd, Andy's magical delivery forces the entire convention hall and the press in attendance to go crazy. The crowd is beside itself with joy. Unlike anyone before him, Andy makes the choice and the election about the voters. From anyone else, this part of the speech might seem contrived, but from Andy, it strikes home with absolute sincerity.

After a long wait for the applause to stop, Andy continues: "So, China thinks they can bully their neighbors and the rest of the world. My opponents in this election think it best to placate China. Mr. Como visited China recently and continues his claim that it is wrong to formally recognize Taiwan. Only diplomacy is required, according to Mr. Como. History teaches us something different. Why does China feel the need to bully its neighbors? Has our country, at times, had the ability to take over the world? Yes. Did we? No. Has our country always had the ability to invade its neighbors and win? Yes. Have we? No. Why not? Because it's both wrong and unnecessary. What justification does China have to invade? None. What belief should we have that China will stop at one border? No belief. History has taught us that lesson over and over again. Once China is taught the lesson of nonaggression, then that should be the last time a nation on this planet will require that schooling. Russia is now part of the family of nations. The nations of the Middle East generally understand that their religions teach peace, and that any jihad should not be to conquer another nation of differing religious perspectives. We are on the cusp of a truly lasting peace if China is encouraged to behave. I will not stand by and fail to do everything in my power to achieve that peace."

Andy makes his case to the convention hall, the press, and the viewing public. The applause starts with the last words Andy speaks. Everyone sees in each other the realization that this man, Andy Brock, is, in truth, leading a nation to a place that is right—even if they do not realize the rightness themselves. When a people suddenly gain awareness of true leadership that they can admire, that awareness is transformative. Everyone in the hall senses the growing awareness of leadership, and the applause grows to a crescendo not heard for Jack's speech, not heard for anything Andy has said before, and in the view of the commentators, is more robust than even the senior commentators have heard in their coverage of conventions for years. As a result, the biggest hurdle Andy and Jack are going to face in the election—namely, taking on China—has been turned by Andy into one of their biggest assets.

Andy's speech builds on that asset, and the surging applause matches his impassioned commitment to his beloved country.

Andy concludes with: "Yes, Jack and I love this country. So do our competitors in the other party. Mr. Como and his running mate are great Americans who have served our country with dignity. This election is not personal. Every election, politicians say: 'This election presents a choice between two different visions.' I think I've heard that a hundred times. What's different is that no one has ever verbalized some of the policies I'm proposing. Maybe some scientist or professor has mentioned some of them, but no politician has ever run on them. How about a water pipeline to irrigate the entire Southwest? Never before."

Some in the convention hall join Andy in shouting, a little late, "Never before."

"How about a buildout of private-government medical facilities across the country? Never before."

This time, the entire convention hall joins in with "never before" and does so louder and louder when called upon to do so.

"How about advanced prison reform creating the option of farming communities that also help the homeless? Never before. How about educational reform implemented by the federal government, reducing the student–teacher ratio and focusing on core classes? Never before. Right. I don't need to tell you these are galactic changes in policy and approach that Jack and I will bring to government. It is self-evident. This is the next evolution of our country and our world. You are ready for it. Many of you have already voted for it. I ask the rest of the country to join us. When we win, I boldly ask for and expect Mr. Como's help in getting the job done. Why? This is not about Republicans or Democrats, as Jack demonstrates. It's about our future together. I humbly suggest that Jack and I can lead you to that future. The beauty of our great nation is that the choice to make that future is ultimately up to you. I'm going to fight for every one of your votes. Don't be surprised if you see me on your doorstep, whether you are in Oklahoma, California, Montana, or Illinois. Your vote is worth it, and I know our country is as well. Lastly, understand that I ask to become your public servant. I do, however, expect and demand that you make the effort as a citizen to participate in this election. If you do, then I promise you that one day, you'll tell your children the following: 'I was there to cast the vote that radically changed our country for good. I was part of a great generation that took this country by storm, and I am so happy with the nation we created for you.' At that point, you will have taught your children the lesson of what is required as a citizen. And I'll be damned proud to have joined you in that fight."

Both women and men in the convention hall are openly weeping, overcome with the feeling that before them is a leader never before seen. Before them is a man who not only provides a new, smart direction but leads with humility and an overwhelming magnetic force of personality. It is a little strange. Normally, the hall would erupt with applause, but after Andy finishes, it is as if everyone is a little stunned. It is as if the crowd is overrun by Andy's performance. The press commentators are initially speechless as well. After a few moments, the applause and shouts are earth-shattering.

Richard Moore, senior political analyst for MSNBC, observes, "OK, so Jack left us breathless last night. We were all saying that Jack almost made it look like he should be at the top of the ticket. We should have known better. I've heard Brock speak before. I know how persuasive he can be, but this was another level. Sometimes, at these conventions, we talk about the candidate giving the speech of their life. This speech was the best speech of any candidate's life. What's so particularly amazing is how positive the message was. I mean, my goodness, Andy Brock went out of his way to make it look like Como is going to be a valuable member of his team. We hardly have ever seen or heard such a completely positive campaign run."

His colleague in the booth, Nancy Albrecht, adds, "I agree, although Andy's so far ahead in the polls that maybe he thinks there is no need to be negative."

"I get that. Anyway, it's still refreshing."

Charles Wilcox of CNN observes at the same time on that network, "What we don't see coming out of Como's camp is the kind of attacks on Brock's policies one would expect. Como has been left flat-footed. The most they are coming back with is that some of the plans will be expensive and hard to implement."

In the booth with Wilcox is Veronica Hernandez, who joins in with, "But then Brock's camp comes back with on-point scientific studies by reputable firms that show not only the viability of each and every one of the plans but that most if not all of the plans will generate savings if not profits for the country. Heck, the water pipeline will make money. The prison reform studies demonstrate billions of dollars of actual savings. The problem for Como is twofold: He now has a tougher time on China, and he's got to make a case for himself. Merely feebly trying to attack Brock's truly fresh policies is not getting him anywhere. It's just not clear how you fight the phenom of Brock."

Wilcox responds, "Here's the other problem for Como that you kinda mentioned: Brock's a rock star at this point. He's Kennedy, the Beatles, and Reagan at his peak rolled into one. The only thing that could bring down Brock now would be a scandal we don't know about. And when I say, 'bring down,' I mean Como avoiding a nearly total landslide."

The rest of the press commentators uniformly state that this is so new and compelling as to be literally incomparable. Andy has found a way not to be overshadowed by Jack, which makes the Brock–Gatlin ticket seemingly unbeatable.

Of course, not everybody in the world loves Andy's success, and a faction believes that the only way to stop Andy and Jack is not through the electoral process.

CHAPTER 18

ONE MORE TRY

"He has to be stopped. There is no way Como is going to beat him. I mean, Jesus, he might get more Democrat votes than Como will. While he might be great for a lot of people, he would not be great for our business."

"I get that. We are not fooling around this time. Everything is set to go. We've got the people in place with the right equipment. He's going to need a miracle to survive this time."

They do have an impressive operation. It is impossible for Andy's team to hide the fleet of three Silverstone motor coaches, joined by four escort security transports: two in front and two in back. Security personnel are also on each of the motor coaches. It is clear that Andy is going to join Jack in LA for a major California campaign stop. They are going to have to travel on I-15 from Vegas. The opportunity itself to attack the convoy is, by traditional measures, viable, but no traditional attack is viewed as truly threatening given the security countermeasures and counter capabilities.

This opportunity is not met by merely a lone gunman. The assassination team is composed of mercenary former military commandos, well supplied with rocket-propelled grenades, anti-tank missiles, and munitions sufficient to take out a battery of opposition vehicles. These are not traditional security concerns, for it is as if a small battalion is lying in wait in the desert along Interstate 15.

Andy's motorcade is moving down I-15 when the first shots are heard. Dempsey is on board, and based on his military experience, he recognizes that there are shots that are administered by army-level combatants.

The motorcade picks up speed consistent with the Special Service escort protecting it. However, both the Special Service and Dempsey know that this attack is not going to be successfully won by merely picking up speed. At some point, they are going to either stop and fight or be forced to stop and fight.

What no one anticipates are the explosions seen and heard yards away from any vehicle in the motorcade. Tom, Andy's campaign manager, swears he sees blue light hit munitions heading for the convoy, with the munitions bursting into flame. After that, Tom hears explosions in the direction from which the attack appears to emanate.

Suddenly, no more evidence of any attack is evident. One of the security transports doubles back to investigate. The second-in-command for Andy's security team, Paul McMichael, is in charge of the reconnaissance and says to his next in-command, "Mack, look at that, man. It looks like that artillery was obliterated. That had to come from the air. I did not see any air cover, did you?"

Mack replies, "I think you are right, and no, I did not see any air cover. I have no idea what could have made those strikes and then silently fly away."

CHAPTER 19

PROTECTION

"**C**aptain Siven, we were able to successfully obliterate the threat to Mr. Brock and Rein. There are thirty-two dead who were part of the attack force, and we have captured thirteen from that force. None remain."

"Thank you, Commander Buman. Good work. Any sense that, other than our captured, your force was seen?" asks the captain.

"No, sir, our stealth measures were in full operation," replies Buman. "And we are questioning the captured for information on who organized this attack. They are remarkably cooperative, given the shock of being on their first starship. We will be able to neutralize the planners of this attack shortly. Obviously, Andy might have other enemies, but at least this faction will not be a factor again."

CHAPTER 20

INTERSTATE 15

R eflecting on the attack, Rein is privately satisfied with the swift and silent handling of the threat. She also wonders to herself how many more threats will have to be dealt with. She isn't worried about the threats themselves but whether the Merkians will be discovered the next time they handle such threats. While she is occupied by these musings, Andy walks over and sits down at the booth in the Silverstone. "What the hell do you think just happened?" he asks. "I mean, Tom and Dempsey are talking about the fact that it looked like we were being shelled by heavy artillery, and then something out of strategic missile defense came in and shot it down. I've called the head of our security team. He said that reconnaissance said that a substantial battery from where the attack was made was obliterated."

"It certainly was impressive," Rein replies.

"I've asked security to put a call into DoD. We'll see what they come back with," Andy says, then continues, "Annie, I haven't had time to get your view on the convention. What are your thoughts?"

"I'll assume you are asking me about where you think the polls are. You heard the response from the hall and the press. I can't wait to get to LA near the ocean and see if it's true that you walk on water. As far as the polls go, you are now up so far that Como may actually be thinking about any chance to join your team. With how well Jack did, I think we even have a chance to carry Massachusetts.

Unbelievably for you as a Republican, you are now ahead by five points in California."

"Let's not let the team rest easy. I want to show everyone that this is just the beginning of our fight."

Annie appears quite comfortable in a silk-cashmere blend outfit. Her bottoms are uncharacteristically loose-fitting and are paired with a matching midriff-bearing top. Andy is dressed in a black Calvin Klein modal long-sleeve t-shirt and white Hugo Boss jeans. Together, they look like they are going to be part of a *WSJ* Sunday Magazine photo shoot.

"So, when we get to LA, would you like to grab some dinner?" Andy offers.

"Sure, so long as the restaurant is near the ocean so that I can see the whole water-walking demonstration," Annie responds.

"Your ever-present sarcasm aside, I was not thinking oceanside. It's been a while since I've been to Lawry's. How's that sound?" Andy asks.

Not knowing what Lawry's is, Rein responds, "Sounds great. As I assume this is a working dinner, what's on the agenda in particular?"

Andy's moment of truth comes, and he says, "Listen, Annie, is it just OK that we perhaps take a little well-deserved break and maybe get to know each other a bit more without constantly working?"

Now, Rein's decisive moment comes, and she replies, "Sure, I'd like that, but if this is a date, I'm not sure how the press is going to respond."

"Well, I'm not much into labels, and on this subject, I don't care what the press says," Andy chides back.

Rein says, "Well, if this *is* a date, then I have some things I would like to tell you. So, be prepared."

"I'm not sure where you are going with this, but I'll be as prepared as possible given it is you we are talking about."

CHAPTER 21

THE AUTHORITIES

"So, General Stratton, what's your explanation for what happened in my state?" asks Governor Gatlin.

"Well, we really don't quite know. Listen, I have been put in charge of this investigation as part of an interdisciplinary force with some of the finest people I know in the DoD, the CIA, the top people in the relevant jurisdictions in California police agencies, the FBI, and others, and no one has been able to determine how a military-type strike was attempted on the Brock procession and then how an even more impressive military-type strike wiped it out. Heck, there are no bodies of the attackers left to investigate. This was the most impressive military strike and cleanup I've ever seen."

"What do I tell Mr. Brock, then?" the Governor responds.

"Tell him we have doubled his security forces, and we are working on the investigation with an army of people at every level of federal and state control. You should also tell him he's one lucky SOB, and you can quote me on that."

CHAPTER 22

THE FIRST DATE

A ndy appears at Rein's hotel room door wearing black athleisure pants, a white turtleneck sweater, and a black sports coat. The sweater is a combination of silk and cashmere and is nearly as thin as a t-shirt.

Rein opens the door, and Andy physically responds at the mere sight of her. "I am questioning whether I am just a shallow cad who merely enjoys stunning beauty, but then I stop myself and realize it is your wit, charm, and energy that I truly find as attractive as your body."

Andy's enhanced security detail keeps a respectful distance but also cannot help but visibly react to Rein's appearance at the door.

The reaction from Andy and the security detail is in direct response to seeing Rein in a peach dress, which strategically covers her breasts and weaves its way down to cover her crotch. All of the fabric is connected, but there is much more skin showing than there is fabric. Of course, she doesn't wear a bra or panties. Her nipples are readily apparent, yet magically and perhaps unfortunately, the well-designed garment reveals no camel toe. She is wearing heels but moves in them as if they are ballet slippers. Andy notices that Rein has not only sculpted abs but also sculpted arm and leg muscles, which are shown off in this dress.

"Thank you. I find you somewhat attractive as well," Rein responds.

"Your dress will certainly put to rest any question in the minds of the press as to whether our dinner is business or pleasure."

"Well, I am hoping it is as much pleasure as I hope to bring you," Rein says.

"Your hopes have already been fulfilled. Shall we go?" Andy asks. "Unfortunately, based upon the most recent incident we had, as you can see, we are going to be escorted by even more security than normal. I hope you don't mind."

"I'm glad they are here," Rein acknowledges.

"Well, let's hop in the limo and get some food, OK?" Andy urges.

"Let's do it," Rein responds.

The limo has a four-car escort—two in front and two in back. Their limo is fortified with bulletproof glass and has additional steel housing reinforcements. It is no ordinary limo.

Lawry's, the restaurant, is well aware of the Brock party reservation. Management had asked if Andy wanted a room to himself and his guest, but Andy declined. He wanted things to be as commonplace as possible.

Dinner is great. The meal starts off with the famous and delicious spinning bowl salad. Both have prime rib off of the cart, mashed potatoes, and creamed corn. Security keeps onlookers away, and Andy and Rein are able to chat in relative privacy. That does not mean the press is not ever-present and that they don't have enough photo opportunities to generate a huge story in their online journals and tomorrow's papers.

Despite the press and the enhanced security, Andy feels that something is a little off during dinner, as far as Rein is concerned. Their previous interactions have been kinetic—they always click—and on the ride back to the hotel, Andy says as much. Rein acknowledges she has something on her mind and asks that they talk about it back in her hotel room. Andy does not protest.

They make it back to the hotel room, and it is finally just the two of them.

"Listen, Andy, you don't fool around, and neither do I. When you are president, you'll have classified secrets that you will have to keep from certain people. In a way, I have been laboring under the same constraints, and I have been trying to determine how to balance the need for confidentiality with informing someone I am growing very attached to about my status," Rein begins.

"Whoa, I can't imagine where you are headed with this since my team vetted you pretty well, and I have no idea what you have hidden. Is this something that will hurt the campaign?" Andy responds.

"It transcends the campaign," Rein answers.

"What the heck does that mean? The campaign is likely not only the most significant thing in the country but also the world," Andy counters.

"True enough. This situation transcends the world," Rein reveals.

"Let's stop dancing around this issue. What is it?" Andy pushes a little.

"OK, I'm from another world."

Andy had to process this. So, here is an extremely intelligent, talented, and thoughtful woman, who has uttered what would otherwise sound crazy. Andy needs to compute this before responding. Rein sees him doing so. Andy initially thinks it is best to believe her. Is it possible? Yes. Does anything else make sense right now? No.

"Which world?"

"It is called Merk."

"And you are only telling me this now because if we stayed professional, then you felt it was not yet required to tell me. However, because you anticipate a relationship with me, you now feel compelled to make the disclosure because being in a relationship changes things." Andy communicates these points as statements even though they can easily be presented as questions.

Rein thinks, *My goodness, this guy is amazing. Instead of being upset, instead of doubting me, he has processed what I have said, rationalized it, and calmly arrived at a logical conclusion.*

"Yes."

"Hmmm. Do you anticipate me keeping your secret?"

"For the moment, I hoped you would for both our purposes. Ultimately, my world was planning on making the disclosure—mainly because of you."

"Because of me?"

"Yes, you are leading the change of this world in a manner that justifies an invitation from my world to join the civilized worlds of the galaxy."

"That's probably the best compliment I've ever received."

"Do you believe me?"

"Oddly enough, I do, but it's a lot to process and still a little hard to grasp."

"Well, would you like to see my ship?"

"It's here?"

"Yes."

"Is it safe for me to go there? Never mind, you would not ask me if you thought otherwise."

"If you have a few moments now, we could go."

"How long will we be gone?"

"A few hours, or more if you would like."

"So, I haven't known you that long at all, and now I should trust that joining you on an interstellar spacecraft is safe, that I won't be abducted or raped."

"Well, the evening was kind of going well. You'll be safe and won't be abducted, but I might sexually force myself on you, and that might be considered rape."

"Nope. There's a thing called consent."

"Alright. Please take all of your clothes off now."

"I thought you wanted to go to your ship now and not make love?"

"Getting naked is required to get to the ship. We are what you understand to be 'transporting' up there, but unlike on *Star Trek*, it does not work with clothes on. Don't be such a prude."

"Listen, sweetheart, I'm not a prude, but I generally don't strip down at the drop of a . . ."

Before he finishes his thought, he notices that Rein (Annie) starts stripping right in front of him. Of course, there is not a lot to take off. Her shoes and nylons go first, then the dress-like thing, and soon, there is a beautiful, totally nude lady standing in front of him. Amazingly, even though what she generally wears does not hide much, her unhidden body is more sensual than what the imagination has allowed him to envision when she is clothed. Her breasts are perfectly formed and sized for her body, and she is perfectly hairless and unabashed in her state of nudity, which makes her that much more sensual.

"Well, I'm waiting."

With that, Andy disrobes. Involuntarily, his nine-inch cock is hard and actually throbbing.

"I find that men from my world don't get hard as fast as you just did, and generally speaking, they are not as large in the penis as you are."

"I aim to please."

"Well, you certainly are aiming . . . Two to Send now, please."

And, within moments, the two of them are on the ship being greeted by Clevin and several attendants with proper attire for both of them. Andy's erection survives the Send and is discreetly noticed by all in attendance.

Rein is provided with her typical grey one-piece suit. Andy's top is made of a modal-type fabric that hugs his torso yet is extremely comfortable. His bottoms are made of identical fabric that does nothing to hide his continued erection or any of his rippling muscles. Like Rein's outfit, his is also grey.

"As I was about to ask before you had us whisked off, your name is not Annie, correct?"

"Rein."

"Like falling water droplets?"

"No. It's spelled in your alphabet, R-E-I-N."

"And your last name?"

"None to speak of. I see that this conversation has lessened your sexually oriented manifestation. I'm both glad and saddened—glad it was inspired in the first place and saddened we were not able to address it at the moment."

"There's a lot of stimuli right now. One, I have never been outside of Earth's atmosphere. Two, I have never met folks not from Earth. Three, the technology that surrounds me is independently fascinating. Annie, er, Rein, we've got a little bit to discuss, don't we?"

"Yes, but first, please meet Cliven, who's been here amongst us awhile."

"Cliven, pleased to meet you."

"Mr. Brock, you as well. Welcome to our humble ship."

"The others who were here have already gone without me being able to thank them for the clothes. Cliven, would you do that for me?"

"Sure."

Rein explains, "Cliven is our cultural attaché for Earth. Essentially, he is your unknown diplomat."

Andy then asks, "And what are you?"

Cliven responds for Rein, "You have been mingling on Earth with the very head of the Merk Earth Assessment team."

"How's Earth doing in that assessment?"

"Not bad, largely because of you and the following you have engendered," Cliven responds.

"Cliven, how do you feel about Rein revealing the ship to me?"

"Based upon your evident current state of mind, I am accepting of it even though it was sooner than anyone here expected. While we anticipated the possibility that you would form a connection with Rein, we did not expect either the speed or the apparent depth of that connection. Also, I think both you and Rein are in for a surprise once you have sex, as your penis is extremely large, and the female Merkian vagina is not as deep as those you find on Earth."

"Everyone is rather cavalier about Rein and I having sex. I think I have something to say about that."

Cliven responds, "Listen, Merkians don't appear to have what you call 'hang-ups' about such things. It is clear you and Rein have a profound connection. You are both mentally, spiritually, emotionally, and physically attractive. You are a fabulous match. It is, therefore, both reasonable and predictable that you will want to manifest that attraction in a physically proximate fashion."

"I am flattered you find me physically attractive. Men on Earth are not generally secure enough to make that statement."

Rein says, "I think you will find some substantial differences between Earth and Merk. We have to get you back, so let me show you a little more of the ship and introduce you to the captain. Then let's get back to the hotel room."

Andy is most interested in the bridge and the navigational capabilities. The captain is eager to introduce him to the basics of FTL travel, the control features, and some of the defensive and offensive capabilities of the ship. It becomes clear how Merk had successfully intervened to protect the Brock entourage on I-15 as well.

Rein shows Andy her living quarters, which he finds amazing. She is also able to show him the dining facilities, associated kitchen facilities (both for fabrication and natural preparation), and entertainment areas (which, by comparison, make cruise ship entertainment capabilities look like a 1950s TV set).

The Merk on board the ship are fairly amazed at Andy's calm and inquisitive demeanor. Most aliens of a pre-FTL world can hardly handle the sheer shock of a foreign world with FTL capabilities. They are terrified, suspicious, threatened, and incapable of taking it in. Andy, on the other hand, is probing, composed, calculating (in a positive way), and good-natured. One might say he fits in as well.

"Well, I must say, you are taking this all rather well, Mr. Brock," Rein says.

"What am I going to do? If you wanted to take over the Earth, you would. If you wanted to hurt me, you could. You appear to be here to engage in good faith with Earth and probably help Earth. Why fight that?" Andy responds.

"I understand, but please understand that most of our new visitors don't react as intelligently as you are reacting, so we have a right to be a bit surprised," Rein interposes.

"But you suspected I could handle it, or you would not have risked it, right?"

"True, but that does not mean I am not somewhat surprised by the fact that my instincts proved true in what you call 'spades.' Regardless, we need to get back, don't you agree?"

"Indeed. Disrobe, please."

Rein does so even though they are in a common area with at least twenty others.

"Your turn."

Andy actually blushes, not being accustomed to nakedness in front of both female and male strangers. It is one thing, in Andy's mind, to be in a locker room, but another to be in a common area full of people and just take your clothes off. Regardless, he thinks, *When in Rome*, and strips. One more time, both at the circumstance and witnessing Rein's nude form, he experiences another massive, throbbing erection.

Rein says, "Well, that's good. It looks like you're ready for the hotel room. We typically perform the Send from the Send platform, so let's make our way there."

Andy asks who he should give his clothes to, and before Rein answers, an attendant is already there to retrieve them.

They make their way, stark naked, to the Send platform. Andy tries to say as many goodbyes as possible, and before he knows it, he and Rein are back in Rein's hotel room.

"Despite being alone with me in my hotel room again, I see you no longer feel inspired as your erection is gone," Rein observes.

"Listen, sweetheart, we scurried to the Send platform through a crowd of people. I experienced the Send process again, and I have a million additional things to process. This would affect any man's penis."

With that, Rein comes over to Andy and kisses him quickly but gently. Andy pulls Rein to him and they exchange the kiss of either of their lifetimes. The kiss runs so deep that they both feel it in their respective abdomens.

Of course, it does not take long for Andy to return to his excited state, which Rein can actually feel on the outside of her stomach.

"This penis size situation is going to be interesting," Rein says.

"I think we will manage. I know we had dinner a few hours ago, but I'm starving as it seems we've been gone a long time. I'm sure you are hungry as well for at least a late-night snack, but any chance we can finally make our way to the bedroom?" Andy asks.

"Follow me," Rein answers.

Predictably, the hotel room doorbell rings. Rein puts her robe on and answers the door. It is security asking if Mr. Brock is available. Rein answers in the affirmative, and before she can get him, Andy appears fully dressed.

"What is it? I trust you realize the hour?"

"Sir, Tom said there were two things happening that he thought you needed to know about right away, so he asked to see if you were available. We'll let Tom inform you of what those two things are. May we escort you to Silverstone One?"

After giving Rein both a longing look and a brief kiss, Andy says, "Yes, let's go." Andy also apologizes to Rein for having to do so, and she says she understands, adding that he should never apologize for such a circumstance ever again. With that, Andy is off. He invites Rein to join him in Silverstone One as soon as she is able to collect herself.

When traveling, there are times when the motor coach fleet has maid service, is detailed, and has other maintenance. During those times, Andy and his team stay in a hotel. Otherwise, Andy prefers to stay in Silverstone One. It just so happens that this evening, all of the team members are in hotel rooms rather than some of them staying in the Silverstone fleet. There is never the occasion that all members of the team sleep in the Silverstone fleet, but there are those who desire to do so, and seniority rules on such occasions.

In any event, Silverstone One is ready for deployment. Both Tom and Dempsey are busy at the consoles, viewing a range of content.

"Andy, good to see you. Sorry to interrupt your evening," Tom says.

"Andy, we actually have a couple of developments you need to know about," Dempsey adds.

"Dempsey's right, but me first," Tom interjects. "This date between you and Annie is blowing up. There are serious press-level communications beginning to suggest that you do not protect professional boundaries. They, of course, refer to both Lisa and Annie. While we obviously don't have poll numbers on this, I think we're going to take a serious hit."

"What's worse is that a Chinese fighter plane shot down one of the Taiwanese fighters over the Taiwanese Strait. Also, Indian troops clashed with their Chinese counterparts along the border. Como is saying it's all your fault because they see you as the next president based upon poll numbers, and therefore, he says they are going to try to take care of business before you get in office," Dempsey adds.

"Well, so much for having a nice dinner and taking a few hours off for a little relaxation," Andy responds.

At that moment, Rein enters Silverstone One and joins the meeting. Andy fills her in on what has happened.

Rein says, "Well, I am going to hold a press conference tomorrow to address the professionalism issue, whether you want me to or not. As far as the China–Taiwan situation, Como's an idiot for admitting that everyone thinks you are going to be president; as such, admission will become a self-fulfilling prophecy. It also admits that the Chinese are afraid of you once you get in office, which is even more reason everyone will want to see you in office. You should also hold a press conference and say that Chinese provocations are nothing more than bullying tactics that the United States of America does not have to either tolerate or cave in to."

Tom, Dempsey, and Andy look at each other for a moment, then each magically, at virtually the same time, state their agreement with Rein doing the press conference and the substance of her recommendation for Andy's press conference.

Dempsey says, "I still don't know where Annie came from, but, man, she's the real deal, Andy."

Andy looks at Rein.

Tom adds, "Annie, you are amazing. Glad to have you on the team. Do you need any help preparing for your presser tomorrow?"

"Tom, no need. I'm merely going to tell the truth."

CHAPTER 23

REIN'S FIRST PRESS CONFERENCE

The hotel's main conference room is set up for a press conference at noon. Press credentials are soon restricted as the overflow demand is more than typically present for a Brock press conference. Of course, every network is there—every cable news outlet is present, every major newspaper has a representative, and foreign national press is also involved. Still, only about twenty percent of the demand for credentials is satisfied.

Tom introduces Rein, indicating she will make a brief statement followed by a limited Q&A session.

Rein appears at the podium, having intentionally chosen to wear a tight-fitting cream-colored turtleneck dress, which shows off her figure and does not hide her nipples (although on camera, they are not readily apparent), though it is otherwise tastefully opaque. She looks stunning. Her makeup is also tasteful and not overdone, while her hair perfectly frames her face. Her stance and posture demonstrate strength and confidence.

Rein begins with a tone that is simultaneously soothing to hear and compelling in its strength. "Ladies and gentlemen, thank you for attending. It appears some of you noticed that Mr. Brock and I had dinner last night. Some of you, based upon that dinner, are suggesting—and some doing more than that—that Mr. Brock is unprofessional. You mentioned he dated Lisa previously and now appears to be going down the same road with me. You are contending that his actions are wrong.

"First, let me say that most of what you are commenting about is none of your business. What I am about to say should not need to be said and is also none of your business. I trust that the reason it is none of your business will become quite evident when I am done.

"For those of you who are contending that Andy's relationship with Lisa was inappropriate, let's examine a moment what you are attempting to say. Are you suggesting that Lisa did not consent? Are you suggesting that Andy somehow wielded undue pressure on Lisa to join him on a date? Are you suggesting that Lisa lacked such a spine as to be overcome by such pressure? Are you suggesting that Andy had trouble finding a relationship, and so he had to coerce a co-worker to date him?

"Well, let me enlighten you. I did not have the great pleasure of ever meeting Lisa, but I certainly have had the opportunity to learn about her after I joined this wonderful team. Lisa was universally seen as one of the most intelligent, strong-willed, and mature women of this world. It is also generally viewed that Lisa had no problem attracting the affection of others. She had the ability to choose whomever she wanted to be with. The fact that Lisa and Andy worked together and an attraction formed was viewed by everyone on the team as a natural and almost expected result.

"With respect to Andy, *People* Magazine, represented by Alice Chambers seated in the front row here, has identified Andy as the most eligible bachelor and 'Sexiest Man Alive' five times in the past fifteen years. In that span of time, Andy was married and has had two dating relationships since his wife died. Lisa was one of them, and with one date, I am the other. To suggest that Andy is a rampant womanizer is not supported by the record.

"Let's turn to me. Andy is the most attractive and amazing person I have ever met. Forget all of the 'sexiest man' stuff. His incredible intelligence, wit, charm, and, most importantly, ethics are what I value the most. Yes, it is nice he is physically fit, I won't lie, but that is not the core of my attraction to him. Andy was as shocked as he could be to find someone after Lisa, whom he also finds attractive. He tells me he feels I possess some qualities he finds attractive as well. The mutual attraction was present from the moment we met. Andy never behaved inappropriately. There was never a hint of him trying to use his position to influence me in any manner. We both realized a mutual attraction, and both came to the point of communicating that attraction in a discreet and calm manner. We behaved as two consenting adults.

"Now, I can confidently tell you that I have received numerous overtures seeking my attention in my life. You will find, as you look into my records, that I have been fairly career-oriented and have had relatively few relations—much like Andy.

"Anyone who would contend that I somehow needed to date Andy in order to have a relationship, to get ahead in my career, or out of some other rationale in desperation has no idea who I am and, frankly, has no right to speculate on such a silly basis.

"Anyone who would contend that Lisa was feebly coerced into a relationship with Andy has no idea who Lisa was and has no right to speculate on such a silly basis.

"Anyone who would contend that Andy ever acted inappropriately with either Lisa or me has no idea who Andy is and has no right to speculate on such a silly basis.

"Now, if anyone in this room has an iota of data to bring forth that suggests otherwise, then I'm all ears. Just make it a fact and not conjecture. Right now, I trust that you all understand I could not be more emphatic in communicating that going to dinner with Andy last night was entirely of my own volition. Right now, I trust that none of you will further impugn the good name of Lisa in suggesting she would engage in anything untoward.

"Listen, I've spoken very directly this afternoon. I don't want to be misunderstood on this point. While I say it is somewhat none of your business, please understand that both Andy and I have deep respect for the role the press serves. Andy is a public figure. His character is something appropriate for discussion and examination. You, ladies and gentlemen of the press, form arguably the most important function in our democracy. That is one reason that on the day after I had dinner with Andy, I stand before you now. Andy and I truly care that the American public understands who Andy is and knows he respects the fact that the press is an important avenue for the public to learn about him.

"There are some limits, however. One limit is engaging in good journalism, which means reporting the facts and not participating in unfounded conjecture. Another limit is respecting that even public figures enjoy some bounds of privacy. A public figure's private inter-actions with their spouse or partner need not and should not be explored.

"So, I respect your journalistic inquiries but reject any inappro-priate prying into private matters.

"Any questions?"

The room is initially silent. The press cannot believe whom they have met. First, and not too long ago, there was Andy's vice presi-dential pick, who gave a breathtaking speech. Then, of course, there was Andy's acceptance speech, historic in its own right. Now, Rein's speech is viewed as nothing less than future candidate material. Rein's confident command of the room is seen as a leadership-caliber per-formance. She is articulate, rational, humble, and intelligent—as well as physically stunning. No one in the room has any feeling that Rein could be coerced into a relationship.

Despite that, CNN's Martha Cohen asks the first question: "Regardless of whether either Lisa or you were the subject of harass-ment, you should appreciate that in today's environment, we have every right to ask about the propriety of a very powerful man decid-ing that the only people he dates are subordinates, right?"

Rein responds, "I am here right now for that very reason. You have the right and perhaps the duty to ask. However, let me read you a quote from one of your colleagues in the press, published last night: 'Mr. Brock has clearly crossed a line. Can't this guy get a girl unless she works for him? Mr. Brock needs to understand that these kinds of relationships are absolutely prohibited. He should now be found completely unfit for office.' Ms. Cohen, that's not asking a question. That's reaching completely unwarranted and baseless conclusions. That is not the appropriate exercise of the freedom of the press. That is an abuse of the power of the press. I respect your question, but I do not respect and will not tolerate your colleagues' unfounded report-ing, as I just referenced."

Once again, Rein knocks the ball out of the park and heads nod throughout the room. One of those heads is sitting on Martha Cohen's neck.

James Culbert at Fox News then asks, "May I inquire what your plans are with Mr. Brock?"

Rein responds, "No."

Mr. Culbert adds, "Well, then, as a kind of follow-up, I thought in your long speech you indicated we had a right to ask that question."

Rein responds, "With all due respect, Mr. Culbert, that is not what I said, and I will humbly suggest to you that part of good journalism is listening very carefully to the facts."

Rein's swift but respectful dismissal of the Fox News inquiry is generally viewed in the room as adept. Part of Rein's appeal is her tone. While her one-word response could be seen as arrogant, the totality of that response and the later response is viewed as almost tolerant in the face of stupidity.

Tom then intervenes, "OK, folks, I think you have a pretty good understanding of what the deal is . . ."

With that, Melissa Brown of *The New York Times* asks Tom, "Are we going to hear from Andy about this?"

Rein retakes the podium and responds, "I hope not. The issue, as Ms. Cohen correctly put it in her thoughtful question, is whether I was harassed. I was not. I am not. Every available data point indicates that Lisa was not. Andy telling you he did not harass me is less informative, and at best merely duplicative, than my statement—as truthfully as I can possibly make it before you today—that I was firmly consensual in my desire yesterday to have had a dinner date with Andy. I am not being coerced. I am not capable of being coerced. Now, Andy can do what he wants, but I hope we have permanently put this issue to rest."

Tom says, "Well, Annie, I could not have said that better myself. Folks, Andy will be having a press conference on recent international events. I hope you all are able to attend. Thanks very much for joining us today."

And with that, Tom and Rein leave the press conference. The post-conference reporting is almost universally favorable. Commentators find Rein believable and are uncomfortable commenting on Lisa's status.

Some commentators go so far as to conclude that Rein and Andy are a match made in heaven. The headline in *The Washington Post* the following day reads: "THE WORLD'S GREATEST POWER COUPLE."

Rein calls Andy after the press conference and tells him there is an emergency on the ship that requires her to return, but she will be back tomorrow. Andy's heart drops as he wants to return to Rein's hotel room more than anything in the universe, but he, more than most people, understands when duty calls. He also has his own press conference to prepare for, so it is probably better that Rein and Andy do not spend the night together as little work would be achieved.

CHAPTER 24

ANDY'S NEXT PRESS CONFERENCE

In the very same conference room at noon the next day, Tom appears at the very same podium and announces Andy. The press credentials requested are double the credentials of yesterday's conference, if that can be believed.

Andy takes the podium.

"I'm here to discuss China's provocations and how my administration will respond to same.

"Let me note that I also appreciate the tremendous outpouring of favorable opinions to Annie's discussion with you yesterday. She is a remarkable woman.

"Now, back to China. I think China's activities demonstrate unequivocally that the only appropriate policy in dealing with them is one of strength. We cannot abandon our allies, whether that ally is India, Vietnam, or Taiwan. Any policy that would appease China with respect to a possible attack on any of our allies would only be a recipe for further attacks and would only lead to further conflict.

"With that, I'll take your questions."

Randy McMichael of Fox News first asks, "So, do you agree that you should be more careful in how you go about choosing dates?"

Andy responds, "First, let's keep our eye on the right ball. Surely, a discussion of China policy is more important than who joined me at Lawry's the other night. Second, I don't feel I chose either Lisa or Annie as dates. I felt more or less compelled by my attraction to both of them in particular ways to join them socially. Was I careful to ensure the communications that led up to those social interactions avoided any undue influence? Yes. In that manner, I was careful."

McMichael follows up, "OK, well, then how did you ask them?"

Andy answers gingerly, "Let me start out by saying I am pretty sure most candidates would not field this question. I will, but I am a little concerned about the precedent. So, while I will answer this question, we are very close to the limit of what I am willing, or I think any candidate should be willing, to answer. In any event, the answer is I don't remember what I said verbatim, but I'll tell you my thought process. First, with both Lisa and Annie, there was ultimately an obvious connection that was mutually felt. Interestingly enough, that connection was not initially sensed with Lisa, but it was with Annie. So, with Lisa, there was a relatively slow process involved in assessing whether there was a mutuality of feelings. Lisa made a sense of interest fairly clear to me before I ventured any inquiry on my part. With Annie, there was immediately and consistently this palpable sense of commonality and profound attraction. It is something words cannot describe. You know, what's funny is that you never can tell for certain whether there is true mutual feeling. So, there is a risk of some level of offense in these situations, but you just have to trust your judgment and your feeling. If I had been wrong about it, if Lisa had been wrong about it, if Annie had been wrong about it, then there could be consequences. As the employer, if you will, the consequences to me are the worst. If I had misunderstood either Lisa's or Annie's feelings and made an untoward advance, then I should and would pay the consequences. What is important is that if either Lisa or Annie rejected any slight advance made on my part, then it would also have been critical for me to ensure they did not feel there would be any adverse consequence to that rejection. Thankfully, there was no misunderstanding with either Lisa or Annie."

Melissa Stork of the *LA Times* next asks, "So you agree that you even asking an employee on a date could and, under the right circumstances, would expose you to liability, correct? If so, let's say things don't work out with you and Annie, and you become president. Will you continue to make advances on women while in the Oval Office?"

Andy responds, "Ms. Stork, those are two great questions. First, yes, workplace romance exposes the employer to liability, which is why the employer must be very, very careful. Second, I would rather not predict the demise of my relationship with Annie—I care for her very much. That said, men have an ability to mess things up all the time; therefore, there is always the possibility for me to mess it up with Annie. In that event, if someone like my deceased wife, Lisa, or Annie were present, under the right circumstances, and I were careful, then I would not change my approach. If I truly believe I could love someone and that person was as good of a match for me as I could imagine, then I would not prevent that relationship from happening based upon the risk of liability—but only so long as I am very, very careful with how I go about it. Annie, as you all have seen, is one of the great women of this universe. There is something quite remarkable about her. While we are still getting to know each other, if I am right about her, then yes, I am convinced I love her. That present or perceived love is something I would risk liability over if I were ever to attempt to court someone."

It seems as if Andy and his team are on a roll with silencing the press. With Andy's last words, once again, the press conference room falls silent. It even takes Tom a moment or two to close out the conference, but he eventually says, "As no one seems to want to talk about China today, and as we appeared to have covered the other area of inquiry, we thank you for your time and look forward to seeing you through the rest of the campaign."

The pundit reaction afterward is mostly favorable. Andy's humility on the subject of being able to mess things up with Annie scores points. Andy's answers also start a torrent of conversations on social media about whether employment romances need to be banned. The developing consensus is that Andy's approach is dead-on: The country is not going to ban employment romances, but that does not mean employers need not be careful, and if employers are not careful, then there could be liability.

The women who are surveyed by the press shortly after the press conference are mostly found to be swooning over the romance. The female population generally thinks Andy's speech is, in a word, "dreamy." To profess his feelings of love for Annie so confidently and forthrightly is so rare, gallant, and true. In their minds, Andy goes from being the world's most eligible bachelor to the now unavailable Prince Charming. Most women can only dream such a man would not only be theirs but appear so publicly dedicated to the woman he is courting. Women's hearts also leap when Andy uses the old-fashioned phrase "court someone." It is what most women say they want but seldom find.

CHAPTER 25

THAT NIGHT

Rein's Send takes her directly to Andy's hotel room. Before the Send, she is able to view and hear Andy's press conference in her private lodgings on the ship. She is not stunned by what he says. It is as if he merely confirms the feelings she already knows, but that does not mean it is not great to hear—he tells his world about his feelings even when he does not necessarily know exactly how she feels. Even Merkians aren't so confident.

Rein arrives at Andy's room shortly after his press conference, before he is even able to get there. She chooses not to call him. She also chooses not to get dressed, even though the second Send provides her with clothes.

Andy calls Rein after the press conference, but she does not answer. At the moment of the call, she is actually in the process of the Send. Hugely disappointed but still understanding, Andy goes with Tom to the central war room in the hotel dedicated to the campaign and talks strategy while getting something to eat.

"Tom, what's the reaction looking like?" Andy asks.

"Andy, you know, I've worked with a decent number of candidates in my day. I've never seen anything like you. It seems you are incapable of not hitting a home run. I mean, they called Reagan the Teflon President, but even he got into trouble from time to time. You just seem unstoppable, and it's mostly of your own doing, although I am certainly willing to take at least forty percent of the credit."

"Well, it's very generous of you to give me the sixty percent," Andy replies, "but seriously, what are the details?"

"Weirdly, if you are worried about the female electorate, don't be. The female reaction is through the roof as if you are some kind of white knight on a steed. So, the vote we were at one point a little concerned about based upon employment harassment has now turned into an advantage. I don't know whether to love you or hate you—love you as the best candidate in the history of the world or hate you just because no man should be able to be as frickin' perfect as you.

"The male vote has not really changed. Men don't seem to see much of an issue here. The polls seem to conclude that Annie is the catch of the century, so men are saying, in the vernacular, 'Yeah, I would try to tap that ass too,' and don't be upset with me by that turn of phrase because that is exactly what is being said in abundance on social media."

Andy takes a bite of his caprese salad, which has the perfect mixture of balsamic vinaigrette combined with buffalo mozzarella and ripe tomatoes. He ordered it seasoned with garlic and Lawry's seasoned pepper—the latter a bit of an odd twist. "Well, listen, I just try to do what's right. Maybe I am a little lucky too. Don't hate me."

Tom joins Andy and takes a bite of his own salad. "See, what might piss off most men is that you are even good at ordering salad, but since I am the current beneficiary of this incredible meal, I won't complain."

"OK, hold that thought. I'm going to give Annie a call," Andy interrupts.

Andy tries Rein once more and gets through this time.

"How's the emergency?"

"It's handled for now."

"When are you coming back?"

"I'm back."

"Where are you?"

"Where you want me."

"Hmm, sounds good. See you in a moment."

Andy re-enters the conference room and tells Tom he has to go. Tom gives Andy a knowing look and says, "Don't do anything I wouldn't do."

"Tom, despite the fact that the whole world now knows about Annie and me, let's not get glib about this, and I wouldn't do anything you would do because I am much more skilled at it," Andy gibes with a sly smile.

Andy silently tries to guess whether Rein is in her room or his room.

CHAPTER 26

ALIGNMENT

Andy guesses correctly: Rein is in his room. Naked. "Rein, I don't know what your expectations are, but I'm not the kind of man who can be toyed with. If you think I am so shallow that showing up in my room completely naked is going to provoke sexual relations, well, then, you'd be . . ." Before Andy can finish, Rein, faster than he's ever seen anyone move, crosses the room to where he stands and kisses him as if it were the last night of the universe.

Rein breaks away and says, "First, I know we have a lot to talk about and do. I'd like to do the doing first and then talk. However, I'd like to do the 'doing' part on the ship in a special place. So, please strip."

"I've never been in a relationship where I am commanded to disrobe as frequently as I am with you. In fact, generally speaking, I don't think I have ever been so commanded to disrobe by anyone."

Regardless, Andy strips. Rein notices he is primed for the "doing," and his nine-inch cock is in full glory. Without any hesitation, Rein communicates the order to effectuate the Send for both of them.

Andy has no idea where on the ship Rein is taking him. Next thing he knows, they are on the transport and attendants are present to provide clothing. Rein waves them off and takes Andy by the hand to lead him to the null gravity room.

Andy still finds it hard to get used to walking around naked. It is even more awkward because he is anticipating making love to

Rein, and his anticipation is readily apparent. So, here is Andy walking through the concourses of the ship completely naked and with a full hard-on. To his amazement, there is no awkward attention paid either his or Rein's way. He notices that most everyone views his penis and remembers that the men of Earth apparently have larger endowments than the men of Merk.

They arrive at the null gravity room, and it is generally empty. In fact, they are the only ones there. There is a well-appointed antechamber into which they enter. "Before we do this, I do want you to know a little something that is on my mind. By your way of thinking, I am very much convinced I do in fact love you. Merkians think about it a little differently. We find the Earth-think about 'love' is a little unsophisticated. Earthlings tend to conflate 'love' with a bunch of thoughts, feelings, physiological reactions, and emotions that are not particularly lasting or meaningful. It is why people of Earth don't stay together very long in relationships and the divorce rate is so high. They don't really understand the relationship they are in, they don't understand what they are feeling, and they are generally very shallow about the whole thing. Merkians have had more time to digest all of this as a society and a culture. It's ironic considering our relationship, but it takes Merkians a bit longer to develop their relationships, and those relationships last exponentially longer than the ones on Earth. The best translation for what I feel for you is that we are 'aligned.' In this case, 'alignment' does not mean we are merely going in the same direction. It means that even though we are separate, we are whole. So, before you 'make love' to me, as you would call it, please know what I feel for you is much deeper than this 'love' concept. I feel we are fully aligned."

Andy responds, "I feel the same way." And then he passionately kisses her.

"Hold on one more moment. You've got to remember one thing and learn another. First, my vagina can probably only take in two-thirds of your penis. The good news is the top, meaning the deepest point, of a Merkian woman's vagina has a stimulating surface for a penis. I promise you you'll know when you reach it. All I ask is that you be careful not to try to break through. More good news is that null gravity will help reduce your ability to thrust. One of the great things about null gravity is that we will truly feel as one, and your ejaculation will take a significantly longer time than if we were in normal gravity, enabling greater friction."

"Rein, the science thing is great, and I'll be careful, but I think I've waited long enough to further align with you."

With that, they leave the antechamber and, holding each other, enter null gravity.

For the first time in their brief relationship, no words are spoken. Their lovemaking is, in a word, compelling. Rein is able to form a seal around Andy's penis with her vagina and stimulate him with vaginal throbs. Andy is able to somewhat stave off an orgasm for a while, but not too long. Their kisses are deep and passionate throughout, and they cannot and will not stop gazing into each other's eyes, which speak more than anything about their feelings. As Andy comes, it is as if his ejaculate is sucked into Rein. He is expecting his semen to awkwardly float in null gravity, but none is apparent.

Out of null gravity and back into the antechamber, Andy says, "I know I should probably say something more romantic, but the science of how no semen was present after I pulled out intrigues me."

"After that, there's no need to apologize about anything. I told you Merkian vaginas are different . . ."

"Yeah, well, you don't have to tell me that based on what I just felt . . ."

"Let me finish, please. To put it simply, I'm able to suck in all of the semen."

"Hmmm, OK. By the way, for two of the most responsible people in the universe, it's amazing we did not discuss birth control."

"True, we did not."

"Are you toying with me?"

"Maybe a little. I don't use birth control. If I have your child, then that would be the most amazing thing that would ever happen to me."

"Are there any genetic concerns of Earthling and Merkian combinations?"

"No, or I should say, not that we know of or that our science has been able to discern—and our science is really, really good. I guess anything is possible, but there are no risk factors currently understood or even envisioned. The only risk is that we probably would have one of the most spectacular babies in the universe."

"I assume you are familiar with Disney. As I suspect that is a safe assumption, you know that what we have going on here only happens in a Disney movie or maybe a Hallmark Christmas movie?"

"Yes, I guess, but none of them compare to the reality of you and me."

CHAPTER 27

THE ELECTION

A ndy is joined by Tom Kynes, Jack Gatlin, and Rein in his living room in his Chicago home. His other team members are in various locations around downtown Chicago, awaiting the anticipated celebration at the United Center. The election sites are about to close in some of the East Coast states and the real question on everybody's mind is how sweeping a victory it will be and what the complexion of the next Congress will be.

"Well, Andy, knock on wood, if the polls that came in last week are even close to being right, this should be a good night," Tom says.

"Jack, what do you think about California?" Andy asks.

"Given you are a Republican, Andy, it is a minor miracle that the polls have us up by seven points, and my own information says that may even be low," Jack reports.

"Rein, ahem, Annie, any thoughts on any changes to the speech tonight?" Andy asks.

"Funny you should mention rain, given the torrent outside. We want to make sure everything goes smoothly in us getting you to the United Center, but no, I think we are pretty set." Rein helps Andy cover with her response and thankfully Tom and Jack do not really catch the slip.

"Jack, what kind of coattails are we going to see in California, in your opinion?" Tom asks.

"You know, that's real hard to figure. California has generally gone so hard Democratic for so long that I would have thought we are not going to see that big of a shift, but the Brock phenomenon is so different that I just can't rule out some nice coattails."

"Jack, let's make sure we understand it is the Brock–Gatlin phenomenon," Andy corrects with a smile.

"Thanks, Andy, you are as generous as you are observant," Jack responds with a bigger smile.

"OK, guys, we've got some results coming in and, Andy, you have not lost a state yet. New Hampshire and Maine are in and it's by a wide margin. Andy, you've taken New Jersey, and it was not close," Tom reports.

"Tom, could we get New York?" Andy asks.

"Polls in New York were pretty close, so yes, but I'm not banking on it," Tom responds.

"We just picked up Virginia, West Virginia, Kentucky, Indiana, Tennessee, and, ahem, Georgia," Rein says.

"Should we be concerned that Florida has not been called yet?" Andy asks.

"No, because in the brief moment Rein was reporting, we just got Florida," Tom says.

"Guys, no one has touched the great food I've had sent in. Listen, I actually had Southside pizza made in my pizza kitchen and had Italian beef prepared as well. Annie, I'm not sure you've had it, and if not, you've got to dig in," Andy implores.

With a mouth half full, Tom says, "Where the heck did you get this Italian beef sandwich? This bread is so amazingly light and the beef is sliced so thin and flavored so well. It's like nothing I've had before."

"I happen to have an in with D'Angelo, and the owner was willing to set up a kitchen here and make it directly for us," Andy responds.

"Andy, I am now firmly in love with Chicago food, and I like you more now that you have introduced it to me," Rein says with a smirk.

"Well, I am glad I finally found a way into your heart a little bit," Andy responds.

"Guys, CNN just called the race. Andy, CNN says you are the next president of the United States. And it looks like you are going to win New York, Illinois, and Minnesota. I can now say this may be the biggest landslide in the history of elections. Right now, I just don't know which state is going to go for Como. It also looks like we will take the House and the Senate. Andy, Jack, you've got the biggest mandate since George Washington," Tom congratulates.

"Jack, we've got a lot of work to do," Andy says.

"Andy, Lance is on the phone," Tom says while holding out the cell.

"Andy, congratulations. You know, you've run a heck of a campaign, you brought the country together, and whatever I can do to help, just tell me," Lance Como says.

"Lance, you have been a gentleman through this whole process. I'd love to talk to you later about a place in the administration if that is what you'd like to think about," Andy responds.

"Andy, apart from the whole Taiwan situation, I'm on board with many of your new ideas. After the dust settles, let's talk about it, OK?" Lance asks.

"Sure thing. Take care, Lance, and thanks again." Andy and Lance end their call.

"Annie, let's get ready to make our way to the United Center. I trust you have not changed your mind on joining me there," Andy nearly begs.

"I have my nice red dress already set out," Rein says.

The United Center in Chicago is much larger than a conference room but smaller than a football field. It is the home of the Chicago Bulls but is staged for tonight's celebration. Without risking a fire hazard, the place is absolutely full of admirers and the press.

"Well, the Brock-Gatlin team pulled off the greatest political victory in American history. I'm not sure what to call this situation, a new Republican Party or something else, but it is absolutely history in the making," observes Sharon Luger of MSNBC reporting in a booth at the United Center.

"The closest we've ever seen to this was the Reagan landslide in 1984, but we've never seen a candidate win every state and win by such margins. Brock took the center majority of the country, got the votes of a majority of the right, and also received a lot of the votes of the Democratic left," echoes Chris Walters, also of MSNBC.

"Well, here is Andy Brock now to greet his admirers, joined by Annie Chandler, whom he referred to as the person he is 'courting,'" says Sharon Luger.

"First, for the seventy percent of the electorate who voted for us, thank you for your support of our ideas. For the thirty percent who did not, it is my job in part to earn your support. I will not forget you and the fact you have a different view that still needs to be heard. I spoke with Mr. Como and congratulated him on being a great American and joining me in one of the greatest and most civil contests we've ever seen. I intend to offer him a position in my administration, and I hope he will accept.

"I have too many other people to thank individually. I will do so privately over the next several weeks.

"I hope you understand this is a humbling victory. I hope you understand even more that Jack and I have a lot of work to do. That is our focus right now. You'll next hear from me at the inauguration—that is my next and only speech planned. In my view, the time for speeches is not as important as the time for us to go to work. My hope is that over the next four years, our actions will speak louder than any speech we might give tonight.

"I thank you all."

"Wow, the man swept the country in one of the most magnificent victories and gave the shortest victory speech ever. It's hard to believe. Well, that's Andy Brock, unconventional as ever. I don't know; it seems like the man teaches the country new things every time he speaks. Equally as amazing is that President-Elect Brock is inviting Lance Como into his administration. What position do you think he'll get, Chris?" asks Susan.

"It won't be secretary of defense given Como's position on Taiwan, but I would not rule out secretary of state, Susan. I also agree that victory speech was almost as remarkable as the victory itself. Andy seems to want to send a critical message: 'I'm done talking, and I plan to focus on getting the job done like I promised.' How many politicians act like this? Well, maybe that is why he carried the entire country. I'm not sure that the thirty percent who did not vote for him are not on his side now," answers Chris.

CHAPTER 28

WHEN TO INVITE

"I hope you are enjoying your oatmeal with blueberries, Rein, but the real star of this show is the thick-sliced bacon covered in maple syrup, right?" Andy asks while they share breakfast at his Chicago condo.

"While I am enjoying the food, I'm not sure that there is not a little smugness in your tone, which is really your racquetball victory speaking as well," Rein answers.

"Well, I am older than you by a good margin, and I still kicked your butt pretty well," Andy says.

"I don't think fifteen to ten is that much of a victory, given that was the first time I've ever played," Rein retorts.

"Listen, I need to savor the one victory I imagine I'll ever get over you, as I have never seen anyone pick up the game as quickly as you did. However, what you wore to the game was unfair. Your shorts exposed plenty of butt cheek, not that it mattered since your shorts were see-through and your sports bra was transparent as well. I don't know where you get your clothes, but they create a lot of distraction."

"The clothes are standard-issue Merkian sports attire, so get over it."

"Well, the men outside the court looking in were very appreciative of Merkian attire. Heck, there were even some women looking on fondly."

"Andy, I need to head up to the ship. I have meetings about Earth, and there are some developments in the galaxy that require attention. Here is a ship communicator. If you ask to speak to a particular person, it will direct your communication accordingly. As you really only know me, Cliven, and Captain Siven, I suspect those folks are the only ones you might be able to reach. If, for whatever reason, you can't reach me and need to, please try Cliven next. If that does not work, then try Captain Siven. I plan to be back in two days, but before I go, should we try some gravity-based sex?" Rein asks.

"You know, it was so good the first time that I just don't think I want to ruin it and change perfection," Andy answers.

"OK, well, then I'll just prepare for the Send and say goodbye," Rein says while stripping down, immediately noticing Andy's burgeoning nine inches of manhood.

"On the other hand, it is possible the first time should be viewed as part of a continuum of perfection, and gravity-based sex could be had in the bedroom right over there," Andy says while taking Rein in his arms.

After their second session, Rein says, "You know, I like this idea of an effort at continuing perfection, and as you know, I will be naked upon my return and see no reason not to pick up where we left off."

"All right, sweetheart, go off to work, and I'll be waiting right here for you."

With that, and with Rein conveniently without the burden of apparel, she executes the Send.

"The Send sensed foreign matter during your transport. Anything we need to be worried about?" Cliven smirks.

"If you believe that fabulous DNA from a truly special Earthling is of concern, then think again," Rein responds.

"Well, I hope the acquisition process was enjoyable," Cliven responds.

"Enough of that," Rein shuts him down.

"Understood. The team is together and ready when you are," Cliven informs.

"I'm going to clean up a bit, and I'll be there in a moment."

As Rein showers, she muses that Chicago is starting to feel like a home away from home. The ship is not home but it is comfortable.

Merk is home, but she is beginning to feel that home is wherever Andy is. She knows she does not have much time for such thoughts given the two pressing matters, but she cannot avoid the feelings that are wonderfully flooding her.

Rein makes her way into the conference room and says, "OK, folks, we've got two related issues: One, when do we invite Earth? Two, how do we deal with the Davark?"

"I'd like to invite Earth sooner rather than later, if for no other reason than we need to focus on the Davark sooner rather than later," opines Captain Siven.

"I appreciate your desire to deal with the Davark, but I think we need to give Earth a little more breathing room," Sorcen says.

"I agree with Sorcen. Andy's administration needs to get its footing before we hit the world with our invitation and intervention," adds Rein.

"That's understandable, but if China becomes any more provocative, then it might be an intervention more than an invitation," says Krin.

"You are right too, Krin, but let's see what the next few months bring and reevaluate. What is the latest on the Davark, Captain?" asks Rein.

"They appear to be reinforcing their positions and actually reaching out to potential allies, so it appears we have some time, but not a whole lot. I would like to go over the entire Davark schema within the galactic quadrant with you. We also need to be evaluating strategic advisors. I hope you are set for a pretty full two days up ahead," warns Captain Siven.

CHAPTER 29

FIRST STEPS

"**W**ell, the previous administration at least did a few things right. I like the fact that we have an entirely new aircraft carrier group coming on line this week and substantial reinforcements to the bomber and fighter crafts. Dempsey, based on the reports I've seen, we need to move forward with another new carrier group and even more fighter craft, right?" President Brock asks.

Dempsey, the newly installed secretary of defense, responds, "Those are, in fact, my recommendations, Mr. President, and I realize it might affect your domestic agenda on the economics."

"Jack, any thoughts?" Andy asks.

"Mr. President, US air and naval power must be maintained as a first priority. I agree that given the lead times for another carrier group as well as the air force enhancements, those expenditures need to be authorized as part of this budget. China will know about our new naval and air capabilities, but I think they should know there is more to come, and this administration is not backing down one degree in our commitment to being the strongest military on the planet."

"Thanks, Jack. Tom, how big of a hit will the domestic agenda take?"

Tom Kynes, former campaign manager and now chief of staff, responds, "Mr. President, my studies indicate we can prioritize all of the domestic agenda with the new military expenditures. A good part of the domestic agenda does not require full capital outlay at the beginning, and some of the domestic agenda can be achieved without serious capital outlays. If we seriously attack waste, I'm projecting a budget surplus in your third year."

"Annie, how is the bill administration process going?"

Annie, Andy's chief speech writer and chief domestic policy advisor, is also in charge of working with congressional liaisons in drafting bills. Andy knows her capabilities are enormous, and she has her own resources to call upon, which seem endless. "Mr. President, with the general mandate you enjoy and the congressional majority, your administration could probably outlaw Christmas and get it passed. I've had tremendous help from my congressional colleagues. I have no doubt bills will be on your desk for signature that cover the water reallocation and improvements for the West, the public-private medical buildout, the federal education infusion, prison reform, and the immigration control and amnesty package in addition to the military revamp. Of course, that's just a start, but I expect all of that to be moving in some form by Q2."

"Thanks, Annie. Dempsey, what are China's latest moves?"

"Mr. President, it's strange. China seems to be wanting to feel you out. That is the best way I can put it. Ever since the election, they have been solidifying strategic positions but have not been as provocative as with the prior administration. Surveillance—both on the ground, satellite-based, and otherwise—indicates they may be preparing for something bigger, but it's not clear what direction that will take. Obviously, they are poised to be able to attack Taiwan, but their movements are not that obvious."

"Thanks. Lance, any thoughts from your front on the China situation and with our allies?"

Lance Como, former Democratic candidate for president and Andy's political rival, was, in fact, invited to become secretary of state and successfully acceded to such position. "Mr. President, my counterpart in China is trying to leverage me. He understands my position during the campaign was not in alignment with your own and is trying to influence me to soften your own position. Obviously, that will not be successful, but it shows us some things. One other undercurrent that my people at state are telling me—along with the folks at the CIA, which I'm sure David will discuss next—is that there is a growing sense of dissatisfaction with the regime within the populace. There has always been some level of dissatisfaction, and Tiananmen Square was the last time there was a real manifestation of that dissatisfaction, but what I'm hearing is that the new under-current might make Tiananmen Square and Hong Kong look like child's play. Not only is there real upset about the number of soldiers at the borders and how long they have to stay there, but that is com-bined with a seriously deteriorating economy. The people also feel like the government's lies are now too much. Independently, Western media influences have successfully penetrated all levels of society. The Chinese see, if you'll excuse me, the rock star president the US has and what you are going to do for the US, and the Chinese popula-tion wants that. The problem, of course, is that the Chinese in power see the same thing, and I believe that is making Chen and his cronies even more desperate."

"Lance, there were a few people in my party who questioned whether I should have you in the administration. As I hear you and as they will hear you, I know they will find themselves mistaken. Glad to have you on board. I also appreciate your concern about my Taiwan stance, and I intend to respect your thoughts on that throughout this process. I'm not going to do anything precipitous. My position remains that we need to stand up to China, however."

"Mr. President, thanks for your kind words. I committed to you when coming on board that I would administer your policy on China as a loyal member of your administration. The funny thing is that my prior stance and relationship with the Chinese may very well help fos-ter a result that avoids conflict. I don't mean that in a smug way. What I'm trying to say is that something is happening that I did not foresee, and that is the uprising of the people that might occur. You see, your strong stance combined with my prior relationship may work together to bring about a result that maybe neither of us saw coming."

"Hmmm, that's interesting, Lance. I'm not going to bank on a revolution anytime soon, but let's see where this goes. David, what's the CIA's view?"

David King, CIA director, is actually a holdover from the prior administration. "Mr. President, I agree with Lance. All information is that there is one heck of an upswell in the common population. Business leaders are also stressed. Crackdowns have increased. I'm not saying it's a powder keg right now, but it could get there. This is both an opportunity and something we need to be gravely concerned about. Chen might be able to brutally control it, or Chen might lash out with the military to divert attention. It's not readily predictable. It is, however, quite dangerous either way."

"Thanks, David. Please stick around with Annie, Tom, and Jack, as there is something we need to discuss. I want to thank the others for their time on this issue."

The others leave, and Andy changes the subject. "While discretion and confidentiality are always required, what I am about to discuss requires the highest level of both. Understood?"

"Yes, Mr. President," all say in unison.

"I have been made aware that there is a sophisticated and benevolent alien presence near Earth. That presence has been in contact with me."

The room is stunned, with the exception of Rein, although even she is taken a little by surprise.

"When did this happen?" asks Tom.

"During the campaign."

"Mr. President, the CIA has actually discovered something we were investigating that we thought merited your attention. The attack on I-15 and the shutdown of that attack appeared otherworldly. There have also been atmospheric occurrences that are difficult to explain. Your knowledge affirms all we were investigating."

"Thanks, David."

"Care to elaborate a little, Andy?" asks Jack.

"The group comes from a planet structure called Merk. They have faster-than-light travel capabilities. They have been monitoring Earth for a long time and are planning to possibly invite Earth into the galactic community."

"And you know all of this—" Jack interrupts.

"Because I told him," Rein interrupts.

Everyone looks at Rein, then everyone looks at Andy.

"I am the head of Earth Assessment Analysis for Merk. We have seen the progress that Earth has been making over the decades to become a civilized society. Frankly, because of Andy's leadership and the fact that the United States and now much of the Earth are following his civilized lead, Merk is prepared to invite Earth into the galactic community. The only thing that has held us back is our desire to give the administration some breathing room. We wanted there to be time to accomplish what was needed before we swooped in and announced ourselves.

"We thought it best not to interrupt the flow of the first one hundred days of Andy's administration. We also thought it best to give the people in China the ability to deal with their government on their own before we entered the scene. David and Lance are correct in their observations about China."

"I knew you were out of this world, Annie, but I did not realize you were out of *this world*," Tom snickers.

"Andy, you do realize you have a real alien as part of your administration?" David observes.

"Hold on, David, there is technically nothing wrong with a non-US national as an advisor so long as they pass examination," Jack advises.

"Sure, but there's no question that Annie falsified records to get here, right?" David responds.

"Technically, the only thing that is obscured in my records is my place of birth. Everything else is truthful, and even the place of birth could be viewed as within arguable limits," Annie says.

"Well, let's start with your name," David says.

"Rein," Annie replies.

"Like water falling down?"

"No, R-E-I-N."

"Folks, let's step back a second. I'm telling you this so that you can guide me on what we should do. Now that I am president, I have a fiduciary duty to disclose material facts concerning this nation. I'm disclosing those facts to you. They can remain top secret, or we can disclose them to the military, to more of the government, or to the people at large. It is also complicated by what I'm about to do."

At that point, Andy pulls a small box out of his Oval Office desk, shows Rein the most elegant diamond ring anyone in the room has ever seen, takes Rein by the hand, and says, "I know your culture has a different way of going about alignment, but I figure you are OK with us bridging cultures and respecting both, so, Rein, I already feel as one with you, but, nevertheless, will you honor me with having that alignment recognized and becoming my wife in the sense that it is recognized on Earth?"

"Yes, on two conditions—that you become my scaron, Merk's version of a husband, and that we have a ceremony both on Earth and on Merk."

"I'm not sure those are conditions, and I never thought this would be a negotiation, but yes, yes, yes."

This scene is way too much for everyone in the room to handle, except for Andy and Rein. Not only did they just find out that Rein is an extraterrestrial, but now Andy will soon be married to her. Almost as significant is that Andy is getting married at all. And even more, he is marrying a member of his administration.

While Andy and Rein are in mid-embrace, Tom says, "Well, first, congratulations to Andy, and best wishes to, ahem, Rein. You guys really know how to load up a meeting. First, galactic surprises and then marriage. While I saw the marriage thing coming, I did not expect it at this meeting and under these circumstances. Well, we are obviously going to announce the wedding. David, from the CIA perspective, how do we handle the Merk disclosure?"

"Tom, you are handling this really well. I'm still trying to get my arms around the whole situation. Annie, I'm sorry, Rein, you have a spaceship in orbit?" David asks.

"My ship is in sufficient proximity to Earth but not in discernible orbit."

"Can I see it?"

"Yes."

"When?"

"Now."

"How long does it take to get to your ship?"

"In real-time, the process takes approximately thirty seconds, but it does not feel that way."

"Andy, any problem with you if I go there and get my arms around it?"

The others in the room immediately add that they would like to go as well.

"I have no problem, but you are going to have to remove your clothes first, and you are going to have Rein with you on the trip," Andy says.

"Do we go into separate rooms while we remove our clothes and transport separately, Rein?" Jack asks.

"No."

"Andy, I assume you are not OK with us seeing Rein without clothes and vice versa," says Jack.

"Actually, I think I'm going to find the experience enlightening. Just so you know, I'm going to stay back in the Oval Office and hold down the fort while you are gone. Please be back within an hour so that things don't get uncomfortable for me," Andy responds.

"Uncomfortable for you, you say, but how about us . . .?" Jack responds.

While Jack and Andy are speaking, Rein removes her clothes, walks over to the armoire, hangs her clothes, and waits in the nude for her travel mates to disrobe.

David observes to himself that it looks like Rein has an even spray tan all over her body, which has a glistening sheen. It is the most beautiful, toned body he has ever seen. Despite Rein now being engaged to Andy, David and the rest of the other men cannot control their cocks—all of which are engorged. None have removed their clothes yet, however.

"Guys, while I appreciate the looks, we should be going. You are going to have to strip now, please, and you should hang your clothes in the armoire like I did, just in case."

"Before I go, I just gotta say, Andy, I knew you were a lucky man, but I did not know how very lucky you were until today," Tom says.

"Thanks, Tom, but Rein's right, let's get a move on. Strip, or you don't get to go. Although I have to say, the last thing I want to see in the Oval Office is your naked asses, but the things I do for my country. That being said, I think I'll keep my eyes on my future wife, which I trust you'll agree is a wise decision."

Tom, David, and Jack uncomfortably disrobe. Rein notices their stiff cocks and also realizes that Andy's penis is significantly larger than any of the others. She commits to discussing this with Andy upon her return and will note her sacrifice for marrying a man with such a large penis.

Now that everyone is ready, Rein is able to have the ship execute the Send after she expeditiously makes arrangements for their reception.

"OK, guys, here we go."

"Wow!" Every Earthling present on the ship immediately reacts the same way.

Each man present is provided standard Merk clothing, which they all gratefully and immediately put on. Rein is provided with her standard, nearly transparent bodysuit, which she chooses to wear. There are other Merkians who were also just the subjects of Sends, and they casually return to their respective quarters, not requiring any clothing.

"Guys, you are on an extraterrestrial spaceship. My bodysuit should not be the focus of your attention. Let's put everything in perspective, shall we?"

Tom says, "I think I can speak for all of us and say that no matter where we are, that bodysuit deserves plenty of attention, even after we were fortunate enough to see you out of it."

"You know, this obsession you have with nudity and sexuality is one of the reasons we've held back on inviting Earth to the galaxy. If you persist in your shallow attention to things of marginal importance, then I may recommend that we reconsider the invitation. Now, if we could get down to business, I'll show you standard quarters, the common areas, and lastly, the bridge, but then we need to get back."

None of the Earthmen are handling the situation particularly well. Jack is the most mature and contained. Meanwhile, Tom is nearly a basket case. David, despite being the head of the CIA and, in theory, more clinical, is also having difficulty adjusting to the new reality.

Rein's strategy is to get them to understand that Merkians are not to be feared. Merk's presence and approach here is benevolent. Once that concept sinks in, Rein hopes these three will help Andy through the difficult phase and decision of how and when to introduce Merk to Earth.

Rein also decides that disclosure of Andy as her effective scaron and that she is effectively, and equally, Andy's caron is imperative as well. There are Merkian protocols involved with extracultural alignment liaisons that formalize into the Caronic relationship.

The group of Earthmen struggle through the introduction to the ship. Though certain probing questions are asked, they are still coming to grips with the new reality and fumbling over themselves, unlike Andy's introduction. It does seem, however, that the Earthmen are grasping the reality that Merk's presence is nothing but positive for Earth, the United States, and Andy Brock—though not necessarily in that order.

Another thing hits each of the Earthmen: seeing Earth from outer space inspires a stunning new perspective in each of them. None have been in outer space before. Seeing Earth engenders the feeling that the territorial squabbling on the planet is just plain silly. The universe is just too big. Rather than spending trillions on munitions, the people of Earth should realize that the planet is a valuable resource not to be squandered by tribal warring. The fact that Earth is one of many places with sentient life reinforces that Earth-domestic squabbling is myopic, geocentric, and simply idiotic. While Earth has come a long way from previous wars and stresses, the China situation needs to be resolved. Presumably, if Merk invites world leaders onto the ship, then the hope is everyone will feel the sense of community that viewing Earth from the lens of the ship brings about.

CHAPTER 30

THE FIRST TASTE

W hile the Send group is on their field trip to the ship, Dempsey makes his way to the Oval Office.

"Mr. President, Chinese and Taiwanese air forces are engaged. Up until this point, the Chinese were merely testing air space, but then, as of 8:57 p.m. our time, a Chinese fighter shot down one from Taiwan. Taiwan responded and the skirmish or air battle so far has numerous aircraft in total taken down by both sides. So far, the Chinese lost seven planes and Taiwan three. Consistent with your orders, I ordered attack craft from the USS Clinton to engage. At that point, the Chinese disengaged for the moment. We were not required to fire on any Chinese aircraft as of yet. That being said, this is the first real engagement between our forces on behalf of Taiwan with Chinese forces."

"Thanks. Have the situation room assembled in a half-hour. Within that time, you are to instruct the joint chiefs and the remainder of the cabinet to be prepared to discuss a plan of action and contingencies. I will have David and Jack meet us there as I have another matter of national security I am addressing with them currently," Andy instructs.

At that moment, Rein and the guys return to the Oval Office. Apart from Rein, it is not a pretty sight. Thankfully, with the exception of Rein, everyone (including Rein) gathers their clothes and gets dressed. Andy briefs them on the need to go to the situation room and indicates that the Merk situation will have to await discussion until later.

Andy, Jack, and David head to the situation room. This crisis is not presently appropriate for Tom and Rein to attend.

"OK, Dempsey, where are we?" Andy asks.

"I, along with the joint chiefs, are so far satisfied with our response. When our fighters appeared, the Chinese backed down. None of our forces were directly attacked, and we did not incur any casualties of any kind. We intend to deploy two more carrier groups to the Philippines, however. Taiwan is on as high of an alert as it can be. The Japanese and Koreans, as well. Japanese naval forces, in particular, have joined our forces in substantial numbers. Despite China having tried to grow the raw number of ships in its navy, the combined deployment of the US and its allies in the Pacific not only outnumber the Chinese navy but are qualitatively vastly superior. The Chinese have two carrier groups, with each carrier having only about two-thirds of the capability of our smallest carrier. We now have five carrier groups in the relevant region. Of course, those carrier groups do not include the land-based air force groups in Taiwan, the Philippines, Australia, Japan, and Korea."

"Thanks, Dempsey, but that's just not good enough. The US cannot be merely reactionary here. We now have a hot shooting war wherein US forces were actively engaged. While, thankfully, the Chinese backed down and there were no US casualties of any kind, that does not complete our analysis of the next steps. Indeed, at a minimum, I want an analysis of what the Chinese backdown means. I want to have an understanding of where this situation leaves us now and what a proactive response should be. David, Jack, you are with me back in the Oval Office to discuss some other matters. Dempsey, I want a better and more complete set of advice in one hour upon my return here. Understood?"

"Yes, Mr. President."

"OK, David, Jack, let's go."

CHAPTER 31

FIRE OR FRYING PAN

A ndy's administration has hardly been instituted, and he already finds himself having to address some of the most serious issues ever faced by any administration. Not only is he grappling with the first known alien presence presenting itself to humanity, but at that very same moment, there is war erupting that involves the Earth's one superpower, the US, and the only other serious power on Earth, China. The combined firepower of these two combatants equally exceeds the combined firepower of all nations on Earth throughout history. The military might of the US alone is awesome, and China's firepower itself could destroy much of the planet. If not for the US, China would be the most significant military power the world has ever seen. While US allies could, collectively, still defeat China without the US, the casualties of such a conflict would be enormous; the combined losses experienced in World War II would be a fraction by comparison. Andy finds himself wondering whether this is merely the frying pan or if he has actually already leapt into the fire.

Tom and Rein join David and Jack in the Oval Office with Andy, who takes a moment to laugh to himself. It is funny that all of them, except for him, were naked in the Oval Office not too long ago. That is the thing about Andy. His ability to compartmentalize is probably his best trait. Here, in the face of great crises, Andy is able to take a second and get a little self-control through internal humor. He knows time is precious right now, but he also somehow instinctively knows that one way to stay cool is to keep an even-keeled outlook. At times, his subconscious approach to this is to add an element of humor into the picture.

Tom recognizes this in Andy. He sees how Andy actually gets cooler as the heat of events intensifies. He also knows that humor is never far from Andy's mind or lips. Tom learns how to keep his own emotions from Andy and tries to adopt Andy's techniques of stress control as much as possible. However, sometimes it just does not work for Tom, and in those times, he often seeks out Andy to help him through the process. Upon reflection, Tom recognizes that when he uses Andy as a crutch under such circumstances, it is both unfair and just plain wrong. In those times, Andy probably bears more of the stress burden than anyone else. Despite handling that load, Andy never hesitates to help Tom through his own challenges. It is the current crisis that makes Tom realize how wrong he is in inflicting such a burden on Andy and how kind Andy is for helping Tom through his rough times. Obviously, Andy is a true leader, but that does not mean Tom should abuse Andy's abilities. Tom resolves to be a better part of the team.

"Tom and Rein, the folks in the situation room basically announced they were satisfied with the status quo. I told them to be prepared with a better answer within the hour. We need to be proactive. The status quo is unsatisfactory. So, before we return to a discussion of Merk, any thoughts from anyone on the China situation?" Andy asks the room.

"I agree that the folks in the situation room need to be more helpful. There has to be a more concerted, forward-looking plan of action," Jack concurs.

"I agree. I think Dempsey needs to push everyone in the room a bit harder. The national security advisor and the joint chiefs have to step up," David says.

"OK, let's discuss Merk. If anyone has a problem talking about Merk with Rein in the room, then please speak up. Trust me, I will not hold it against you," Andy says.

Andy looks around the room. No one says anything, and no one's body language indicates they have a problem.

"Andy, I'm not going to put anyone in that position. I'm going to the anteroom. After you guys confer on this, please come and get me," Rein interjects.

Andy is about to speak and ask Rein to stay, but her swift departure precludes that.

"In all the years that people have wondered what alien contact might be, this is the very best scenario anyone has ever imagined," David chimes in.

"Not only are they pro-US, but they are pro-Brock. I hope I'm not going to be perceived as too crass, but it's not a bad thing that the leader of our country is going to be married to the leader of their advance team," Tom says.

"Gentlemen, the immediate question is when we make a further disclosure and to whom. There is no question that Merk is benevolent. There is also no question that a Merk-Earth liaison is a good thing. Merk does not pose a defense risk. So, from that standpoint, there does not appear to be a need to make further disclosures from a national security perspective. The CIA has been informed. Check. A disclosure with the knowledge that Merk is on America's side could be either really good as applied to the China situation or really bad. If China knows what Merk is and is aligned with us, it could engender a preemptive nuclear strike, no matter how foolish that would be. On the other hand, if China knows Merk's capabilities and that it's a possibility Merk would intervene on the side of the US, that could be the ultimate deterrent. That being said, I think we should ask Rein to have Merk announce itself to the world at the United Nations. We can facilitate that introduction. Despite Rein's pending nuptials, it is best for a Merk representative to be present at the UN and appear objectively not in favor of any one country on Earth but merely offer an introduction to Earth as a whole," Jack says.

"To be followed shortly by Andy and Rein's wedding announcement?" asks Tom.

"The wedding will have to be explained. More importantly, Rein's participation in this administration will need to be explained," Jack agrees.

"I tend to agree the best scenario here is a Merk announcement at the UN," David says.

"I agree," Tom concurs.

"Let's bring Rein in and see what she has to say. If she agrees, then I think Jack should introduce the Merk representative at the UN," Andy states.

"I see where you are going with this, Andy, and I'm OK with the direction, subject to further thoughts," Jack responds.

With that, Tom invites Rein back into the room.

"Rein, any thoughts before we share our conclusions?" Andy asks.

"I think as soon as possible, Jack should introduce me at the UN so that I can present Merk to Earth," Rein responds.

"David, is it possible that Rein has a listening device to the Oval Office or that she heard us from the anteroom?" Tom asks.

"Not one currently known to man, and the anteroom does not enable audio reception to the Oval Office," David responds.

"Well, David, I've got news for you. Rein's not from this Earth," Tom says.

"Guys, I did not hear what you said. I came to my conclusion on my own," Rein says.

"Well, then, great minds think alike," Jack says.

CHAPTER 32

THE UN

Since the incorporation of Russia into the West and the reunification of the Koreas, the UN has taken on an even bigger role in the international community. UN agencies are better funded and perform more duties. From disaster relief to artificial intelligence issues, the UN addresses at a basic level the kinds of issues and emergencies formerly left to individual countries or allied relief. Since the US remains an unquestioned world leader and the only true superpower, there is less need for the US to exert its power. The UN assumes many of the intervention duties the US used to engage in. This is of enormous benefit to all. The burden on the US is lessened greatly, both economically and practically, and the organizational infrastructure of the UN enables rapid relief and/or attention without having to go through the US Congress. Even China sees the advantage of working cooperatively with the UN. On many occasions, whether it be earthquake or typhoon relief or other humanitarian aid, China directly benefits from the more robust UN presence. China, still retaining a seat on the Security Council, however, continues to throw a wrench into some processes, but not enough to dilute the growing influence of the UN.

The new UN Tower in Manhattan is magnificent, soaring 250 stories tall and boasting a central auditorium that makes the main UN sessions extremely comfortable. The building also hosts a hyper-secure hotel, restaurants, incredible office space, and diplomatic residences.

The US ambassador to the UN makes an announcement requesting a full session of the General Assembly. While cryptic, the announcement gives sufficient gravity to the need for such a session that the US ambassador's office, as well as the White House, is flooded with requests for elaboration. Andy's instructions are to respond that the session involves a matter of the greatest international importance and that anyone who chooses not to attend would be foolish. Andy even authorizes the use of the word "foolish," even though it is viewed as improper in diplomatic circles.

Jack and Rein are poised to appear at the podium before the General Assembly. The normal news outlets are present—Fox and CNN—but not the major networks and not all international outlets.

"High-ranking administration officials have only told us it is a really important speech, and the vice president will preside at some level. Candidly, I've never seen two things operate before the UN like this: a combination of mystery and statements of preeminent importance," says Abby Stenstrom of CNN.

"It is odd. Well, here come the vice president and—wow, is that the president's girlfriend?" asks Carl Crystal, also of CNN.

"It is. Let's listen in," Abby responds.

Jack and Rein do, in fact, approach the central podium. Jack speaks first: "Ladies and gentlemen, I'm here right now only to give complete legitimacy to what you are about to hear. I have experienced firsthand certainty of the facts about to be spoken. I will also attend, in the central news conference room, a news conference shortly afterward. It is at that time I will try to answer all reasonable questions put to me. Right now, I'd like to introduce to you someone you somewhat already know. She is an exceptional person. Her name is Rein."

The audience in the auditorium cannot begin to understand what is happening. They know the woman standing in front of them as Annie, part of Brock's administration and his girlfriend. They cannot imagine why she is appearing before the UN General Assembly and why the vice president of the United States has referred to her as a weather phenomenon. The UN General Assembly is a place for momentous international concerns, not a place for the US president's girlfriend to make a speech. These are the nearly universal and instantaneous thoughts of everyone in the room, including the press in attendance and those listening through news broadcasts.

Rein takes over the microphone and speaks. "Thank you, Jack. Many of you know me as Annie. It is true my real name is Rein, spelled R-E-I-N. You also know I am part of Andy Brock's administration. That is the truth, and what I'm about to tell you does not change that fact. You also know I am friends with Mr. Brock. I'm not here to announce I am engaged to marry Mr. Brock, but that is true as well and will not change after what I am here to tell you."

At this point, the room is in what could only be called a stupor. They are being hit with the disclosure that the world's most discussed couple is getting married while being told that this is minor news. While they are in this stupor, the projection screen behind the podium shows the image of Earth from space.

Rein continues, "What you see right now on the screen behind me is the view of your beautiful planet from my ship."

At the same time Rein shows the image of Earth, Andy is in the White House with a group of government leaders. Immediately prior to Jack speaking, Andy reveals the Merk situation to them. The speaker of the House, the Senate majority leader, the leaders of the military, and the full Cabinet are in attendance, among others. Andy gives this group little time to react and instructs everyone to watch Jack's introduction to Rein and her ongoing speech. The group is in relative shock and remains riveted by what is happening at the UN.

Rein continues at the UN. "On the screen right now is the view of my ship from a shuttle external to my ship." On-screen at that time is a gorgeous image of the amazing Merkian ship—a modern-looking skyscraper floating in the sky. While the material of the ship appears glasslike, it is nothing of the sort. The closest material on Earth would be titanium, but the ship's material includes additional strength by orders of magnitude as well as heat resistance, impenetrability properties, and viewability properties unknown to Earthlings; plus, the underlying materials and fabrication techniques are not available on Earth and are both unknown to Earthlings.

At this point, everyone viewing the screen and listening to Rein is in a state of shock. In addition, all television and cable news networks in the United States and around the world stop their programming and break into the UN feed. Social media handles the others. Anyone who has a television, a cell phone, a computer, or any other device allowing public interface is now glued to Rein's speech. As such, her speech becomes the most viewed event in the history of the world. She isn't done.

"We come in peace. I am from a place called Merk. It is light-years from Earth. Merk is part of an advanced group in the galaxy that invites other planets to the galactic group when it is believed that a given planet is sufficiently advanced to merit such an invitation. Generally speaking, we seek a threshold of civilization that advances science over religious myth or superstition, bases ethics on principles of noninterference, and otherwise understands the need to treat all sentient beings with respect.

"We have been studying Earth for a long time. Recently, we have seen Russia become part of the family of nations, the Koreas rejoined, and generally, all nations of the Earth—except perhaps China and holdouts in the Middle East—come together for the general betterment of Earth.

"More importantly, and I say this not because I'm going to marry him, Andy Brock's policies, which have been resoundingly well received in the United States and throughout much of the rest of the world, demonstrate an advancement of society that tipped the scales in favor of inviting Earth.

"Some of you in the United States may be wondering how I worked my way into the government and when the president gained knowledge of Merk. After Lisa died and Andy was shot, Merk decided protective efforts were required. Four of America's greatest leaders were assassinated: Lincoln, two Kennedys, and Martin Luther King Jr. The loss to Earth was enormous with each of their deaths. Merk found it was in the best interests of all that Andy be protected. There was an attack on Andy's motorcade on I-15 recently. That attack had military-level attributes. Merk thwarted that attack and had an insider, in the form of myself, assist in that effort. It was also decided that an insider could further Merk's evaluation of Andy's policies and motives.

"Now, Andy is obviously an attractive person. There appear to be few females on the planet who do not find him attractive. I confess that while on my ship, I observed Andy and understood that attraction. It was not until Andy and I met in person, however, that the real attraction was realized.

"Andy learned of Merk prior to the election but made the decision that shortly after taking office, namely about now, it was critical for him to reveal Merk to certain information-oriented and defense-oriented leaders in the government. It was then quickly decided that all of America, and therefore the world, should become aware of Merk, so Andy pushed me, and Merk, to have the invitation occur faster than Merk wanted. Andy felt it was his fiduciary duty to reveal Merk to the citizens of America—no matter what Merk might do and when Merk might do it.

"I also felt a duty to Andy to reveal my origins when we became romantically involved. In doing so, I put Andy in a tough spot.

"It is certainly my hope—and, I can report, Andy's hope—that members of the administration and the citizens of America and the world understand that this situation is one that no one has ever had to deal with. It is our further hope that everyone understands this disclosure is happening, per Andy's desire, as quickly as possible.

"Now, where do we go from here? Merk hereby invites Earth to the galactic group. Merk policy is to treat the issue democratically. If the nations of the Earth that constitute the majority of the Earth's population vote in favor of our invitation, then Earth will join. Those nations that vote against such a joinder will be treated with respect, and nothing will be forced on them.

"What does joining the galactic family do and/or entail? Earth would become entitled, or at least those nations voting in favor of joining, to a wide array of disclosures from Merk. Merk has advances in medicine, agriculture, meteorology, general science, and many other areas that would be disclosed and massively benefit the planet. Depending upon how Earth's entry takes place, without upsetting a balance of power, it is also possible that disclosures associated with space travel and defensive military capabilities would be made. Also, depending upon how Earth's entry occurs, Earth would be invited to become part of the defense of the galactic group against galactic agitators. For the most part, I can tell you that Earth remains vulnerable, and it is in Earth's best interest to join the peace-oriented planets in the galactic group.

"I hope I have answered some of the key questions you all must have. Jack and I will now move over to the press conference. After that, Jack and I will be willing to meet with UN delegates at their US offices. We will stay this week. Delegations may schedule time to meet with Jack and me at the US offices in brief increments and on a first-come, first-met basis—nations of the Security Council will be given priority preference. Cliven, whom you now see on screen, is the main Earth liaison. We will publish details for how you can schedule meetings with Cliven in your own government offices from this point forward. We will not refuse any invitation and will therefore be willing to meet with representatives of every nation's government on Earth. Merk will entertain the entry vote in due course. If the nations of Earth want to take a vote on their own and that vote is unanimous for entry, then Merk will respect that vote. Merk just wants to ensure every nation has due time for reasonable evaluation regarding the decision to enter.

"Obviously, to say this is an exciting time for Earth is an understatement. Merk is excited to welcome Earth to the galaxy and share with the people of Earth the great advances the galaxy has to offer. Earth's worst fears about extraterrestrial life were just that: fears. The reality is that Earth is not going to be taken over by ET, but rather is going to be welcomed while remaining an independent planet. Yes, it will be expected that Earth helps the galaxy in any way it can and helps in the defense against galactic agitators, but that is for Earth's benefit as well.

"Earth has become my second home. It is exceedingly rare that anyone from Merk becomes romantically involved, particularly early on, with anyone on the planet under study. My marriage to Andy is remarkable, to say the least. Andy is remarkable, and I say that in having a broad view of the galaxy. I am lucky to have him, and you are too. I hope you will welcome me to Earth and help me solidify Earth as my second home."

The combination of Rein's message, presentation, and charisma results in her receiving a loud, prolonged standing ovation from the General Assembly. Everyone in the room who had joined Andy back at the White House witnesses that ovation. Whether due to Andy's political power or the reaction to Rein, the government leaders with Andy join in the ovation. At some level, most in the room are ultimately so struck by the deluge of news that they aren't sure where to put their focus—on Andy's marriage or the issues associated with Merk. Andy has enough political and social awareness to understand the awkwardness of the position in which most find themselves. He ends the meeting by telling everyone he will meet them separately in due course; he understands this news must be jolting and not to worry about extending personal greetings at this time. After that, most fumble through leaving the meeting and nevertheless attempt to congratulate Andy.

The press shifts their attention to the press conference. Rein and Jack make their way from the General Assembly auditorium to the press conference situs. In the meantime, the news networks are hardly able to maintain a sense of control and decorum. They do not have the ability to schedule experts in the field to question. All they can do is try to catch up and summarize. The coverage prior to the press conference generally discusses the standing ovation and then the conclusion that maybe the world is coming together. A good percentage of the press comments on musings as to what China will do. Executive producers around the world scurry to get relevant "experts" in place to comment on the situation after the press conference. The real question is deciding who is an expert on what is unfolding.

Rein and Jack finally find their way to the press conference situs. If Rein and Andy weren't a couple, Jack and Rein would be a great match. Both wear suits of black with grey pinstripes and white silk shirts underneath. Jack has on a green tie and Rein's shirt is unbuttoned. Rein's pantsuit, which looks a bit like athleisure, is cinched at the waist, with the pants showing off her muscular legs and cupping her ass. There are several camera angles of Rein and Jack—the straight-ahead view from the rear of the room and a side angle that shows them entering the room and approaching the clear podium. As such, the side angle, which some news networks linger on, robustly reveals Rein's feminine form.

Andy is watching the press conference and has mixed thoughts. First, he's one lucky guy. Second, he thinks it is remarkable that Rein shows as much restraint in her attire as she does, yet even with that restraint, she shows more sensuality than others would probably find acceptable. Finally, he thinks, fuck them. Rein can do whatever the fuck she wants. It is liberating. Even though he is president of the United States of America, she makes him feel young and free, not constrained. She makes him feel anything in the universe is possible and that they do not have to obey stupid societal conventions at any level.

The press conference starts, and Jack speaks first. "Well, I imagine one or more of you may have questions. Please feel free."

Satoyo Yamakawa of the *Mainichi Daily News* asks, in remarkably perfect English, "Japan remains very concerned about the conflict with China surrounding Taiwan. As you must know, recently, that conflict erupted into a serious air battle. That battle ended when the US Air Force intervened, but that was too close for anyone's comfort. Japan is prepared to assist the US in protecting Taiwan's interests. If that happens, then there are substantial concerns that the conflict will soon involve the Japanese homeland directly. With that in mind, does your ship have the capability of deploying overwhelming force to stop the violence, and under what circumstances, if any, would you intervene?"

"If Earth desires to vote in favor of joining Merk, then Merk will disclose Merk's capabilities. For now, you can safely assume Merk has tremendous defensive and offensive military assets on board. To answer the other aspect of your question, Merk prefers not to become the police force of worlds it interacts with. I'm not saying Merk would never intervene—you've already seen Merk is willing to do so in particular circumstances—but that intervention should not be taken for granted."

Maria Alvarez of CNN then asks, "May we safely assume that you personally would urge Merk to intervene if Andy's safety was ever at risk?"

Rein, without any hesitation, responds, "Yes, I would."

Maria follows up with, "Would an attack on US forces be considered putting Andy's safety at risk?"

Rein, again without any hesitation, responds, "A mere attack on US forces would in and of itself not be deemed a risk to Andy's safety. I can say that Merk has abilities to assess military and/or other offensive risks at a level currently unknown to anyone on Earth. Merk's abilities in this regard would shock folks at the DoD, the CIA, the NSA, and their counterparts in other countries. Merk could intervene early in a risk dynamic and could also intervene substantially later in a risk dynamic with confidence that such intervention would be effective."

"One last follow-up: Are you admitting Merk's response to the US-China conflict would be different if it were just the US generally involved as opposed to Andy being at risk?"

Rein responds, "I thought I made that clear. Merk will be hesitant to be Earth's police force, but there may be circumstances where Merk might intervene. That being said, if my future husband is at risk, then I'd move heaven and the universe to not allow that risk to actualize itself."

Mark Andrews of Fox News asks, "So, despite being able to do so, Merk might not intervene even if millions of lives might be at stake. Is that correct?"

"There is no bright line test. There are two principles at play here. First, it is rare for someone from Merk to become romantically involved with a member of the target planet. My relationship with Andy is way beyond the norm. Second, if and when Merk intervenes involves many different considerations, much of them opaque to others. Indeed, if Merk telegraphed precisely when it might intervene, then the party inflicting damage might inflict only so much damage up to the limit of that line of intervention. Merk should and will keep aggressors guessing as to when and how Merk might intervene. That being said, I can personally say that if anyone threatens my future husband, I will see to it Merk does everything in its power to prevent that harm. Moreover, if harm were to come to my husband, let me be clear: I will not rest until Merk justice is done, and Merk justice in this regard will punish the harm-doer gravely."

Alicia Valdez of MSNBC then asks, "Has a date been set for the marriage ceremony?"

"No."

Felicia Wright of BBC News asks, "Jack, how concerned is the US with the Taiwan situation? It would appear that if the Chinese did not back down in the latest air battle, the US and Chinese, at a minimum, would be engaged in a full-blown attack and counterattack, risking substantial escalation. Is the US prepared for that escalation?"

"The US is deeply concerned with the Chinese aggression toward Taiwan. The US has been clear that we will come to Taiwan's aid, and we are fully prepared, with our allies—including, without limitation, the United Kingdom—to engage militarily if required."

Wright follows up, "Will Andy ask Rein to ask Merk to come to the aid of the US in such a fight?"

"The United States will respect Merk's policy of nonintervention. Moreover, the United States and its allies believe we have sufficient firepower and resources to deal adequately with Chinese aggression."

"One last follow-up: Wouldn't it be smart to ask Merk to intervene to preclude nuclear war?"

"Based on what you heard from Rein, if it came to nuclear war, then I don't think the US would have to ask Merk to intervene, as Andy's safety would be implicated. Independently, US nuclear defense is the best in the world, better than anything China has, and is designed to substantially preclude the effects of a direct nuclear attack. Obviously, that defense would not stop radioactive cloud drift, and the results would be the same, but China should know it would not survive a preemptive strike, and the US would likely have the ability to do so.

"I know you folks have a lot more questions. We could probably be here for hours. We do need to get back and address the very issues you have been asking about. As Rein said, Cliven, the Merk-Earth liaison, will be coordinating visits to governments around the world. You can safely assume President Brock will have a press conference in the near future.

"Let me sum up: The greatest wishes of the Earth have come true. We have made first contact with an extraterrestrial civilization. That civilization could have been one that wanted to conquer and use Earth. Merk is the opposite. If Earth decides correctly to accept Merk's invitation, then the people of Earth will enjoy the benefits of advancements in medicine, science, energy, and a host of other disciplines that will likely make the history of all prior advancements of civilization on Earth pale by comparison. I have been to the Merk ship. To say it is remarkable is an understatement. Let me say one last thing: Looking at Earth from space made me appreciate even more how the people of Earth should not squabble among themselves. I have seen images of Earth from space, but actually being there has a psychological effect that is hard to put into words. It reinforced that we need to treasure our planet and that we are all part of humanity together. It's crazy to fight among ourselves, especially when there is so much more out there—as Merk and the rest of the galaxy represent. I suspect that even the Chinese leadership would be impressed by a trip to the Merkian ship. I don't know if they'll get an invitation to go up there, but I think it would have a profound effect."

Wright follows up one more time, "Rein, will Merk welcome a trip by Chinese leadership to your ship?"

"Merk is prepared to and will be extending an invitation to the leadership of every nation on Earth to join us on my ship. It is only fair and proper that every country has its leadership represented, no matter how large or small that country is. We also find, in our experience, that what Jack said is true. When one views one planet from a galactic perspective, it has a remarkable ability to have the impact Jack spoke of."

Jack concludes, "Well, folks, that's really all we have time for right now." And with that, Jack and Rein make their way out of the room with a tremendous security detail—a beefed-up Secret Service contingent is present and a Merkian undercover security presence is also stealthily deployed.

CHAPTER 33

THE DEBRIEF

J ack and Rein return to a senior meeting in the Oval Office with
Andy, Tom, Dempsey, and David. Andy briefs the room, "While
some of you were on vacation in New York, Dempsey and the
rest of the situation room developed additional proposals. As I understand it, those proposals have changed since the revelations at the UN.
Dempsey, please summarize where you think we are."

"The first thing I can report is that Chinese attention right now
is on Merk. They have effectively stopped all military action everywhere. They have made no statement of a ceasefire, but they have
nevertheless not only stopped firing but have stopped any further
mobilizations. Now, they haven't scaled back their former mobilizations, but no further actions have been taken. Moreover, we are
informed by a very good source that their UN delegation has reached
out to Cliven to schedule a visit to the Merk ship.

"As far as our protocols and engagements, we have increased air
and naval patrols by twenty percent in the strait. Japan and Korea have
also increased both their air and naval presence by the same amount.
We have affirmed the rules of engagement with our Chinese counterparts. Any attack on any US, allied, or Taiwanese aircraft or naval
craft (or otherwise) shall be deemed an attack on each and responded
to accordingly."

"Thanks. For now, I think we need to watch China closely and see how the Merk situation plays out. Tom, where's Lance? We need to get him in here now," Andy says.

"He's on his way—and ah, here he is," Tom answers.

"Lance, welcome. What's the feeling at state on how the world is reacting to Merk?" Andy asks.

"Honestly, a good part of the world is reacting more to a couple's upcoming marriage than just about anything else, and much of the rest of the world is acting like it's a world holiday. Talking to my counterparts around the globe, they feel as if the world has just received the biggest present they've ever seen. So far, not a single country has indicated they currently intend to vote against the Merk invitation—and that includes China. Most government representatives can't wait to book a trip to the Merk ship."

"Thanks, Lance. Rein, how are the folks on the ship taking everything?" Andy asks.

"Actually, they seem quite excited. They are enjoying the prospect of the various visits by government representatives and are very happy with Earth's reception of me and the Merk so far."

"Tom and Rein, where are we at with the Senate confirming treaty acceptance of the Merk invitation?" Andy asks.

Tom answers, "We expect unanimous support by next week. Jack and Lance have secured all Democrats, and I've been pretty successful with the Republicans. I have left Rein out of it because I find that people don't respond to her very well. I think they just don't like her, Andy."

"Funny you say that, Tom, given I've seen the latest approval polls. While I am quite happy with my seventy-seven percent approval rating, Rein's approval rating is at ninety-five percent, as I am sure you know through your brimming sarcasm."

While looking into Rein's eyes, Andy continues with a broad smile, "I suspect many men would have some competitive feelings about that disparity. That thought never entered my mind. I don't mind at all that I've been on this planet for decades, fought battle after battle to get where I am, and won the presidency by the largest landslide in the history of elections in these fifty states, yet with all of that, Rein, a newcomer, is loved by nearly all people. When I saw the poll results, these thoughts never even occurred to me. Tom, I'm not even sure why you brought up the poll numbers."

"Sorry, Andy, from now on, I'll make sure to only report your own personal poll numbers to you, but to be fair, with respect to the ninety-five percent favorable rating Rein received, the other five percent was noncommittal for whatever reason: They have been in a hole and have not seen any news or, I guess, have been otherwise distracted. There is an argument that Rein, over time, will be universally loved. And to be clear, you had a sixty-two percent very favorable rating and a fifteen percent favorable rating. Rein's ninety-five percent was all very favorable. Just saying. Oh, and I forgot, Rein was just voted America's best-dressed woman."

"Thanks, Tom; I always knew I could count on your support. Clearly, the folks voting on best-dressed woman should call their superlative, 'best hardly dressed woman.'"

Rein has to intervene, "Well, I'm glad the man I am marrying is such a self-assured, confident person. With all of that confidence you have, I'm looking forward to our second racquetball game later today."

"Rein, if we can keep our personal life separate from affairs of state while we are in the Oval Office, I'd appreciate it. That being said, I trust you all are ready for the wedding next week," Andy says with a grin.

"What wedding?" David asks while also grinning.

"David, as the leader of the Central Intelligence Agency, you seem remarkably out of touch," Jack says.

CHAPTER 34

THE WEDDING

"Jack, you are not only the greatest vice president ever, but you have become a great friend of mine. I am so sorry we've decided you need to stay back with Dempsey and not attend the wedding. Dempsey, no questions on the 'Execute' command, correct? You understand that either Jack or I can give the 'Execute' command. You are to exercise your discretion. If conditions are satisfied, you feel it inappropriate to reach me, and Jack is confident enough to give the 'Execute' command, then Jack's order will be sufficient. Understood?" Andy asks.

"Yes, Mr. President."

"David, the exact same instructions are true for you as well. Understood?" Andy asks.

"Yes, Mr. President."

"Once again, gentlemen, I value you all as vital parts of my administration and greatly value you as my personal friends. I deeply regret that the status of foreign affairs precludes you from attending my wedding, but thems the breaks," Andy says while leaving.

Andy flies Air Force One to Chicago in anticipation of the wedding being held at the Field Museum of Natural History in downtown Chicago. The Field Museum sits majestically at a gorgeous curve on Lake Shore Drive. The Roman columns are clearly visible while driving down LSD and signify the entry to museum park, which also holds the Adler Planetarium and the magnificent Shedd

Aquarium—all set against a backdrop of beautiful Lake Michigan and the line of parks that form Chicago's front lawn.

Over the years, the federal government has worked with several Midwestern states to focus on a massive cleanup of the Great Lakes, including Lake Michigan, which abuts Chicago. Years and years ago, Chicago changed the flow of the Chicago River to flow out of Lake Michigan rather than into the lake. Recent efforts have ensured that no effluent travels into any of the Great Lakes. Massive modern filtration devices that protect aquatic life were used to minimize contaminants in the lakes, and physical cleanup efforts were undertaken to rid the lakes of garbage, refuse, and other unnatural items. The result is that the Great Lakes, while not pristine, are likely cleaner and clearer now than they have been since the 1700s. Fish life is abundant, Lake Michigan has clear water, and people can safely swim without worry. All of that further enhances the wedding venue which is located right next to the lake.

Chicago also maintains its leadership role in world architecture. The city has recaptured the distinction of having the world's tallest buildings, boasting five of the tallest twenty buildings in the world. The former Sears Tower is dwarfed by these new structures. The construction boom in Chicago has made the view from the Field Museum that much more impressive to wedding attendees. The much-anticipated wedding ceremony occurs in the middle of the museum park against the backdrop of gleaming towers and the now-clear lake.

The wedding turns out to be the biggest social event of the millennium. The most popular president ever is engaging in an intergalactic relationship with arguably the most popular and charismatic person known on Earth. The Merk contingent is surprisingly large, given the distance they had to travel. Another three ships arrive from Merk, two of which enhance security, and one carries Rein's family and friends. While another ceremony has been planned for Merk, Rein's family and friends cannot wait to meet Andy in person, become acquainted more directly with Earth, and merely join in the merriment.

For security reasons and the constraints of the Field Museum's interior capacity, the wedding attendees are limited to five hundred very lucky individuals. Narrowing that list had been challenging, to say the least. Nearly every world government leader sought to be in attendance. The White House social office was able to accommodate fifty such leaders and their plus-ones. Another fifty national leaders and their plus-ones were invited as well. One hundred Merkians were in attendance, leaving only two hundred of Andy's and Rein's closest friends.

Thankfully, the reception will be held at McCormick Place Convention Center, and the venue will then accommodate five thousand individuals, increasing the guest list tenfold.

These numbers did not include the attendance of massive security details and the press. Security details are present for foreign dignitaries, there is a substantial security presence by the Merk and the Chicago Police Department, and the Secret Service contingent assembled is historically record-breaking. All of this security constitutes not merely a substantial police force, but a small army. The Secret Service members are particularly interested in what arms the Merk force carries. Merk forces are instructed by Merk leaders to politely decline revealing too much until the acceptance vote is finalized. That being said, it is impossible not to notice the house shields covering the Field Museum and McCormick Place. While the technology is not completely understandable to non-Merkians, it is clear that some kind of magical force field has been remarkably placed over both venues. There are also separate shields covering the interior spaces in the Field Museum wherever the engaged couple would be present, and similar shields are strategically placed within the reception hall. The interior shields are not only protective but are designed to provide a decorative ambiance for the ceremonies. The shields reveal images of the Chicago skyline, the skies above Chicago, and magnificent views of Amberan, Rein's Merkian place of birth and home city.

The Field Museum is full of lavender, which happens to be Andy's favorite flower and is also adored by Rein. Bunches of lavender are placed in urns lining every walkway, hung from interior columns, and are otherwise strategically and tastefully placed as accents throughout the venue.

While the full-blown Chicago Symphony Orchestra will play at the reception at McCormick Place, a limited string section and a pianist of the CSO will play at the wedding. The song list includes takes from *Rhapsody in Blue*, the theme from *Somewhere in Time*, and "My Kind of Town." Rein plans on surprising Andy with a Merkian musical group at both the wedding and reception. Rein's choices, she hopes, will allow Andy to hear some of the most beautiful sounds he will ever experience. The Merkian instrumentation, oddly enough, incorporates forms that are variations of strings and keyboards but with completely different materials and orientations. The materials come from a combination of indigenous sources found on Merk as well as synthetically fabricated quasi-metallics.

The chief justice of the Illinois Supreme Court, Andy's personal friend, is set to receive the vows and officially marry Andy and Rein.

There is no wedding party—no maid of honor and no best man. Andy does not wait at the end of a walkway for someone to give Rein away.

Those in attendance for the wedding are all assembled. The chief justice is at the end of a magnificent walkway lit with vertical columns of violet light. The light twinkles to the sound of mystical pieces played by the Merkian orchestral group.

Rein and Andy appear together at the beginning of the walkway. Rein wears a grey satin minidress with a remarkably short hemline. The minidress hugs her body and, while not completely transparent, does very little to hide her feminine features. It barely meets the standards for what is legally permitted in the state of Illinois. By Merkian standards, the minidress is looked upon as elegant, if not a bit overdone, as many a Merkian wedding finds participants without apparel of any kind. Andy obviously did not have the chance to see the minidress prior to the wedding ceremony, and his eyes remain fixated on his bride—and not just on her eyes.

At that very moment, the Chinese foreign minister finds himself without apparel on the Merkian ship.

Also at that very moment, the Chinese military leadership gives the order to have various air force squadrons fire their engines and for the vast naval forces to ready their pre-attack position places. That military leadership has also tuned in to the American president's wedding footage.

Andy and Rein make their way down the walkway and reach the chief justice.

"Rein, pursuant to and consistent with the laws of the state of Illinois, do you without any reservation whatsoever unconditionally accept Andrew Sheridan Brock, standing before you, as your lawful husband?" the chief justice asks, her voice projected by microphone to all in the wedding venue and to those listening by way of the broadcast.

"Yes, I do," Rein says, also on microphone.

At that moment, the order is given by Chinese President Chen to launch a full-scale attack against US and allied forces in the Western Pacific. It appears to the Chinese a brilliant surprise attack. Not only is President Brock in the middle of his wedding and away from his military leadership, but most allied heads of state are in attendance as well.

"Andrew Sheridan Brock, pursuant to and consistent with . . ."

"Madame Chief Justice, please hold that thought a moment. Yes, Dempsey and Jack, I hear you. Yes, I understand, 'Execute.' Madame Chief Justice, you may now ask the rest of that question," Andy says, with everyone able to hear his every word.

"Consistent with the laws of the state of Illinois, do you, without any reservation whatsoever, unconditionally accept Rein, standing before you, as your lawful wife?"

"I do."

"Then, with judicial notice of adequate witnesses to this undertaking, I hereby affirm you as husband and wife, pursuant to and consistent with the laws of the state of Illinois."

"Thank you, Your Honor. Everyone, I need to run. The Chinese have mounted a full-scale attack on the United States and allied forces in the Western Pacific. I want everyone to know there is a bit of a situation room that I have access to. Please make your way to the reception and have a great party. I hope Rein and I can join you sometime tonight."

With that, Andy kisses Rein and grabs her hand before they are whisked away with a Secret Service escort to the temporary situation room on-site at the Field Museum.

Having reached the Field situation room, Andy is linked into the White House situation room. "Dempsey, please advise," Andy says.

"We have initiated our own attack, Mr. President. Presently, there are thousands of sorties by US and allied aircraft engaging airborne and Chinese land-based targets. The Chinese feigned an attack on Taiwan, but your prediction came true that at the very moment of your exchange of vows, the Chinese attacked our forces instead."

Thinking it a surprise attack, the Chinese appeared to be targeting Taiwanese assets and then broke off into various directions, specifically focusing on the US and some allied targets. The Chinese, through the years, have expanded their air force greatly. They have built an additional five thousand fighters and an additional two thousand bombers, a good percentage of which are long-range. The Chinese did not dedicate resources to aircraft carriers as they felt long-range fighters and bombers could do the trick.

They did not expect the many Russian and Indian aircraft attacking from the north and west. Andy coordinated brilliantly with his counterparts to have those counterattacks occur instantaneously as the Chinese launched their own attack.

The Chinese will have no choice but to redirect a healthy percentage of their forces to the Chinese northern and western frontiers.

Dimitri Petrov, the Russian president, and Mehta Gandhi, the Indian president (a distant relative of another famous Gandhi), both in attendance at the wedding, are also both invited into the Field situation room.

"Dimitri, Mehta, everything is going according to plan. Your forces are doing more than just diverting a good percentage of the Chinese attack. Your friendship will never be forgotten."

Dimitri speaks first, "Mr. President, you are not just a leader of your great country, but I consider you a leader for our new world."

Mehta then adds, "By the way, congratulations on your wedding, Rein and Andy. It was a lovely ceremony, if not a bit brief by Indian standards."

Everyone in the Field situation room laughs heartily at Mehta's jibe, including Andy and Rein.

Andy says, "I see that dry British humor continues to have its impact on India, for better or worse."

Charles Rockwell, the British prime minister, is also invited into the Field situation room and chimes in, "I can confidently say for the better."

Mehta responds, "Well, we have been able to jettison most detritus of British influence over the years. I prefer to view my humor as apt Indian irony."

"David, what's your status?" Andy asks his head of the CIA while shifting back to more serious matters.

"The Taiwan president, Deng Xi, and the Chinese foreign affairs minister are now both on the Merk ship. They are coordinating with their rebel leaders and forces in Hong Kong, Shanghai, and Beijing, as well as numerous other locations in key industrial sites along the Chinese eastern seaboard. Internal Chinese clashes are happening in all aforesaid locations. We have received commitments from all rebel leaders to have Deng recognized as an interim Chinese leader of both mainland China and, of course, Taiwan. Ironically, the calculated risk you have undertaken may very well bring about the Chinese reunification of mainland and island that China desired to achieve through warfare."

At that moment, Chinese President Chin recognizes the threat to his leadership. He sees that some of his military leaders sense defeat and abandon their positions, instead joining the rebel camps. While Chin is, for the moment, somewhat secure in his own situation room, he feels the world closing in, though his arrogance refuses to allow him to accept a total defeat.

The air and naval battles continue. US forces are able to break through and attack Chinese airfields. The enormity of air, naval, and land forces has never been seen before on Earth. Thousands of aircraft are engaged in massive battles on various fronts, while hundreds of naval forces are locked in violent sea battles. Large land forces are facing off against equally massive enemies. The scale of these operations indicates extensive planning over many years. Japanese and Korean forces have suffered losses but have managed to hold off a significant portion of the Chinese attack on their homelands. The US forces join a revamped Philippines military to protect the Manila region entirely, with only some of the outlying islands experiencing some bombing runs. A few long-range bombers approach Oahu but are cut down.

Russian success in the north is substantial, and India now absolutely secures the western front. While the Chinese forces are considerable, they simply cannot come to grips with the enormity of forces simultaneously responding to the attempted Chinese sneak attack. The Chinese air force is being decimated, and the Chinese naval forces are not doing any better. Modern munitions are able to do massive damage in a matter of minutes, let alone hours.

Chin, of course, is watching the growing defeat of his forces. Reports from his various forces make clear there is no way that the combined allied air forces are not going to overwhelm the Chinese air force. Chinese air space is no longer controlled by China. The Chinese surface ships in its navy are also in dire condition. Russian forces have been blitzing the northern front. The Indian forces are managing their own blitz in the southwest. Chin realizes there is no scenario in which even he can see a win. Chin did not imagine that an allied defense would look like the counteroffensive currently being experienced. He also did not conceive that such counteroffensives could achieve such rapid results. Launching the thousands of sorties was not logistically difficult for the allies. The Russian and Indian troop movements with armored columns were also not surprising. Bursting through defensive lines and gaining thirty miles of territory while devastating Chinese combatants is apparently now a very viable result of new military technology. It is also not surprising that Chinese naval forces were so quickly decimated. Chin is myopic and arrogant—two horrible qualities going into war.

Not wanting to concede defeat, Chin issues the order for submarine-based nuclear-armed missiles to be launched and, at the same time, orders a land-based missile launch.

Moments before, the head of the Chinese Navy sought asylum after being put in direct contact with Deng. CIA assets secure that asylum within the hour. The submarine-based launch is stopped in its tracks.

Only a few diehard Chin loyalists follow the launch orders. Others either see the writing on the wall and join the rebel forces or just do not want their children to live in a world of nuclear winter. Of the thousands of nuclear bombs at Chin's disposal, fourteen are launched. All happen to be US targets. Chin is actually pretty lucky in the targets he is able to successfully include in his order: New York; Las Vegas; Seattle; Washington D.C.; Houston; oddly enough, Huntsville, Alabama; Denver; San Francisco; San Diego; Norfolk; Philadelphia; Boston; and Chicago.

The Merk captain is able to instantaneously see the Chinese launch, and two Merkian forces are sent to deal with the launched missiles. The first force is designed to intercept each missile in flight. That interception is a tricky maneuver for Merkian forces. There is the risk of radiation emission even with the most careful interception. That is why a second force immediately follows, which is the radiation sweep force that effectively vacuums in any trailing radiation caused by any such interception.

Chin is not able to see the results of his launch. The CIA's coordination with rebel Chinese forces is very effective and is helped tremendously by the massive information flow coming into newsfeeds of every nature featuring the miserable showing of the Chinese military forces. The CIA is able to enable these newsfeeds to come into a variety of Chinese media outlets and through internet access points. Encouraged by the news, rebel forces successfully overtake the government leadership offices. Rebel forces also gain control of key media outlets. Deng is patched in and implores Chinese citizens against further violence. He announces himself as interim leader and immediately indicates that democratic elections will be held in six months. An initially unbelieving Chinese public begins to take to the streets en masse. Demonstrations grow faster than expected as the dam bursts. The Chinese people have had enough of authoritarian rule. They see the opportunity to revolt, and they take it. Demonstrations are initially the largest in Hong Kong, a city always waiting and prepared to be free again. In seeing the success of the demonstrations in Hong Kong, cities around China rose up with cries of freedom and, rather than shout Deng's name, began to shout another name as part of their rallying cry. "Brock, Brock, Brock" is heard throughout China.

Back in the Field situation room, Dempsey links in on-screen. "Mr. President, we have confirmation of nuclear warhead launches by the Chinese."

"How many?"

"It appears there are fourteen land-based missiles, Mr. President," says Dempsey.

"How much time do we have?"

"Unknown exactly, but I'd estimate about fifteen minutes?"

"Do we have any concerns about intercept?" Andy asks.

"Andy, I can answer that question. Merk should intercept these missiles prior to your strategic defense kicking in. By the way, the Chinese rallying cry is one word right now: your name. So, it looks like that Chinese vote you were after has been locked in," Rein says.

"Rein, I'm looking at a nuclear attack within maybe fifteen minutes, and you're going to joke about the Chinese vote?" Andy responds.

"Yeah, I thought it was funny," Rein answers.

"Rein, seriously, when do you—and therefore we—get word from your captain on the intercept?" Andy asks.

"Now. All missiles were intercepted so far except one—the one headed here for Chicago, apparently. I'll have to talk to my captain about his sense of priorities," Rein says.

"Yes, I agree, if we happen to survive the nuclear missile currently on schedule to meet with us. Rein, I appreciate how cool under literal fire you are, but everyone in this room would appreciate a little more elaboration on the missile you just mentioned. Does US strategic defense need to intervene?" Andy inquires.

"No. I just heard from the captain. They were not able to intercept the Chicago missile prior to explosion, but it exploded at 35,000 feet over the Pacific. Merk sweeper ships, for lack of a better word, were able to remove the radiation cloud. By the way, I am allowed to now tell you, husband, that Merk also has radiation sickness therapies and cancer immunotherapies that would address any effects of radiation."

"Let's go get Tom, as I probably have to address the country now and give them an update. Let's set up a podium at the wedding reception, and I'll give the address from there, if you don't mind, Rein. That, actually, will be the fastest way for us to join our party tonight. It is pretty amazing how many people have stayed through the hours of this battle, but I guess the party is pretty good, and world war keeps people from going to bed. By the way, do I refer to you as Mrs. Brock from now on?" Andy asks.

"Remember that Merk protection of you I spoke about earlier? Well, my name is Rein, your name is Andy Brock, and that's how it's going to stay, or I'll remove the promise of protection," Rein—not Mrs. Brock—replies.

CHAPTER 35

THE WEDDING RECEPTION

*G*arlic. *What's a wedding reception dinner without garlic?* Rein thinks. She knows there is a reason she loves this man. She wants her parents to love him just as much as she does. Thankfully, her parents have not been extensively exposed to Earth's indigenous garlic-based recipes. Moreover, Rein is able to tell her parents that Andy is the driving force in choosing the non-vegetarian menu: prime rib infused with a garlic marinade, Caesar salad with a heavier-than-usual garlic-laced dressing, garlic croutons that are yummy on their own, asparagus sautéed in olive oil and garlic, garlic-infused mashed potatoes, and other items.

Thankfully, as Rein is starving, she is able to eat with Andy prior to his televised address from the reception hall.

While they are eating, the television crews are busy finalizing the set, which is actually placed on a dais next to the couple's sweetheart table. The press is allowed three camera angles intermixed between dining tables. It looks like a hybrid Academy Award ceremony.

Before the cameras click on, Andy assumes the dais and speaks only to those in the reception hall, "Sorry to interrupt the party, but I have to make a little speech. I'll try not to make it so long so that we can start dancing to this beautiful music soon."

Even with Rein's assistance, Andy does not have time to prepare a speech for his televised address. For better or worse, he will effectively go off the cuff for a televised address about one of the most significant events in human history.

Cable news is enamored with the Brock administration. Since he came on the scene, ratings of every network have gone through the roof. The conservative-leaning networks like him because he is a Republican. More liberal-oriented networks love him because he brought on Jack and Lance and because his policies are poised to actually advance a somewhat liberal agenda. They all love him because he is immensely popular, and they know that typical agenda-driven bashing is not going to work. It is not that the networks are gushing over him, but it is getting pretty close. In addition, events that appear to be driven by him are creating, in and of themselves, news coverage rarely ever seen. There have been conflicts before that resulted in robust news coverage, but the recent battle between China and the US is the largest conflict since World War II. On top of that, Andy's history-making rise to the presidency has resulted in political coverage on steroids, particularly since he is the rock star of politicians. It is not only news junkies or politicos who watch news about Andy. Twenty-somethings follow coverage of him as closely as they would follow pop music or movie stars. Adding fuel to that fire is, of course, the hottest female in the known universe marrying Andy, not to mention that she comes from another planet that is about to bring a host of beneficial advances to the human race. This is beyond the golden age of news coverage. News anchors, with all that in mind, are in enraptured anticipation of Andy's press conference. To their credit, the circumstances deserve that attention. The interesting problem for Andy is that recent events make the press conference low-hanging fruit: What transpired was so great that it is hard to fail. On the other hand, the expectations are so high for another amazing Andy performance that anything less than spectacular will be viewed as a failure—not of his recent performance as president, but of his performance at the press conference.

Andy is oblivious to the expectation game. He is in the middle of his wedding to one of the universe's great beings, has just won a major war by way of an amazingly rapidly executed multipronged attack, and is riding the wave of the Merk engagement. He is relatively unconcerned with how people are going to rate him. That, people like Tom tell him, is one reason he performs so well—he doesn't get in the way of himself and refuses to allow stress to burden his performance.

Andy is given the signal that the cameras are rolling. "As you know, I'm coming to you from my wedding reception. In fact, I'm coming to you in the *middle* of my wedding reception. My wife is not only very beautiful, but very understanding.

"I ask you to forgive me if what I say is not as polished as you might want from your president. I have not had the time to prepare a speech, and there is no teleprompter. So, this is off the cuff.

"I also speak to you now not just as your president but also as a fellow member of Earth, having just gained some in-laws from another world and being a member of the Merkian family.

"First, I must give you some reports.

"While I was in the middle of trying to say, 'I do,' the former Chinese government launched an attempted sneak attack on US forces. The timing was not coincidental. Our sensors detected that the Chinese were warming their engines in order to time their attack exactly when I was in the middle of our wedding ceremony.

"We anticipated that attack. Our forces and our allied forces were prepared to move exactly at that time. For those of you watching my wedding who heard me say 'Execute,' that was an instruction to the secretary of defense and the head of the CIA to move forward on attacks and actions that anticipated the Chinese attack.

"To put it simply: We, with our allies, won one of the most amazing and rapid military victories ever. The US itself was able to launch thousands of air sorties from both naval assets as well as air bases in Japan, Korea, Russia, Australia, Vietnam, Thailand, and a host of other locations. We also deployed drone and missile attacks from similar locations. Our allies launched land-based attacks simultaneously. This combined effort made the German blitzkrieg pale by comparison in scope and speed. All of this was no accident as we have been training to execute this effort ever since I took office."

The wedding reception party is occupied by world and business leaders, dignitaries from Earth and Merk, and leaders from education, sports, and entertainment. This is a room of more who's who than ever seen before. Despite being otherwise thought of as high society, with Andy's last words, the room explodes in applause and screams. Yes, it is a standing ovation, but even more than that—a mini party breaks out and interrupts Andy's speech. People are kissing, dancing, whooping, and generally behaving in a less-than-controlled manner. The Merkians are less vibrant but nevertheless applaud loudly. Many Merkians sit back and grin broadly at the mirthful rancor occurring before their eyes. This uproar lasts for ten minutes despite Andy's efforts to control it. He finally succeeds.

"Our forces and our allied forces performed brilliantly. Because those thousands of aircraft were attacking virtually instantaneously, hundreds of naval forces were engaged at the same time, and allied blitzing land forces overtook Chinese land forces so quickly the Chinese military faced defeat as rapidly as anyone might not have previously imagined but as swiftly as we planned.

"The former Chinese government has resigned and is no more. The Chinese people are free and are now part of a united Earth."

Once again, the room goes crazy, but—sensing the need to give Andy some courtesy this time—follows his request to settle down.

"For the results of winning the war and freeing the great Chinese people, there are many to thank.

"Let's start with our Russian ally. Dimitri, my dear friend, your efforts in coordinating your attack with our forces were nothing less than tremendous. Your team worked with ours seamlessly. Russia executed its mission from the northern front perfectly. The Russian efforts saved many American lives and helped bring about the swift victory we achieved."

Sustained applause.

"Mehta, the only reason I started with my thanks to Dimitri was that he promised a case of vodka, and I am going on record to say there are certain ways to bribe me."

Laughter and applause.

"Seriously, the coordination of the simultaneous attack from the west by India with the attack from the north by Russia was nothing less than amazing. India's efforts were flawless and contributed equally to saving many Americans. We are in both your and Dimitri's debt."

Increased applause.

"It would be tremendously unfair to mention our other allies in this fight to any lesser degree. The coordination with Japan, Korea, Taiwan, the Philippines, and Australia, as well as their precision participation from the east and south, was critical to our success.

"From afar, the British, French, and Brazilian forces participated magnificently."

Sustained applause.

"For the first time in our history, we were the subject of a nuclear attack. Fourteen ICBMs targeted fourteen of our cities. Our new Merk allies took out all of these missiles. While our own defense might have achieved a similar result, the Merk defense left no radiation debris in our atmosphere. It is likely our Merk friends saved hundreds of thousands of lives."

The room gives a prolonged standing ovation in recognition of the Merk effort.

"Make no mistake. This was a war, even if it did not last long. While it ended quickly, it was nevertheless a full-scale attack on the United States of America. It is now time to thank those brave souls who perished in our fight. While the count is not complete, we know we lost one hundred and seven souls. Their sacrifice should never be and will never be forgotten. I ask you not to applaud but merely join me in silent recognition of our thanks to them and their families."

The room went quiet.

"Now, the former Chinese government was intent on ruining my wedding. Between the time I said 'I do' until a few moments ago, we fought a war. We fought a war in the middle of my wedding. I know it is quite late now, but I plan to party. I hope those in this room will join me. I hope you folks not in this room have your own party. Now, if you'll excuse me, I believe my wife owes me a dance."

A raucous ovation ensues as the cameras click off.

"Before our dance, the first thing you need to do is finally let me meet your parents."

"That's kind of a big step, isn't it? We really have not been seeing each other all that long."

"True, I'm not quite sure I'm prepared to make much of a commitment to our relationship just yet either."

"By the way, nice speech, I guess. Well, it was a little rough at the edges. Nothing a professional speechwriter could not have made better."

"You know, I see no reason not to add one-on-one basketball to our racquetball contests. Are you available tomorrow?" Andy asks.

"No problem, old man," Rein answers.

"Well, hand me a cane to help me walk over with you to your parents so that I can finally meet them," Andy beseeches.

Rein and Andy make their way over to Rein's parents' table. In Merkian, Rein tells her parents she will use English to introduce her husband and that it will translate as somewhat familiar through the universal translator. She explains that Andy has never heard her speak Merkian and that having the translator interpret what Rein says for Andy probably will not work as well.

"Mom and Dad, I'd like you to meet my husband, Andy," Rein says.

Striking complete surprise into Rein, Andy says, in unaccented Merkian, "Pervoran mustavia accendan." This is the classic greeting in Merkian, which translates to: "It is my great honor to start our relationship."

Triven, Rein's father, responds in Merkian but is otherwise immediately translated through the universal translation device, "The honor is mine. It has always been a great mystery to me whom Rein would align with, but I knew one thing, he would have to be special. From everything I have heard and seen from you, Rein could not have made a better choice." Triven extends his arm, which Andy takes as they grasp their arms together.

Planan, Rein's mother, says in Merkian with immediate translation, "Welcome to the family."

Andy responds in Merkian, "Rivak, supernan essenk csiaonk dresskin," which, in English, roughly translates to, "Thank you, you are as beautiful as your daughter."

"OK, let's stop right here. When have you had time to learn Merkian?" Rein asks.

"C'mon, it's just a few phrases. It was the least I could do," Andy answers.

"I'll give you that, but your pronunciation is perfect. That takes time to pick up. Who taught you?" Rein asks.

"Cliven's assistant, Shenin, was very kind to help me. She's an attractive young lady, by the way, and she likes Earth clothing even less than you do. In fact, we had three sessions together, and she was naked for two of them. She wore clothes the first time but asked me if I would mind her naked body for the final two sessions. I told her I had no problem whatsoever, and she should make herself comfortable."

"I'll have to make time to congratulate Shenin on her excellent tutorial efforts. Shenin is considered one of the most beautiful women on the ship. I'm comforted that you were able to control your male urges while in her naked presence."

"What made you believe I controlled anything?" Andy asks with a smile.

"I imagined you understood what 'aligned' means," Rein responds.

"Ah, I do now," Andy says and smiles again.

"I hope you had fun with this little discussion. I plan to address your smiles on the basketball court. Oh, sorry, I forgot to tell you. Part of Merkian physiology has enabled a substantial vertical leap capability. I am being quite generous since my plan was to put a wager on our game before you learned that news. You lucked out, but that won't diminish the sweet taste of victory. Actually, we can still wager on how many points you'll get. What say you?" Rein asks.

"I'm so glad we had this conversation in front of Mom and Dad so that they are aware of your treatment of me from time to time. Mom, Dad, if Rein abuses me, may I call you for help?" Andy asks.

"Rein is incapable of abuse," Triven says.

"Andy, you can call me at any time for any or no reason. That being said, Rein is and will be blameless at all times," Planan says.

"Wow, family solidarity is a great thing to see," Andy responds.

"Seriously, when can we plan for your ceremony on Merk? We really don't want to wait too long after alignment," Triven says.

"Dad, Andy and I spoke about this. Please trust us; we will get there as soon as possible and give you as much advance notice as possible. I know you are sympathetic. Andy was just elected president, fought a war, is in the middle of Earth's acceptance of Merk's invitation, has a country to run, and is now arguably not only the leader of what on Earth is known as the 'free world,' but the leader of Earth itself. That being said, I think we can carve out time soon," Rein says.

"As the Merk chancellor, I can empathize. As you know, we have our own Davark situation, but despite my status and our situation, I did make it here, so I expect reasonable accommodation as well," Triven says.

"What is the status of chancellor on Merk?" Andy asks.

"He is the leader of the planet," Rein says.

"Well, you might have told me that so I could have mentioned it out of respect," Andy replies.

"Dad did not want to be a distraction."

"Dad, first, may I call you 'Dad'? Second, may I introduce you to Earth's world leaders in attendance?" Andy asks.

"Yes, and yes," Triven responds.

Andy takes a spoon and hits the glass before him on the table. He also waves to the room to get their attention, finds a microphone, and says, "Ladies and gentlemen, please allow me to introduce my humble, unassuming, and unpretentious father-in-law, Chancellor Triven, leader of the planet Merk."

Sustained applause breaks out.

"Thank you, son. I did not imagine when Rein was assigned to explore a relationship with Earth that not only would she find one of the most special planets in the galaxy but that she would add to the family a most cherished son found here on Earth."

Rein takes the microphone. "While my father is, in fact, the leader of our planet, what I have not been able to tell Andy yet is that my mother is what you would call the 'maestro' of the Amberan Symphony Orchestra and, given Merkian's love of music, her renown on Merk equals or exceeds that of my father's, but no one would ever say that in public. Mom, please take a bow and say a few words."

In auto-translated Merkian, Planan says, "Yes, Rein, no one would ever say that in either public or private. Let me just say this: we are overjoyed at welcoming Earth to the galaxy and Andy to the family, but not necessarily in that order. I am also extremely impressed with the performance here today by the Chicago Symphony Orchestra. It is said that the CSO is one of the greatest orchestras on Earth. I'm willing to confidently state that it is one of the greatest musical groups in the galaxy. I have had occasion to study some of Earth's notable compositions and recordings, and it is my hope that someday I might be able to work with Maestro Giuliani at some level."

Maestro Giuliani, the world-renowned musical director of the Chicago Symphony Orchestra, in attendance at the wedding reception and conducting the orchestra during the party, walks over to Andy, Rein, and Rein's parents shortly after Planan's speech.

"Planan, you are too kind. It is my great pleasure to welcome you to Earth. May I inquire which composition has interested you the most?" Maestro Giuliani asks.

"There are several that caught my attention. I can say that Beethoven's Fifth is the last one I focused on."

"Well, I hope you will accept the baton and run my little musical troupe through the first movement. What do you say?" Maestro asks in jest.

The request is palpably unfair, as there is no suggestion that Planan has done any preparation whatsoever. Even the most skilled conductor would need hours upon hours of preparation for a public performance of that movement.

To Maestro Giuliani's shock and amazement, Planan responds, "I'd love to. I have it memorized. Does the orchestra?"

"Well, no. We would need the sheet music printed, and we have no way to do that tonight."

"Rein, please have the first movement sent through Send."

"Yes, Mom."

Within five minutes, appropriate sheet music for the orchestra arrives.

Reeling from the additional shock of having fully appropriate and distributable sheet music produced in such a short period of time, Maestro says, "I can see there will be some real advantages of having a relationship with Merk."

With that, Maestro asks various members of the orchestra to help distribute the sheet music.

Planan makes her way over to the podium with Maestro Giuliani, who takes the microphone and announces, "Ladies and gentlemen, it is with great pleasure and no small degree of shock that Planan has agreed to conduct the first movement of Beethoven's Fifth Symphony for us this evening. Magically, our guest was able to whip out from the sky the appropriate sheet music for the orchestra. Apparently, Planan will not need any sheet music herself as she has committed this work to memory—somehow. With that, I give you Planan, guest conductor of the Chicago Symphony Orchestra."

By way of auto-translate, Planan says, "Thank you, Maestro. It is, in fact, my great pleasure, and I thank you for this opportunity. I obviously did not plan on this this evening, so please give me a moment to chat with the orchestra."

Planan huddles with the members of the orchestra—a quarterback describing the next play. She describes in detail which aspects of the first movement require emphasis and reviews pacing, places for pronounced pauses, and other aspects of interpretation. The CSO is no stranger to this symphonic work, having played it countless times and having one of the world's finest recordings of same. No one, however, is familiar with the particular interpretation Planan requests. More than one violinist inquires whether they understand the instructions correctly. Upon Planan's affirmation and further guidance, all of them thought it through and began to understand how well the interpretation will flow.

Planan asks the maestro and the orchestra whether they would mind adding a section of players from Merk to the orchestra. The maestro and the orchestra cannot imagine what Planan is doing, but they are so intrigued that they readily agree.

Planan decides to add two sets of players. One consists of Merkian instrumentalists using cranor, a beautiful instrument with a similar sound and function to the violin that adds a soothing background sensation to the violin section. The other set consists of a supplement to the cello that also adds background. Planan believes such background will round out the sound and make it fuller—something Beethoven would have wanted if he had access to such instruments.

After running through final preparatory instructions and confirmations, the orchestra is in place. Planan lifts the baton.

What follows is a thing of auditory wonderment. Without the encumbrance of viewing any sheet music in front of her, Planan directs the first movement with great acuity and emphasis. Those familiar with the music in the audience recognize they are hearing not just something special but music that combines interpretation, fullness, and a weird combination of Earth and Merk instrumentals never heard before. Those unfamiliar with the music are enraptured by it.

Planan finishes. Those in attendance, having already applauded more in one evening than they ever have before, are compelled to stand, applaud, hoot, and yell, "Encore!"

Planan, not familiar with requests for an encore, takes the microphone and apologizes that she does not think it appropriate to perform further but says she'd love to return another time and place.

Also, at this point, Andy and Rein are looking for some alone time. They invite everyone to stay and party but announce their thanks and their departure. A honeymoon is out of the question, given the crush of national, world, and galactic events coupled with Andy's and Rein's relative positions. They take Air Force One back to Washington D.C., then a helicopter to the White House. Thankfully, Air Force One has delightful bedroom accommodations. Despite the events of the day and the hour, however, there is not much sleep on the return trip.

CHAPTER 36

EARTH'S ENTRY

S everal months have passed since Rein and Andy's wedding, but given the events that have transpired since then, it seems like years. China's transition to democracy is in full swing. Elections are scheduled, and the Chinese are experiencing a freedom of choice that has never been seen before. The burst of energy and enthusiasm for the new China within China itself and around the world is remarkable. New trade deals are being signed, new investments are streaming into every major Chinese city, and tourism both flowing into and out of China is at levels never experienced before. China's interim government holds a referendum on China's vote regarding Merk. The referendum passes in favor of Merk entry by a wide margin, allowing the Chinese interim government comfort in affirming the Chinese favorable vote regarding entry. China, therefore, joins the rest of the nations of the world in unanimously voting in favor of entry. While there are one or two countries that muttered initial thoughts of not voting for entry, they did so only to attempt to win some concession from the US and other world powers. Any naysayers were quick to change their tune when the US and others indicated that not only would there be no favorable treatment of any nation inclined to vote against entry only to win such favorable treatment, but rather, any country voting against entry would become a pariah and not be allowed to participate in any of the benefits of Merk's disclosures and would be cut off from world trade.

On the domestic front, Andy's policies are being enacted swiftly, and the results are already being realized.

New medical complexes are being constructed across the country, and recruitment for staffing those facilities is in full swing. Upon formal entry to Merk, which will occur in one week, a Merk medical representative will be staffed in each new medical center to help with the learning curve when Merk introduces new medical technology to Earth.

The mass irrigation of the American West is beginning to show results as well. Flood water from the Midwest is being piped in, rain reservoirs are being built, and desalination plants are pumping out streams of potable water. While certain desert wildlife preserves are being maintained, the American West is turning green, and the cities in the American West are becoming water-rich. California farmers no longer have to worry about water. Farms around Phoenix have expanded, and there is a new farming corridor extending from Las Vegas to Victorville, California, which can easily be seen from the high-speed trains linking Las Vegas with Los Angeles.

Along with those new farms are the first rehabilitation settlements for those individuals who have formerly occupied the nation's prisons. The annual cost of maintaining a single prisoner had been two hundred thousand dollars. Andy's plan, however, has cut that cost in half and provides each prisoner with a small house, a plot of land upon which to garden, an employment opportunity within the settlement, and the means to earn credits toward freedom. Prisoners are allowed to train and become employed in computer science, agriculture, clothing fabrication, one or more of the performing arts, and a range of other pursuits. Upon graduation, prisoners are then deployed in work-assisted enterprises within the settlement. Incentives are infused into the process. Prisoners who participate in the education and work programs are provided with entertainment facilities in their homes, better food choices, and other perks. Participation rates are, as a result, extremely high.

Safely adjacent to these prison settlements are growing bodies of homeless and unemployed worker settlements. Homeless individuals found in the urban centers are provided a home, a plot of land larger than the prisoner garden plot and means of transportation within what is informally called the Brock Cities. Andy does not care for that name as he does not think the work of many who brought this project into being should be diminished, but he cannot stop the name from sticking. The Brock Cities have become economically self-sufficient operations. Homeless and unemployed individuals are given the means to live and help themselves. The education and employment programs are similar to the programs deployed in the prison context, but because there are no prison safety concerns, the programs are even more robust. Agricultural operations in Brock Cities are sufficient to support the food needs of their residents, with an excess for sale to local communities. Clothing manufacturing has also become a vital element of Brock Cities industry. Medical training is yet another example of a key educational pursuit. A healthy number of physical therapists, medical technicians, and nurses are graduating from the educational institutions in Brock Cities—and a good number of those graduates serve residents of Brock Cities.

With prisoner recidivism declining due to the prisoner settlements, the homeless and unemployed populations being given huge opportunities in Brock Cities, and federally mandated drug and prostitution legalization occurring, crime rates plummet.

Moreover, the revenues earned and saved from the prisoner settlements and Brock Cities, along with the tax revenue gained from taxing recreational drugs and prostitution, are in part allocated to increase police numbers, particularly in urban areas. Gang violence is no longer tolerated. Armies of police appear with federal financial assistance to go after gang leadership and their members. Gangs are treated as enemy combatants and are actively sought out, caught, and prosecuted. Gang activity that affects schools is aggressively pursued. In fact, school bullying itself is the subject of enhanced prosecution, with bullies being removed and placed in other educational institutions with stricter supervisory capabilities.

The country and the world are transforming themselves. The US, with a GDP growing at an annual 10 percent rate, is one of many countries leading the world in an economic boom. Other nations across the globe are following Andy's policies of enhanced irrigation, medical innovation, and crime reduction. Even before Merkian intervention, a global renewal was being experienced. There is a vastly reduced need to invest in the military, as many nations realize. Instead, taxes are reduced, and government programs targeting Andy-type policies are increased. At some level, rationality is winning over stupidity. What is good for the whole is understood as good for the individual and vice versa. Smart money spent on social programs incorporating incentives is now viewed as the rule, not the exception. Flabby government bureaucracy is attacked while market-driven government intervention is instituted. Discrimination against minorities is not tolerated, but discriminatory programs favoring minorities are also not allowed.

In addition, the ravages of climate change are being more positively addressed. Desalination is allowing for more water to flow inland, thus reducing flooding, and the further greening of the planet is adding to the reduction in CO2 emissions. Plant oxygenation is literally springing forth. Cloud creation and control technology also enhance rainfall totals more uniformly and as desired. The press actively comments that dystopian movies and books require a suspension of disbelief because a dystopian future seems too far-fetched.

Against this backdrop, world leaders, including Andy, gather at the United Nations to formalize acceptance of Merk's invitation. Triven represents Merk and the other galactic planets. The Merk Alignment document was previously sent to world leaders, and the terms that are readily understood are nothing more than what has already been revealed by Merk. There are the basic principles of cooperation, mutual security, and industrial sharing. Both Merk and the United Nations, by resolution, agreed that the controlling document would be set forth in English. In alphabetical order, each leader of each nation of Earth came forward to sign the Merk Alignment. Finally, Triven affixed his signature by way of a Merkian stamp.

In the succeeding weeks, Merk began to make disclosures to Earth's leaders. Cancer, in all its forms, will now be a thing of the past. Medical advancements treating a plethora of maladies, such as Alzheimer's disease, muscular dystrophy, and even blindness, are disclosed. Agricultural innovations that will vastly increase crop yields are also part of the disclosures. A revolution in renewable energy beyond the imagination of Earth is about to be realized. These are but a few of the advancements that Earth will enjoy.

Triven joins Andy and Rein on Air Force One on the trip back from New York City to Washington, D.C. Rein is in the seat next to Andy's and Triven sits across from them. Triven says, "It looks like my daughter was right. She believed Earth was ready for Merk. She said you would be a singular force to make Earth ready. Son, I've got to congratulate you. I'm also going to congratulate my daughter for helping to bring this about."

"I agree that it was mainly Rein's intervention and influence that brought this about, but I thank you anyway, Dad."

"Guys, there's no need to outlove each other here. Dad, I know there's more you'd like to discuss."

"Well, yes. Andy, now that the Merk Alignment is signed and Earth is progressing so well, I hope you realize it is time to have your Merk wedding ceremony on Merk. Moreover, it is customary for an Earth representative to visit Merk after Merk Alignment. You are clearly the best representative of Earth for this purpose. And, as they say on Earth, 'What the heck?' You'll already be there for the wedding. What say you?" Triven asks.

"I agree that you have been more than patient with the wedding ceremony. I also agree that it is the perfect time. I don't agree that I can appoint myself Earth's representative. I intend to reach out to the UN and seek approval to be that representative."

"Fair enough. I would have expected nothing less from you, son. Are you sure you don't have Merkian DNA in there somewhere?" Triven asks.

Andy just laughs.

After his return to the White House, Andy has Lance, his secretary of state, set in motion communications with world leaders, informing them of the need to have an Earth representative go to Merk and formalize Earth's entry into the Merk Alignment. Most leaders laugh at Lance and say Andy should be the only person who should go and ask why Lance was even entertaining the prospect of someone else. Other leaders do not laugh but say their vote is for Andy, Earth's leader, to represent Earth. A resolution was made by India and seconded by Russia at the United Nations proposing the election of Andrew Sheridan Brock, president of the United States of America and designated leader of Earth, to be the Earth's representative to Merk. Every representative of every nation on Earth votes in favor of that resolution.

Lance advises Andy of the vote and asks whether he accepts his newly elected status of "leader of Earth." Lance says the last part with a smirk while dramatically positioning himself on bended knee. Andy tells Lance, also with a smirk, that he gives Lance permission to rise and that he accepts being Earth's representative.

Newspapers worldwide feature a headline announcing Andy as "leader of Earth." At the United Nations, serious consideration is being given to a more federal system of Earth governance, with current nations ceding power to a central governing body much more powerful than the United Nations. Along with that consideration is a growing consensus that as long as Andrew Brock is the first president of that federation, the world will be in safe hands.

CHAPTER 37

FOLDING SPACE

"**S**trip," Rein says.

"I saw that coming from a mile away. You know, I thought Merkians were generally more clever given how allegedly advanced they are."

"Strip," Rein repeats.

"You first," Andy says and turns around, realizing his request is too late as Rein is, of course, already naked.

"You know, no matter how many times I see you, it just doesn't get old. Is it possible, though, that you got even more definition in your abs?" Andy asks.

"I'm glad you noticed. I've been working on my vertical leap, and I think it has had an impact on my stomach muscles. You have been scoring more points during our one-on-one basketball games than I would like, so I thought I would practice a bit more intensely."

"C'mon, you have beaten me in every game we've played. You beat me by two points in our first game and by an average of eight points since. I think your vertical leap is just fine where it is."

"I appreciate the victories, but I just cannot let some Earthling get that many points. I don't care if he's the so-called 'leader of Earth.' Anyway, you're stalling, strip."

Andy does just that, and then he and Rein perform the Send. A day earlier, Andy's entourage arrived on the ship. That entourage included a required Secret Service detail; Secretary of State Lance

Como; Vincent Potenza, one of the most famous chefs of Italian cuisine on Earth; Francois Dubuque, one of France's renowned chefs; Xio Bei, a famous Chinese chef; and Maria Reyes, from the Philippines and generally recognized as the finest female vocalist on Earth. Maria agreed to sing at the wedding on Merk, and Andy thought Merk would enjoy the recipes prepared by the three chefs at various functions. Rein insists, however, that only Merkian cuisine will be served at the wedding reception on Merk.

Andy and Rein arrive on the ship. Only Merk staffers and Andy's security detail are present. All members of Andy's security detail wear Merkian outfits—grey bodysuits. Rather than dress in the Send vestibule, Andy and Rein make their way to Rein's quarters, where Andy dons a Merkian grey bodysuit as well. Rein then shows Andy to his private quarters. Although Andy and Rein are now aligned, it is likely that he will need private quarters to conduct Earth business. As such, Andy's quarters amount more to an office than a bedroom, although a bed is provided. There is also a fully computerized communication interface located in his quarters. Rein works with Andy to effectuate the interface programming that will respond to Andy and then let him control the systems through voice and motion commands. Prior to FoldSpace, Andy is able to communicate with Earth remarkably well.

"Jack, you obviously have complete discretion to effect decisions you deem best. While I understand that when I am on Merk there will be communication, there will also be delays, so do make decisions, keep me updated, and good luck."

"Thanks, Andy, and please allow me to compliment you on your attire. For an old man, you have really maintained your abs."

"Thanks for noticing, Jack. I'm glad you find me so attractive. Anyway, hold down the fort until I get back. OK, Rein, so based on what you told me, we actually fold space, which means we get to Merk instantaneously?"

"Not exactly; the fold only allows us to get within about a couple of billion miles. We are able to hyperdrive from there. So, the total trip time for FoldSpace preparations, the FoldSpace operation, then the hyperdrive (and related operations) takes, with direct routing into Amberan, about two Earth days."

"Not bad. I remember going from Chicago to Tokyo back in the day, and it took almost 18 hours."

"I think we will be set for FoldSpace shortly. You won't really feel anything with either FoldSpace or the hyperdrive, as the ship maintains a self-contained and space-impervious environment. As you've also noticed, only certain rooms have null gravity, and those really are for entertainment purposes."

"Yes, I remember that our null gravity experience was quite entertaining. One I will never forget."

"I hope not, although I am hoping for a repeat entertainment experience in a couple of hours."

Andy settles into Rein's quarters and sleeps the sleep of the dead. The events of the past two years have caught up with him now. Moreover, for the first time in memory, Andy effectively has nothing to do for two days. He hits the bed after further manifesting alignment with Rein, who sleeps next to him. While not exhausted, Rein realizes how much she needs the additional rest. It is also amazing to be able to sleep with her husband. For the longest time, she had wondered if she would ever find her mate. Now that she has found him, she has found herself.

CHAPTER 38

MERK ARRIVAL

The spaceport is enormous. After FoldSpace and the hyperdrive, Andy sees that the ship is to dock at a gigantic structure in space. It is effectively a huge wheel that is five miles thick and two miles deep with a circumference of, he guesses, two hundred and fifty miles. The entire structure rotates but permits ship docking. The spaceport appears to have an atmosphere as abundant plant life is evident. It isn't clear how the atmosphere is maintained, but Andy guesses some form of shielding mechanism is being used. Architecturally significant buildings with walkways, pathways, and plazas emanate from the interior of the circle. The architecture is fairly consistent in orientation, made of what Rein says can only be described in bastardized English as tekglass, a material similar to glass and titanium. The orientation is more rectangular than Andy had imagined, but he sees that the flat roofs accommodate shuttle ports, so he thinks they are more utilitarian than fancy.

Andy is very thankful he and Rein are able to catch up on sleep. In fact, apart from a few meals and frequent manifestations of alignment, sleep is about all they do on the trip to Merk.

Andy is awake before Rein and is able to observe the spaceport clearly from their shared room. Rein wakes shortly after Andy. Both slept naked and remain in that state. Rein orders Andy's breakfast to be delivered, which includes pancakes served with butter and syrup, crisp bacon, scrambled eggs, and Cream of Wheat with brown sugar and a side of milk, as well as freshly squeezed orange juice, ice water, and coffee with cream and sweetener. She orders the same for herself.

Rein lets the delivery person in while both she and Andy are unclothed. The delivery person is not fazed by their nudity. Andy still finds it interesting that his wife appears naked in front of strangers and finds it almost as strange that he does as well.

"So, I got a health status report this morning while ordering food. What names interest you for a boy and a girl?"

"What!" Andy exclaims.

"You know, for the leader of Earth, you can be a bit—what do the English say? —'daft,'" Rein says.

"Sorry. No excuses. I should have been quicker."

With that, Andy runs over to Rein and passionately hugs and kisses her. One thing leads to another, and Andy insists they refer to what they are doing as making love, not just manifesting alignment, but it is not like he has a real problem with the alternative Merkian phraseology.

While still in bed but after their prolonged love-making session, Andy finally tells Rein he has some thoughts about names but wants to be sensitive to the fact that he is not as familiar with Merkian names as she is and does not want to assume they would be names of Earth.

"I'll use your term: This is one reason I love you. You are remarkably culturally sensitive for not having been part of the galaxy until this year."

"I try."

"Anyway, I'll show you on-screen a list of Merkian names. I already have access to Earth names. I'm not wedded to either. I'm just looking for names that sound great and maybe carry some meaning we both like."

"Sounds like a plan to me. By the way, what's the gestation period?"

"About six Earth months."

"Hmm, you said a boy and a girl. I could take that one of two ways. One, you don't know the sex, or two, you know we have twins. Care to tell me which one?" Andy asks.

"Twins—one boy and one girl."

"And you know this now? How long have you been pregnant?" Andy asks.

"I am pretty confident, based upon the data I've seen, that it was on the trip on Air Force One after the wedding. You ejaculated twice. I'm not able to narrow it down to which of your orgasms impregnated me—they were, after all, only twenty minutes apart."

"I was the happiest person alive when you married me, but this news takes my happiness to another level. Words fail me."

"Me too."

"I assume this will be the first Merk-Earth combination in history, yes?"

"That has been confirmed."

"I think I asked something like this before, but any medical issues your folks say we should anticipate?"

"No medical issues. Our kids might not have the same vertical leap capability their mother enjoys. I suspect, however, they will both be quite intelligent."

"By the way, I saw the spaceport. It's fantastic. I could sense amazing plant life. If I am not mistaken, instead of green, there's a lot of lavender. Am I seeing this right?" Andy asks.

"Yes. When you told me your favorite color was lavender, I thought it was too good to be true. While much of Earth's plant life is green in color, Merk's plant life is usually lavender. Our soil is more orange than brown. Our water is more of what you would call a sky blue. As you will see, our sky takes on a little bit of a blueish-violet tint. It's quite beautiful, although I love Earth's colors as well. Anyway, we need to be on the shuttle in an hour, and you'll see everything I'm talking about shortly. By the way, we are on Merk now, so I'll be converting time frames and similar concepts to Merk soon if that's OK with you."

"I don't know if I'll be able to follow the references immediately, but I'll try. I guess the timekeeping devices aren't the twelve-hour clocks, right?" Andy postulates.

"Correct. You'll get the hang of it, though. You'll see. Do you want to get dressed for the shuttle, or would you like me to stay as I am?" Rein asks.

"I would like to get dressed, and I'd like you to stay as you are, for obvious reasons. By the way, my being dressed does not say much. I saw my outfit in the mirror; you can basically make out my full anatomy in this bodysuit."

"Yes, I know."

"Anyway, I'll get dressed, if you can call it that."

Andy and Rein make their way to the shuttle, which is the size of three Air Force Ones, both in length and width. It has luxurious restroom facilities, a concession area where hot food and drinks are available, lounges, and meeting spaces. Andy does not know whether every shuttle is like this or whether this shuttle is a VIP craft.

"So, this shuttle is quite impressive. Are all shuttles this well-appointed?" Andy asks Rein.

"No. Shuttles come in various sizes and capacities. You are an honored guest and are being treated accordingly."

"Please advise me to whom I should show my gratitude."

"Me, and I plan to ensure your expression of gratitude is very satisfying."

"Well, I'll say thank you for now and reinforce my sentiments of appreciation later."

Merk comes into view. The planet is gorgeous. Hues of lavender and sky blue are prevalent, and shades of orange are also visible. As the shuttle descends, the city of Amberan comes into view as well. Amberan is Reagan's shining city on a hill, literally. Amberan appears to sit on a plateau that reaches up from an ocean, with hills surrounding the plateau. The buildings glisten in Merk's sun, predominantly yellow, with a fair amount of orange mixed in. Andy guesses that the city's buildings spread out to more than twenty Manhattans. It is truly awesome.

The shuttle lands in a large plaza surrounded by water features and expertly maintained landscapes.

"Rein, this is beyond my imagination. You never even hinted at the beauty of your world."

"It's not our way. I'm glad you like it."

"Like it? You have a penchant for understatement."

"Anyway, welcome. Our second wedding reception will be in that tall building over there. The height masks the large size on the bottom. It's quite wonderful. But first, let's get you home."

Rein respects that Andy's security detail desires to be with him at all times while outdoors as well as in the same buildings he occupies, so her private shuttle craft is large enough to accommodate them as well as her and Andy. The group is able to make their way from the landing zone to Rein's residence.

Rein's residence is a short flight from the landing zone and in bucolic surroundings. While she maintains a residence in a large tower in the central government and business district, her main residence is on about two acres and is lush with vegetation. There is a version of grass on about half an acre in front of the residence. The shuttlecraft is able to land atop the residence, which is quite large.

After exiting the shuttlecraft, they are able to enter the residence from a foyer at the top of the structure. The foyer is huge and adorned with what looks like the counterpart to Earth's marble and granite, but not really. The material has a more metallic and less organic feel and look, but nevertheless is hard and glistens. The interior design hues are cream and dark brown, which give off both a warm and elegant look.

From the foyer, Andy can see the surrounding grounds. "Is that an encircling river with an entry bridge to the front door?"

"Yes."

"Did I also sense correctly that the façade of the house is covered in what I would call castle stone on Earth?"

"Yes."

"I'm also sensing this is a five-story house, right? So, you have a castle with a drawbridge and moat that you never told me about?"

"Yes," Rein replies, this time with a big smile.

"While I appreciate the efficiency of monosyllabic answers, a little elaboration would be welcome from you."

"No elaboration is required."

"OK, nice castle."

"Thank you. I hope you're comfortable here for a while, but if you're not, I think you'll like my place in the city."

"I think I'll muddle through here."

"Andy, is it OK if we go over the schedule? There have been some changes."

"Sure."

"The formal wedding procedure will now be tomorrow. The counterpart to an Earth hour on Merk is forty-two minutes, and as such, the wedding procedure will be at twenty. The wedding party will be at twenty-one. The next day, we will have the formal introduction of the Earth representative—namely, you—at twenty-three. Sorry for the changes, but some issues have resurfaced with the Davark that have required Dad's attention—and mine."

"No problem, I understand. That leaves us with some time to enjoy your castle tonight. Just out of curiosity, when I go to a foreign country, I'm always fascinated with their arts—television and arts programming, in particular. I assume you have that here?"

"Yes, we do. Complen kend rivan," Rein instructs the auto-device. Upon Rein's instruction, audio-visual equipment descends from the ceiling of the living room and tunes automatically to Rein's typical programming, which, on this occasion, is a news report.

"Thanks. Does it have subtitles in English?" Andy asks.

"No, but you can use the auto-translate device I gave you."

"Ah, I didn't need it because everyone else was using theirs. Sorry."

Andy then deploys his device and is able to hear the news in English—and it is fascinating for what it is not. No crime to report and no weather reporting as the weather is controlled. There is extensive reporting about Andy and Earth, the upcoming wedding, and Davark issues.

"So, I will leave you in great hands with Aver, my house manager. Unfortunately, I have to head to a meeting concerning Davark with Dad and the military heads. I'll see you at twenty or just about, OK?" Rein pleads.

"I understand, dear. Have a good day at work. Sorry I didn't pack a lunch for you," Andy replies.

Rein hugs and kisses Andy on her way out the door. Aver shows Andy the remainder of the house, particularly the bedroom. Aver mentions that Rein has ensured Andy has his own office to work from, which is outfitted with all the communications equipment Andy could ever want as well as all the processing power he could ever need. Andy asks Aver if he knows how communications are routed to Earth so quickly, and Aver mentions that relays are set up to allow communications boosts along the way. While Aver indicates he is not an expert in that technology, it is fairly common knowledge, at least in Merk, that at some level, these boosts operate similarly to FoldSpace technology.

With that knowledge, Andy sends what amounts to an email to Jack asking for a status update. Within a half-hour, Jack responds that everything is moving smoothly and calmly on Earth and that Andy should enjoy himself.

With that, Andy asks Aver to show him how to use the exercise equipment that he had noticed earlier. Rein's house gym is what appears to be at least two thousand square feet of what would be considered beyond state-of-the-art equipment on Earth. While some of the equipment looks intuitive to use, Andy wants to make sure.

Andy is trained by Aver, gets a good workout in, showers, watches more Merk TV, and hangs out awaiting his bride's return to their castle on Merk.

CHAPTER 39

THE STRATEGIST

R ein enters the conference room on the two-hundred-and-second floor of the chancellor's tower. Floor two hundred and four houses Triven's offices and those of his direct staff. Floor two hundred and three is where the key domestic managers have their offices. The two-hundred-and-second floor is dedicated to military affairs.

Triven and the military leadership, including, among others, Admiral Riven, head of the space fleet; Commander Denk, in charge of military intelligence; and General Pross, leader of land forces, are all in place in the conference room.

"Chancellor, during your trip to Earth and within the span of your return, Davark has now attacked three more allied planets. While they were not full-blown assaults, they did substantial damage to one or more major military outposts on these planets. Thankfully, there have been minimal casualties, and Davark forces were turned back, but that does not diminish the fact that Davark is becoming more aggressive," says General Pross.

"These assaults appeared to be probing attacks designed to assess our responses," Denk interposes.

"While our responses were apparently successful, it is not clear to us what Davark's ultimate initial target will be," Riven surmises.

"With due respect to everyone in this room, that is one reason I have called for an outside strategic consultant—someone to give us an alternative view. Denk, who are the candidates for that outside consultant?" Triven asks.

"We've got four candidates who have been fully vetted, with one who has not been. All of the four fully vetted candidates came to no conclusion on Davark's ultimate initial target other than what I told you: They were merely probing attacks. Those candidates then identified a range of possible additional targets, none of which is particularly compelling. Moreover, between our internal military and intelligence personnel combined with those four candidates, the general conclusion is to continue monitoring the situation and strengthen defenses in the periphery planets closest to Davark's home territory. So, none of these fully vetted candidates is, so far, adding anything above and beyond what our present intellectual resource is arriving at."

Triven asks, "Who is the candidate that wasn't vetted?"

"Andrew Sheridan Brock."

"Ah, my son-in-law. Tell me more."

"We've analyzed his analytics. He appears to be a real savant when it comes to strategic planning. His ability to predict the timing of the Chinese attack during his wedding was nothing short of amazing. It was not just the timing—it was the method and nature of that attack. He also coordinated the response to that attack, which was flawlessly implemented. Understand, this was a full-scale war that was over in a day. The coordinated response involved the military as well as an internal rebellion—both of which were expertly timed. I grant you that China was able to launch nuclear weapons that Merk intervened to control, but it was likely that even if Merk assets were not present, American defense would have stopped the nukes in flight with only radiation emission issues potentially present. Human losses would have been substantial, but that should be measured against the alternative of a Chinese nation bent on warfare that would likely have cost millions of lives. In addition, President Brock's policies have come to fruition in a very successful way. His strategic planning has borne fruit in prison reform, medicine, energy, immigration, and economics. There is a history of policymakers coming up with good policies that might have an effect. His policies and implementation have transformed society, his country, and his world. It is a more powerful

renaissance than ever before seen on Earth and is making Earth progress as a planet faster than we have ever seen, even considering the
growth trajectory of other worlds. If I didn't know better, it is like he
can see the future."

Triven asks, "Rein, he's your husband. What say you?"

"I'll try to be as objective about this as possible. I agree completely with Denk. Andy's ability to assess data and logically apply
strategic planning to that data is like nothing I've ever seen. It seems
automatic. We all know and have heard the music of Earth's Mozart—
similar to our own Sassin. Both Mozart and Sassin wrote music in a
first draft as if merely taking dictation. The beautiful music just came
to them. Andy's ability to logically assess and plan appears to automatically come to him."

"I've heard enough. The Davark threat is immediate. Denk,
please get Andy over here now," Triven instructs.

"I thought you might say that. A shuttle is at Rein's home ready
to bring him here. Assuming Andy's willing, he can be here shortly."

"Rein, please see if he can join us," Triven instructs.

"Already on it."

Andy is in the shuttle within five minutes, happy to see Rein
but wondering why he was invited to a high-level executive meeting
on Merk at this time. It is plausible that there might be an Earth-
related issue down the road, but he does not expect that meeting to
take place so soon, especially not while he is getting ready for the
wedding.

Andy is shown the conference room and takes a seat next to
Denk, which is the only seat made available to him. Rein looks at
him from the opposite side of the table. Unlike a typical conference
room on Earth, everyone is seated at what could only be called mini-
sofa units, within which are embedded computer interfaces. These
mini-sofas are placed within peninsular desks jutting from the table
so that everyone has an amazingly comfortable seating arrangement
that is also remarkably functional.

"Andy, thank you for coming. Sorry to ask this the day before
your wedding here in Amberan, but we need your help. As you may
know, Davark has been making probing attacks. We have no reason
to believe those attacks are anything but the beginning. We would

appreciate your assistance in formulating what Davark might do next," Triven says.

"In watching the news and speaking briefly with Rein about this situation, I've gained an understanding consistent with what you just told me. I need more data, though. The data that is of particular interest to me concerns the specific nature of Davark's previous probing attacks, the current defensive posture of Merk's forces, Merk's critical military and intelligence infrastructure, Davark's known offensive capabilities, and what would be considered Davark's vulnerabilities as well as all known sociological tendencies and leadership psycho-strategic profiles."

"Denk, how long will it take to get this information to President Brock?" Triven asks.

"I was queuing it while President Brock was speaking. We have set up an office for President Brock down the hall. It can be there in twelve units."

"Dad, I'd like to join Andy on this to help him with any logistical and operational needs he might have," Rein says.

"Granted."

"Andy, by the time we make it to your new office, most, if not all, of the data will be there," Rein says.

"Denk, what volume of data are we talking about here?" Andy asks.

"In Earth's terms, it has been reduced to about two hundred pages in summary fashion with linkages to details that are uncountable as there are linkages within linkages. That being said, I suspect the two hundred pages will suffice for your immediate needs."

"Andy, based on that, when will we be able to hear from you, do you imagine?" Triven asks.

"Chancellor, I hope you don't mind me being direct here as I am still learning Merk culture. Based on my instincts on this, we are out of time. The next Davark attack could happen at any moment. I don't plan on sleeping tonight. Please plan on meeting here again in what on Earth would be nine hours—forgive me, I have not mastered the timing dynamic here perfectly."

"Mr. President, you'll find we are very candid and direct here in Merk. We'll reconvene at the time you indicated. If you come to a conclusion earlier, then contact me," Triven says.

With that, Andy and Rein make their way to Andy's new office. Andy soon discovers that calling it an office is a gross understatement in Earth terms—it makes the Oval Office and the West Wing look inconvenient. There are four work centers with several consoles permitting a variety of audio-visual and computer interfaces. Each of these work centers is outfitted with ergonomic seating that incorporates heating, ventilation, and massage capabilities independent of embedded audio functions. Andy can understand the rationale for having two or maybe three interfaces but can only imagine this office space is intended for a particular Merkian team approach, given the additional consoles.

In addition to the dedicated workspaces, the so-called office also has what is essentially a food and drink bar. One can order virtually any food desired (with more than a few Earth-originated selections) and a range of beverages from a replicator. Two dining tables and comfortable seating are provided as well.

In addition, a spa bathroom provides commodes in separate interior rooms, showers, vanities, a sauna, and a water-massage pool. The vanities are fully stocked with all necessary toiletries, including shampoos, soaps, and colognes.

The office views are spectacular as well and are accommodated by an exterior balcony with ample sofa seating accessed through self-opening doors. For the first time, Andy sees a flag, which features a beautiful lavender on the bottom half, white on the top half, and a black triangle in the middle.

"Rein, is that a Merk flag or an Amberan flag?"

"We only go by one flag universally, and that is for Merk."

"I assume the colors and the triangle have meaning. I guess the lavender is a celebration of the beautiful natural color of Merk. I'm not sure about the white and the triangle."

"Yes. I'm impressed you used the word 'celebrate' because that is exactly the way we on Merk use that color in the flag and what it means to us. The white is our color of peace, which is what we strive for. The triangle represents the three pillars of our society: scientific thought, honesty, and your concept of love, for lack of a better word in English."

"It is a truly magnificent symbol—one I'd be willing to fight for."

"Ironically, we hope never to have to fight for it militarily, only culturally."

"I'm on board with that. Well, let's see if we can get to work."

Andy is able to access the data shortly after settling into one of the work consoles. Rein ensures he has full access to all of the data. Having experienced Merk technology, Andy is not surprised the data files arrive on his console in perfect English.

"You know, Rein, when we have more time, I really need to get briefed on the universe. There are so many questions and issues we have not had any meaningful time to discuss—for example, is everyone out there humanoid, who is the most advanced civilization out there, what's the expanse of the explored universe, and how old is Earth's civilization compared to the others?"

"I know. Things have been moving a little fast, you know."

"Yes, they have. By the way, the wedding is tomorrow, and we may not sleep tonight. Any thoughts about putting it off a day or two?"

"I've been thinking about that. If necessary, let's talk about it first thing in the morning. I just want you to know that putting it off can be achieved, but not that easily—even for a family as well connected as mine. How's the file structure look to you?" Rein asks.

"Very intuitive. I should be fine to review everything without having to call upon you. In fact, in looking through some of the initial results, I'm beginning to form some conclusions."

"OK, anything you want to report now?" Rein asks.

"Not yet, let me settle in, and I'll tell you when I'm done. It's better I keep everything in kind of a mind-flow."

Andy settles into the data files. Rein intuitively brings him the Merkian equivalent of hot tea and protein snacks to keep him going.

In about four hours, Andy tells Rein he is done. Given the urgency, Rein calls her father, and everyone assembles in the conference room.

Andy gives his assessment. "Davark appears to be materially weaker as an opponent to Merk. It further appears that Davark is threatened by Merk as recently, certain Davarkian allies have switched sides or at least claimed neutrality. Davark's behavior then is one of a scared bully. Davark's probing attacks were both meant as a distraction and a test of its powers. Davark has apparently two choices: to seek to join Merk, or to effect a devastating blow on Merk to regain some of its former allies and perhaps bring Merk to terms. My assessment is that Davark will not seek to join Merk. Therefore, it is my assessment that Davark plans to attempt a devastating blow to Merk as it cannot sustain a prolonged war with Merk. As most, if not all, of Merk's leadership—governmentally, militarily, culturally, and societally—will be gathered here in Amberan for the wedding, Davark would be well situated to launch an attack here today during the wedding party. I understand there are considerable defenses that Davark would need to plow through to get here, but Davark is less concerned about the tremendous losses it would suffer if even one offensive ship was able to get through and attack the wedding celebration."

"With all due respect, President Brock, that seems completely unlikely. As you said, Davark's military capabilities do not measure up to that kind of attack without Davark sustaining devastating losses. It is extremely doubtful that any Davark ship would get by our defenses," Denk says.

"True, no one anticipates Davark ever engaging in such a measure to sacrifice so much of their people and assets," Admiral Riven says.

"With all due respect, in return, you are thinking like a Merkian rather than a Davarkian. Merkians treasure every life. Davarkians do not. Davarkians are jealous of Merkian culture and power. They want what you have without joining you. They also want a variant of what you have: That variant keeps the Davarkian leadership in control of their culture without realizing that such control is the antithesis of such culture. They are self-defeatists—never, ever able to achieve Merkian levels of societal improvement because of the leadership's selfish adherence to their own power structure. They just get in the way of themselves. Davarkians only understand that a power move will bring about their goals. They cannot share the universe with Merk. They can only attempt to further their control. It is also not a problem for them to effectuate that control at the expense of their own people and assets—so long as there is enough universe left for them to control. So, a desperate attempt to take Merkian leadership out and show the universe how strong Davark can be is worth the risk. Davark also does not believe that Merk will do anything more than contain Davark—Merk is perceived as too noble to wipe out an enemy. Therefore, again, their desperate attack is entirely worth the risk."

"I see. What's your recommendation, then?" Triven asks.

"Now—and I mean, right now—an announcement needs to go out saying the wedding is postponed due to my sickness—something about me not adjusting well to my foreign environment. After that, Merk needs to attack Davark at the following four locations: Sarik, Travak, Amjular, and Boric. After that attack, Merk should infiltrate Davark's command and control structure. With that infiltration, olive branches should be extended to enough in the upper reaches of the government and the military to make them understand the benefit of joining Merk and the ultimate destruction of Davark's current path. Without hoping to sound conceited, I need to be part of the infiltration team."

"Denk, get the wedding postponement effectuated now," Triven orders.

"Yes, Chancellor."

From his console, Denk immediately effectuates the postponement and the notices of same.

"Riven, what do you think about this strategy? Can we win those battles?" Triven asks.

"To answer the second question first, yes, Chancellor. To answer the first, I think President Brock has shown us a different way of thinking about Davark, which is exactly what we needed. We do need to stop Davark's harassment. We've operated under the egalitarian feeling that containment is more ethical. It's not, and President Brock has helped me realize how abhorrent Davark's way of thinking is to us and that we have not really come to grips with the notion that sometimes you need to fight evil with tremendous force rather than merely keep it at bay. So, Chancellor, I'm on board with President Brock's approach."

"Rein?" Triven asks.

"I think Andy's strategy here is sound. I'm not wild about him being part of the infiltration team. I understand the rationale behind it, but he'll need someone attuned to our level of technology and methods, even though he is clearly a quick study."

"I don't suppose you have anyone in mind who could hold his hand?" Triven asks.

"Cliven and myself. Depending on how the infiltration goes, Cliven might be with Andy on the ultimate team, but I'd like to be there as long as possible."

"I'm OK with Rein coming along on the travel to Davark, but I do not want Rein in situ. I think Cliven, Denk, several combat technicians, several hand-to-hand combatants, two communications experts, and two medical personnel are who I would envision as part of the away team. I'm assuming you have the medical technology to allow me and the away team to look somewhat Davarkian?" Andy ultimately asks.

"I'm on board with that plan, and yes, President Brock, we have the ability to help you blend in," Denk responds.

"You know, son, it's funny. You have been with us for mere moments, and you have come up with a plan, which was conveyed with great confidence. I just want to confirm with you, and I want everyone in this room to understand that what you are really advancing is a strategy that is nothing more than a calculated risk," Triven says.

"Yes. I appreciate that those on Merk do not face as many risks as we do on Earth. Merk's advancements have lessened the day-to-day risks people are subjected to. That being said, I doubt Merkians face zero risks, though risks in life are greatly reduced, perhaps. For those of us on Earth, I'll maintain that every step in life for those who actually live life is a calculated risk. There are those out there who say they will 'go with the flow' and passively let things happen to them, neither appreciating the risks nor evaluating them. There are also those out there who don't really think about risks and simply engage in risky behavior—in other words, they don't really do any meaningful calculations associated with those risks. For those with any chance at lasting success and happiness, logically evaluating and acting upon calculated risks is the only option. On Earth, at least, it's remarkable how many people don't take the time to evaluate and then take calculated risks. To do what logic dictates while still having empathy for the sociological conditions. It also seems Merkians have stood on their successes and myopically failed to evaluate calculated risks. In my experience, without risk, there is no reward, and without a reward of whatever nature, there is no meaningful advancement in life. Life in the universe is ultimately a state of nature; everyone lives from one risk scenario to the next. The best we can do is make our own luck, as it were. Face the risk factors ahead of us, measure those factors, and take a logically calculated risk for our next step. If you do that, then you optimize the ability to control your own destiny. Fail to do that and you don't make a move that is a calculated risk, but rather, you let the universe have its way, unfettered, upon you. I have trained in the process of calculated risks, and I'll wager with anyone that a logically calculated risk is all we have before us now."

"Well spoken. Maybe Merkians have been a little passive. So be it: a logically calculated risk it is," orders Triven. "By the way, you know, Merkian civilization has been around millennia longer than that of Earth. I don't know whether to be a bit embarrassed by being taught lessons from you, son, or downright impressed with the choice my daughter made."

"I am humbled by your thoughts," Andy responds.

"Riven, coordinate and commence the attack President Brock described. If you think there are better targets, then advise me immediately," Triven says.

"Yes, Chancellor, but may I ask President Brock why he chose those locations?" Riven responds.

"In one moment. Denk, while President Brock works with Riven on the attack strategy, assemble your infiltration team and be ready to go as soon as possible," Triven orders.

"Yes, Chancellor," Denk says and leaves the conference room to get his team assembled.

"Son, I have an idea why you chose those targets, but I'm interested in your thoughts," Triven prompts.

"Merk data shows that two of those targets—Sarik and Travak—house forward-deployment capabilities, while the other two—Amjular and Boric—are centers of primary military-industrial capabilities. I want to show Davark we can take out their immediate ability to put together an attack and also stunt their mid-to-long-term capabilities. These concepts will be part of what we communicate to potential Davark rebels when conducting our infiltration attempt. When I say 'rebels,' by the way, what I mean are individuals who can remain loyal to Davark but see a leadership future for themselves within a Davark that is part of the galactic community."

"General Pross, what do you think of those targets?" Triven asks.

"Sensible. Actually, they represent remarkable observations by President Brock in the course of the few hours he's had to make the recommendations. I've reviewed our previous analysis of critical Davark military centers. In that analysis, twenty-three centers appeared as priorities. President Brock actually identified four of them that tactically reach the upper tier of targets, and based upon President Brock's approach, I have to admit those four targets are exactly the targets we should be focused on," Pross says.

"Riven, do you agree?"

"Yes, Chancellor. Interestingly, we have monitored that the most recent attacks emanated from Sarik and Travak. I suspect that is the reason for President Brock's choice, and with that, I concur," Riven says.

"Well, meet with your team, do a further assessment, and report to me any alteration. If there is no alteration, then prepare and execute your attack on those locations," Triven orders then continues, "Everyone else is dismissed. Andy, Rein, please join me in my office for a moment."

Triven, Rein, and Andy make their way up to Triven's office. While there are some personal touches, Andy is impressed that the office is appointed in a similar manner to the temporary workspace provided to him. Triven does not engage in pretentious or selfish embellishments. Everything is functional and convenient. The technology interfaces are robust, and the same restroom and food/drink accommodations are present. There is a larger conference room structure, and the balcony view is impressive, but the office is generally on par with what Andy has seen in other places in the building.

"Daughter, son, I cannot express to you how proud and pleased with both of you I am. I am sure other daughters and sons would be less understanding of a wedding postponement. You both, on the other hand, are the ones effectuating the plan to do what is necessary. Words fail to convey the depth of my appreciation for you both. Now, first, Rein, you be careful with yourself and my grandchildren.

"Understood."

"Andy, I care about you more than you probably realize. I've known you a brief moment, but you have joined my family with a force and depth that has entirely gripped me. I am gravely concerned about your infiltration. If anything should happen to you, I will be inconsolable. Make sure that does not happen."

"Yes, Dad." Andy then hesitates a moment and regains emotional control. It is apparent to both Triven and Rein that Andy is deeply affected by Triven's sentiments. "Let me be clear about something. I have been blessed with marrying the finest female alive in the universe and have no doubt she attained that status through a deep connection to her parents. I will be careful, if for no other reason than I hope to spend as much time with my new family as possible."

"For the leader of Merk and the so-called 'leader of Earth,' you two spend more time on sentimentality than is permitted by the circumstances. Let's get back to work. Andy, we've got an infiltration to plan. Dad, cricken sprangin," Rein says. She explains to Andy on the way out that "cricken sprangin" is the Merkian version of "I love you," but is otherwise untranslatable. In fact, auto-translate does not work to interpret "cricken sprangin" when Rein says it. Between romantic partners, "alignment" is translatable into the concept of "love." In Merk, the parent-child relationship of "love" is not alignment so much as a pure depth of feeling for which English does not have an equivalent expression.

CHAPTER 40

SHIPS PASSING IN THE STARS

A more-than-modest Merkian armada commences their attack run simultaneously on the four Andy-named targets.

Unfortunately or not, Andy is right. In approximately the same time frame that Merk is on its way to conduct its attack, Davark's attack force commences its attack toward Amberan. For whatever reason, Davark apparently does not follow the postponement news or thinks it is a ruse.

The infiltration team also undertakes its mission simultaneously and in conjunction with the Davark attack force departure. Before leaving, Andy meets with Triven and the military heads to discuss his belief that Davark may very well think the postponement is a ruse; therefore, he wants to ensure sufficient defensive capability remains despite the counteroffensive. Andy does not need to express these thoughts, however, as Triven and the other military heads reinforce for Andy that under no circumstances will Merkian territory be left undefended and, in fact, reinforced defenses are being instituted around Amberan.

Merkian forces, generally speaking, are prepared for defensive operations. As such, the counteroffensive is a somewhat uncharacteristic operation. That being said, the rank and file are eager to finally take the battle to the Davark. There is plenty of discussion in the ranks that containment operations are more costly in lives and equipment than ending the fight by going on the offensive. There is also a rumor passing through the ranks that the Earthman, Brock, is the driving force for this offensive. Most believe the rumor, knowing that no Merkian would have probably instituted an offensive. It is not clear how the rumor started, but some are told the source may have been the chancellor himself.

Back in Amberan, Triven gives the order to evacuate all operations in the capital. In a matter of hours, shuttle after shuttle are able to escort a large percentage of the population to outlying areas of safety. The military command center is established within a mountain core, safely away from an attack zone.

The Davark offensive forces are substantial and well-trained in offensive maneuvers. These forces first attack the Merkian initial defensive front maintained at Turink. There are anti-ship installations and attack fighters ensconced as well. Davark attackers are able to avoid most of the anti-ship installations and simply outnumber the Merkian forces. Davark's goal is to bypass Turink in order to get to Amberan.

The fighting is furious. Out of the twenty squadrons defending Turink, all but five are wiped out by the Davarkian forces. Davark loses a mere ten squadrons, and none of their five destroyers are touched. The hardened and battle-tested Davarkian forces are proving themselves worthy of the fight.

At nearly the same time as the Battle of Turink, Merkian forces arrive at Sarik. Davarkian forces at Sarik are taken by complete surprise. The Merkian craft swiftly dispenses with the anti-ship ground installations and decimates the two squadrons that are left as part of the forward deployment. In fact, the two squadrons that are housed at Sarik appear to be older units or recently under repair, as Davark has committed nearly all of their elite attack aircraft to the offensive strike on Amberan. Having completed the devastation of all installations at Sarik, these particular Merkian forces, nearly unscathed, return to help with the potential defense of Amberan.

The Merk attack on Travak goes much the same, except there are even fewer Davark aircraft there. Once again, Merk is able to destroy all Davark forces and decimate the forward-deployment installations. The Merk attack force commander estimates it will take at least six months for Davark to rebuild its facilities. Merk forces in this attack swiftly regroup and turn to rejoin the defense of Amberan.

Within the same time frame as the decimation of Travak, Davark attack forces approach the inner Merk defensive system at Burin. Burin is proving a lot more challenging for the Davark. Merk houses two of its own destroyers at Burin and twice the squadron strength than that at Turink.

The commander at Burin is Streven, one of the oldest and most experienced commanders in all of Merk armed forces. Streven trains his forces hard and privately hates that an offensive attack on Davark has never been ordered. Streven's attitude today is that the battle must stop at Burin and that no Davark force will leave Burinian space. Streven times his defense perfectly, hiding his two destroyers on the far side of the only Burinian moon along with two squadrons of attack craft to protect those destroyers. All other squadrons are left to battle Davark's forces attempting to bypass Burinian anti-ship installations.

The Davark destroyers give a wide berth to the Burinian orbital space, avoiding all anti-ship ground installations. Merk attack craft near Burin engage the Davark destroyers and their protective attack craft perpendicular to the Burinian airspace. These Burinian attack craft are trained and honed by Streven. They harass the Davarkian forces and hold them in place until the Burinian moon's rotation reveals the hidden Merkian destroyer attack forces.

The Davark force is thereby faced with a frontal attack by the formerly hidden Merkian destroyer groups while also being harassed on the Burinian side by the Merk attack craft.

Further, at that moment, the Merkian forces formerly decimating both the forward deployments at Sarik and Travak, having learned of the path of the Davark's attack toward Amberan, appear at the Davark group's flank nearly simultaneously. Nearly surrounded and knowing their forces are fighting an equivalent number of craft without even having reached their intended main battle objective, the Davark commander orders a hyperdrive retreat of the entire force to Davarkian territory.

Meanwhile, Merkian forces reach both Amjular and Boric virtually simultaneously. These forces are composed of one destroyer each with two squadrons of attack craft each as well. At both locations, the destroyers take out anti-ship batteries. Thereafter, the relatively undefended military-industrial complexes are quickly destroyed by Merkian forces.

The infiltration team's ship is embedded with the destroyer group that just attacked Boric. After destroying Boric, that attack group joined the force that destroyed Amjular. The combined force, with the infiltration team embedded, makes their way to Davark's main planet, aptly named Davark.

The Davark forces that have retreated from Burin make their way back to Davark, having heard about the offensive operations in Davarkian territory. Once reaching Davark, they find the attacking Merkian forces.

Despite having lost a large number of their craft, the Davark force substantially outnumbers the Merkian forces that approach Davark. A fierce battle ensues. Merkian forces are on the brink of becoming overwhelmed but still fight bravely.

The Merkian commander of this combined force, Drekin, has to make a split-second decision to fight on or hyperdrive retreat. At the moment of decision, Streven's Burin group comes upon the Davark's flank, having followed the Davark's hyperdrive from Burin.

Streven assumes command of the entire Merk force and engages the Davark force with a fury. It is as if the Merk forces unleash their pent-up frustration at not previously engaging in an overall offensive. Streven immediately instructs subordinate officers to keep things cool but persistent. The Merk forces focus on squadron elimination, knowing the destroyers could come later.

The Davark forces are more concerned with the Merk destroyers and are sacrificing their attack craft at an appalling rate. As the intense battle draws on, the tide turns heavily in Merk's favor, and the Davark force has nowhere to go. Streven's tactics and hard training of his fighters is proving the basis of victory.

Sensing an imminent victory, Streven hails the Davark force and offers terms of surrender. The Davark commander, Verk, requests a ceasefire while terms of surrender are discussed. At that point, Streven agrees to the ceasefire.

Right before the ceasefire is instituted, the infiltration team's ship is struck by a Davarkian attack craft. While not entirely disabled, the Merk ship is forced to nearly crash land into the Davark countryside. All on board survive the landing. Prior to crash landing, Denk is able to hail Streven and report their probable landing site.

Davark land forces track the Merk ship and swiftly intercept the infiltration team. The team, including Andy and Rein, are immediately taken prisoner. All on board, except for Rein, are disguised as Davarkians. Rein, daughter of Chancellor Triven, is famous throughout the galaxy and readily known in Davark. The Davark that takes Rein prisoner knows exactly who they have.

Streven makes clear to the Davark commander, Verk, that a key to surrender is the return of the prisoners just taken.

Verk consults with the Davark leadership and is instructed to tell Streven that no surrender is possible. Merk forces are to be ordered to exit Davarkian space, and if—and *only* if—that happens, then the prisoners might be returned after Chancellor Triven meets with the Davark leader, Berok, at the neutral planet, Sorian.

Streven relays these terms to Triven, who instructs agreement but only if the prisoners are brought to Sorian as well. If any harm comes to any of them, then no deal will be possible.

Berok instructs Verk to agree to such terms.

CHAPTER 41

SORIAN

The Davark are generally misogynistic. They believe women are second-class at best. Foreign women are ranked only as high as livestock. Rein is separated from the rest of her team and put into a separate brig. Davarkian culture is also not enlightened philosophically. Davarkians generally believe in a male higher power figure whom they pray to. It is a religiously conservative society that believes women should respect men, be ruled by men, and should be modestly dressed at all times.

Given those views and given that Rein is a foreign female prisoner, the Davark prison guards think it is appropriate that she is stripped of her clothes. She does not deserve the modest treatment of Davarkian society. She is merely a prison animal who does not deserve clothes. She is given water in a bowl on the floor and told to relieve herself in a hole in the corner. There are no accommodations to wash or wipe herself in any manner.

Despite their demeaning treatment of Rein, one (or more) of the prison guards are noticeably aroused by Rein's femininity and nudity. Rein takes careful note of which of the guards display such arousal.

The male prisoners from Merk are not treated much better than Rein and are, in fact, treated much worse than typical prisoners because they are recognized as spies, given their attempted disguises. Andy, Denk, and the others are also told to strip and prepare to have their disguises removed. The guards are not careful in doing so, using bruising tactics to bring Andy and the Merkians to their natural undisguised state.

Still, the male prisoners are provided the ability to wipe themselves (but not wash otherwise), are provided fresh prison attire, and are allowed food and drink at a central table within their combined confines.

Rein's guards challenge each other to the classic Davarkian dice game. The winner of the game will be the first one allowed to rape Rein while the others hold her down. While there are four guards, there are only two who plan to participate directly in vaginal penetration.

Rein's cage is unlocked, and the first two of the four guards, including the dice winner, enter it. Rein stands her ground in the rear against a concrete wall. The first two guards charge her while the other two follow into the cage. The first guard to reach Rein is met with a roundhouse kick to the head that knocks him to the ground. The second guard fares no better, receiving a follow-on kick to the kidney from Rein's other leg. The last two guards charge Rein and are able to grab her arms—one on each. By that time, the first two guards are recovering and come to the aid of the guards who have her by the arms. Rein is somehow able to loosen their grasp on her arms and turns to meet all four men. She does the math and thinks about the children inside her womb. There is a chance she can beat these brutes, but there is a greater chance that in doing so, her children will be injured. At that point, she changes tactics, perceiving the need to either buy time or stave off greater brutality.

"All right, gentlemen, that fight was fun, but you won. I'm sensing one, if not all, of you would like to have sex with me. I have to admit I have been looking at you there on the right. I'm going to lie down, and if you can do me first, I think it will go easier on the rest. Don't fight over me; you'll all get your chance. This situation of a prison gangbang is kind of a fantasy of mine anyway."

The guards have no clue what to do at this point. They all look at their companion to their left—the guard Rein refers to on the right. He says, "Well, if she wants me first, then that's how it should be. Let her have her fantasy. It's still best to hold her down, guys. You two take her feet and spread her legs. You hold both of her arms above her head while I give her what she wants."

Rein, naked and spread eagle with three men holding her down, hears a group enter from the hallway.

Verk has volunteered and accepted the job of supervising the gathering and transporting of the prisoners to Sorian. Approximately two hours after Rein is imprisoned, Verk himself makes his way to her cage.

Verk overhears the instructions just given by the guard about to rape Rein and sees the guards holding her down. Knowing Rein's status as the daughter of the chancellor of Merk, Verk understands the jeopardy Davark will be in—and how much he will be in personally—if Rein is further abused.

With that understanding in mind, Verk, with his personal guards, rushes into the cage, throws the rapists aside and frees Rein. Verk instructs that Rein is to be clothed immediately and provided an appropriate toilet and suitable food and drink.

Rein is escorted to a guest room at the prison, where she will be allowed to shower and dress. Food and drink are provided to her as well. Verk supervises all activity to ensure no further misconduct on the part of any Davarkian.

After Rein has showered, Verk walks into the guest room and asks her how she is doing.

"Thank you, Verk. I'm fine. Let me also thank you for rescuing me from your apparently sexually deprived colleagues."

"Once again, I am very sorry about their conduct. I will personally see to it they are severely disciplined."

"I thank you for that as well. On another front, before we crashed and on comms after the crash, the reports indicated the Davarkian forces were effectively defeated. It is my understanding and deduction that talks of surrender were underway and that your government was going to mainly use me as a bargaining chip."

"Your summary is and remains basically correct. I am instructed to deliver you to Sorian, where your father and the Davarkian leader will negotiate terms."

"It is my further understanding there are certain elements in Davark that don't agree with how things are being handled generally. Is that fair?" Rein asks.

"There are those elements."

"My sense is you hold a position of power and influence in Davark, and with that power and influence, you can make things better for the people of Davark under the right circumstances."

"To which circumstances do you refer?"

"Right now, Davark is effectively in a position of surrender. The current Davark leadership is hanging on by a thread. I appear to be their only bargaining chip. That's pretty weak. Merk is not the aggressor in this relationship and never has been. All Merk wants is a peaceful galaxy occupied by free peoples who are allowed to make their own choices regarding governments. I sense you are one of the more rational and enlightened members of the Davark community. The bottom line is that Merk is prepared to support those in Davark who want what is best for Davark. That support can start with granting asylum to you and whomever else you want. In return, you don't allow me to be held hostage. Without me as a hostage, the current Davark leadership will have no alternative but to surrender to Merk's offensive forces. One of the terms of surrender will be that Davark holds free and fair elections. Merk would provide protection to candidates in those elections—whether you run or not. You can choose to remain in Merk as an immigrant with full asylum or stay in Davark and help free its people and cease this senseless pattern of war instituted by power-hungry Davarkians such as Berok."

"For someone who just went through the trauma of a near gang rape, you have remarkable self-control. Moreover, everything you said makes great sense. I am, in fact, disheartened by the way Davark has maintained a warring agenda and that those in leadership are not freely chosen, but I never really thought the opportunity you have just outlined would come. Frankly, I never understood why Merk tolerated Davark's behavior these past few years in particular. Whoever anticipated Davark's attack on your wedding day and then also decided to mount an offensive counterattack at the same time was brilliant. No one in Davark saw it coming. Anyway, I accept your offer. Let's get you home. By the way, you might be happy to know that neither the guy you kicked in the head nor the guy you kicked in the kidney are doing well. It appears there are latent effects of your—how shall I say? — defensive maneuvers. They were likely fueled by adrenaline wanting to rape you and did not fully appreciate the extent of their injuries. One guy's jaw is broken, and the other has a punctured kidney with internal bleeding and possible sepsis. Well done, you."

"I try. By the way, obviously, my request is not merely to return me, but my shipmates as well. Understood?"

"Yes. In fact, here they are now."

Denk, Andy, and the rest of the crew come into the guest room, their timing impeccable.

"Verk, can you give us a moment?" Rein asks.

"Sure."

Andy kisses and hugs Rein. The rest of the crew also share friendly hugs with Rein. She then describes to Andy the deal reached with Verk.

"Do you think we can trust him?" Andy asks.

"Yes. No matter what, the Davark regime is done. If they tried to hold us hostage, Merk would never stop efforts at forcing Davark to release us. There's no way the Davark could successfully maintain the hostage environment. Holding us hostage is the dumbest thing in the universe. That approach would only drive Merk into a more offensive position and reinforce the ability of rebels within Davark to overturn the regime. Moreover, it is a no-lose proposition for Verk; he wins through being a hero to Merk. He, therefore, either gains asylum benefits or becomes a hero in Davark by forcing the horrible regime to fail. So, I trust him to act in his best interest."

"I agree. Still, nice work. By the way, they treated us pretty badly when removing our disguises. I hope they treated you better," Andy says.

"I'm fine. In fact, I don't want to brag, but I think a couple of the guards were attracted to me, and their treatment reflected that attraction," Rein says with a smile.

"I'm glad they treated you well. You are, in my opinion, a very attractive woman," Andy says.

At that moment, Verk reenters the room and informs everyone they need to get on the transport ship on the way to Sorian. Verk says he feels he will have control of his chosen crew, and on the way, he will enable everyone to be delivered to Merkian forces while he and the crew seek asylum.

CHAPTER 42

A HERO'S RETURN

A Merkian armada waits at Sorian. The Davark fleet pales by comparison. There is no question who has the superior force. The Merkian fleet is quantitatively superior, and Merkian technology is vastly better at firepower, shielding, and maneuverability.

Verk waits until the transport ship is one hour from the rendezvous point and gathers his senior staff in his stateroom. Verk sets forth the asylum proposal, which quickly receives universal acceptance. All that is needed now is a directional command to be followed by the senior navigator to have the transport ship go behind the protective lines of the Merkian armada.

As the transport ship approaches Sorian, Verk hails the Merkian flagship. "We seek asylum and are prepared to return your people. We need your permission to pass across your lines and then protection from any Davark attack. Over."

Streven, given honorary control of the fleet due to his efforts at the Battle of Burin, replies, "You have permission. Execute now. We will fly to you as well and provide cover."

The Davark fleet commander hears the request for asylum and gives the order to fire upon Verk's vessel.

At that moment, three squadrons of Merkian attack craft fly toward Verk's transport ship, which flies between those squadrons to go behind the Merkian armada's lines. The Merkian attack craft takes out the Davark squadron attempting to fire on Verk's ship, which is safely behind the Merkian craft in a matter of seconds.

Verk's transport ship again hails the Merkian armada.

Rein rushes over to the communication panel. "Dad, we are fine. We are all here. Everyone survived the crash."

"A shuttle should be there in a moment and will take you to my ship," Triven replies.

"Dad, please provide asylum and comfort to all Davarkians on this transport ship. They are true heroes for their people."

"Assure them we will. They have my word," Triven answers, then turns his attention to the Davarkian leader, hailing him. "Berok, you took my daughter captive, you engaged in unprovoked attacks on Merk, you fired on my daughter's ship while it sought refuge, you have ruled your people as an authoritarian, and you have brought nothing but havoc to the galaxy. Those days are over. I will give you and your cronies a choice: Surrender to us and spend the rest of your years in comfortable exile on Salust under our watchful eye or fight us now. Don't confuse our previous generosity and peacefulness with a willingness to ensure you never threaten another planet again."

Berok is left with no choice, and he cannot believe how lucky he is. If Davark had won this day, he would have killed all Merkians in his presence.

Berok responds, "We choose Salust."

"Good choice. I'll not make a martyr of you today," Triven responds.

At that moment, Rein, Andy, and the crew board the Merkian flagship.

"Dad, we are aboard."

"Great. Rein, Andy, and Denk, please report to the bridge immediately," Triven says.

After Rein, Andy, and Denk make their way to the bridge, Triven hails the Davarkian flagship and ensures that the entire Merk fleet hears his words. "Berok, you have taken all of my direct personal time which I will allow and more than you are worth. Denk, the gentlemen to my right, will supervise your removal to Salust. I'd like to introduce to you another two people before I never speak to you again: my daughter, whom you took captive, and my son-in-law, whom you also took captive. First, my son-in-law is the main reason you are in the position you find yourself. It was his strategy that brought about your defeat. By the way, he's from Earth. Second, my daughter discovered him, so she gets some credit as well. Enjoy your stay on Salust and don't cause any trouble there. If you do, then you'll have my daughter to answer to, and I have a feeling she's not going to be in a very understanding mood.

"Denk, please transfer to the Currilon Destroyer with its escort group and take over the administration of your new friends to Salust. I am going to take my flagship and its escort back home," Triven instructs.

With that, Denk's shuttle comes, and he effectuates the transfer. Moments later, the Merkian flagship and its escort execute the hyperdrive back to Merk.

Still on the ship, Triven invites Rein and Andy into Triven's private quarters, which are different from the well-appointed captain's quarters. While Triven has a starship of his own that is the Merkian equivalent in status to Force One (but makes Air Force One look like a propeller plane by comparison), the battle flagship they are presently on is designed to house the chancellor for events such as these, and more often than not, peacekeeping activities that might require a little more muscle than the chancellor's starship. Therefore, there is both the aforementioned captain's quarters and the even more robust chancellor's domain, as the English translation would have it.

The chancellor's domain is, indeed, well-appointed. There is a conference room with an adjacent food and drink serving station, a private office, an assistant's office, two full bathrooms, what can only be referred to as a library/living room, an audio-visual center, and private dining. Triven chooses the library/living room to chat with Andy and Rein.

"Rein, Andy, how are you?" Triven asks.

"Thanks for putting me in charge of dealing with any misbehavior on Salust. While in prison, they stripped me down—which they did not realize was in and of itself not a big deal—as well as failed to give me a proper toilet and washing capabilities, really did not afford me proper food or drink, and tried to gang rape me. I won't hesitate to deal with these guys with due justice."

Triven and Andy both stand in shock.

"Dear, first, I'm going to hug and kiss you in complete sympathy and sorrow for what you went through, then I'm going to complain vigorously that you did not tell me this before," Andy says.

"I'll accept the hugs and kisses," Rein replies.

Without hesitation, Andy smothers her in hugs and kisses.

"Now, why did you not tell me before?" Andy asks.

"I knew it might hurt you, and since no lasting harm was done to me, and it was not relevant, I thought not to bring it up. When Dad told me I was in charge of these idiots, then I thought at least Dad should know the circumstances surrounding why I would not hesitate to be strict. You should also know, for your own sake, I injured two of the guards, one in the head and one in the kidney."

"Well, then, that makes it all better. I know you don't need me to protect you, and I respect that you are a strong person, but I hope you understand I'm somewhat strong, too, and you don't need to protect me from being hurt. I'd like to know these kinds of things and always be informed of anything or anyone that might hurt you."

"Understood. By the way, I had a chance to shower and brush my teeth while on Davark. You, however, as my olfactory senses are indicating, did not have the chance to do either of those activities. Since we are going to tell each other everything, I just wanted you to know."

While walking away from both Triven and Rein, Andy says with a broad smile, "Triven, I'm going to use your guest bathroom now. Rein, thank you for your forthright willingness to inform me of things."

"No problem," Rein says.

"I have to agree with my daughter about everything," Triven says.

"I know, I know, I know," Andy replies.

Triven and Rein begin to share a meal while Andy showers. Rein ensures Andy has a replacement set of clothes and proper food and drink once he is out of the shower. She leaves a note on Andy's new set of clothes saying she is going to send the old set out the air lock into cold space due to the smell.

Andy comes out of the bathroom with his new grey bodysuit.

"Thanks for the clothes and for removing my old set. Maybe there will be a homeless person in space who won't mind a hand-me-down."

"You're welcome, and I doubt even the cold of space will cure what troubled those clothes. Even a homeless person floating in space would have better taste and standards than to wear something that smelled that bad."

Triven intervenes, "You both know I'm right here and can hear all of this, right?"

"Yes, Dad," says Rein.

"Yes, sir," says Andy.

"Well, Rein, if you think I am going to sit here and let you abuse my new son, you've got another thing coming," Triven says.

"Wow, finally a break through the family wall—now I feel special," Andy says.

"Don't, I was joking. Rein was right; you really needed to bathe. But on to more interesting topics. Andy, Merk and I owe you a debt of gratitude. Your remarkable strategy not only saved thousands upon thousands of lives, maybe even millions, but also ended up freeing the Davark people. I intend to visit your United Nations and report on what happened. Earth should also know you saved them from ever having to deal with a stronger Davark in the future."

"It worked out well, didn't it? Except for the whole attempted gang bang of my wife," Andy says.

"Well, we haven't had a manifestation of alignment in hours, and we were apart, so I had to achieve satisfaction somehow," Rein says.

"First, probably not the best topic to discuss in front of Dad, and second, not funny," Andy says.

"Actually, you should know by now that Merk does not have Earth's hang-ups, and it was a little funny," Triven says.

"A gang bang is not a hang-up, but I guess humor arises from irony, and Rein's comment was beyond ironic, so I will concede that maybe there was ironic humor," Andy replies.

"There's a couple of other things we need to discuss. We need to decide when the wedding will happen on Merk. I'd also like to know where you both plan to school my grandchildren. In addition, I'd like to know what Andy plans to do about the burgeoning artificial intelligence threat hitting Earth. Lastly, Andy, I understand you play chess. I've recently taken up the game as it is a variant of my favorite game on Merk. When can we play a game?" Triven asks.

"Hold on a moment. What AI threat are you talking about specifically?" Andy asks.

"Our surveys have indicated Russian-based AI, in particular, has autonomously taken over certain Russian commercial sectors in the past week. That AI would appear to have the potential of seeping into the Russian military-industrial complex and spreading through Earth. If something is not done fast, then even Merk intervention might not be enough to stop widespread damage."

"On Earth, we call that burying the lead. When were you going to tell me about the AI threat?" Andy asks.

"Now, especially since you were previously in the middle of battle, held hostage, and failed to stop my daughter's attempted gang bang," Triven says.

"Well, apparently, since I don't satisfy her, it is something she wanted," Andy replies. "Anyway, I need to get back to Earth and deal with this situation. I assume when we are out of hyperdrive, I can contact Earth," Andy says.

"Yes, but what about that game of chess?" Triven asks with a smile, then says, "We'll be to Merk in a moment, so chess will have to wait, but get back to me on the other points, please—as soon as possible."

Rein and Andy are able to disembark. Given the urgency of the AI threat on Earth, they go to Rein's condominium, which is a shorter trip for the shuttle than her castle.

Rein connects Andy to the White House.

"Jack, what are you hearing about the AI threat?" Andy asks.

There is an understandable time lag before Jack responds. "We just got wind of it today. It appears Dimitri may be containing it, but it's just not clear."

Another lag.

"I trust the heightened protocols have been executed domestically, correct?" Andy asks.

A longer lag.

"Yes, but we're not stopping there, as you can surmise," Jack says.

Another even longer lag.

"Jack, while I know the military sector is mostly air-gapped under these circumstances, my biggest worries are the energy sector and the financial sector. Please keep those closely monitored," Andy says.

Another longer lag.

"Jack, are you there?" Andy asks.

The lag continues.

"Rein, can you determine why we lost Jack?" Andy asks.

"I'm checking."

The lag continues.

"Andy, it's not Merk technology. Jack has been cut off. The first diagnostic indicates it may be AI interference," Rein says.

THE END